THE SOULMATISM SAGA

OUR POISONED LOVE

ISABELLA
AYUBI

Dedications

For my mom and dad. Thank you for being my first and biggest cheerleaders. I love you more than words can say.

CHAPTER ONE

Julie

A gift can also be a curse. Two sides of the same coin, two ends of a string that Julie Seir no longer possessed. The faint echo of a playful, mysterious song met her ears as she rustled the glittering scarlet fabric around her, straightening her appearance. Visitors of the *Circle of Lights* would be arriving soon. They expected an act, a show meant to distract and dazzle. Little did they know that underneath her sparkly, alluring exterior, she was only trying to survive. Julie stretched out her hands in front of her, frowning at the way the candlelight tossed reckless shadows across her gaunt wrists. The stage cosmetics they applied to her skin aided in hiding the fingerprint-shaped bruises she wore like a bracelet. A punishment for getting caught while swiping more food than was her ration. The familiar ache of hunger clawed at her insides, and she knew her sister's stomach was just as hollow. The circus held the promise of food over their heads. Touted as some great prize to win rather than basic human decency to sustain those in your employ. Julie's jaw ached as she thought back to how harshly the ringmaster, Pierre, had grasped it. He spoke in a voice nearly cat-like, *'If you're good, you'll be taken care of. My Doves don't break the rules, or I rip their feathers.'*

His *Doves.* A sordid nickname for the female performers he was the fondest of. A not-so-subtle threat towards her sister, whose task was to tame those very birds and perform acrobatic tricks like she was one herself. Julie tucked her legs underneath her as a blast of chilled night air roamed through the gap in her tent. The gesture caused something metallic to scrape against the wooded platform she was stationed upon. She bit back a groan, arranging the length of her skirts to mask the chain attached to her ankle. Now, no one would know that she was bound to the table. Pierre didn't part easily with his possessions, especially not after Julie had used up her two chances to escape. Everyone had two, or at least Pierre let them think they did. The first, was typically used to scout. To memorize the ebb and flow of the circus until one found a crack just large enough to slip through. The taste of freedom would barely linger on their tongue before they were hauled back in a show of kicking and screaming. It was pure desperation that caused one to take that second chance and attempt to steal away into the soundless night. They became smarter on the second try, once they knew where Pierre hand-placed his security. Yet, he only allowed them to get so far before he personally appeared to applaud their ingenuity and bravado. He then brought them back to the *Circle of Lights* in chains like cattle being led to the butchering block.

"I heard somebody needed a magician's assistant." A sweet voice like a lullaby filled Julie's ears and her hazel gaze snapped up to the woman who'd just slipped into the tent.

"Maggie." Julie didn't try to fight the smile that bloomed on her lips. "You're not supposed to be in here." Julie eyed her sister's wrists and ankles, which were thankfully shackle-free. Though with Maggie not being where Pierre demanded, Julie wasn't sure how long that would last.

"The old goat gave Sasha my performance tonight. I think he believes that it'll hurt me to watch someone else in the spotlight." Maggie waved a casual hand and a fluffy white feather fell from her costume, landing on Julie's table.

"The Prince of Mind Games." Julie swept the feather into her hand, pinching its quill between her forefinger and thumb. *It left a sour taste in her mouth to refer to him in that way, seeing how much he prided himself on the title.*

"I don't mind. I'm still sore from the last show. The birds were in a mood." Maggie rolled her shoulders, the gray glass beads on her costume reflecting the candlelight. "Besides, I never pass up the chance to watch you work." Dark curls bounced with the tilt of her head as she offered Julie a mischievous grin. "Speaking of..." Maggie's smile switched to one more theatrical as she swept her arm out wide. "Welcome, welcome to the Seer's tent. Whether you be lovestruck or *deathly* curious, may you find all the answers that you seek in her Sight."

Julie resisted the urge to giggle. Her sister was a far better show-woman than she. Looks of delight and awe lit the features of the three women who had entered the space. One of them eagerly rushed forward. "We've heard all about you." She exclaimed, blue eyes alight with anticipation.

"Good things, I hope?" Julie offered a smile. *That was always a slightly unnerving sentence to hear from the lips of a stranger.*

"Wonderful. I want to know where my soulmate is too, please." The woman rustled around in her purse and unfurled her fist, revealing three shining, gold aurums. Julie's fingers itched to snatch the coins and hide them somewhere Pierre couldn't reach. But the punishment for stealing from the circus was much greater than no food and heavy ankle chains. He might take Maggie away and punish her instead for Julie's insubordination. That thought alone was enough for Julie to plaster on another smile. The woman dropped the coins into the designated cup on the table.

"May I see your left hand?" Julie questioned, holding out her flattened palms face-up.

"Absolutely." The woman said, nearly giddy as she placed her hand in Julie's.

Julie drew in a calming breath as her eyes settled on the woman's ring finger. She watched the slim, scarlet thread loop around her fair skin and form a delicately floating cord that stretched beyond the confines of the tent. Maggie brushed the tent flap aside, so that Julie could track the direction of the string. "Your soulmate thread is strong, healthy, and it points to the north."

"Esterod is in the north." One of the woman's friends nudged her shoulder knowingly. The woman blushed and told Julie, "My fiancé lives there."

"Ah, I wish you both every happiness." Julie knew of the multitude residing in the northern kingdoms. While she hoped this girl's fiancé was connected to the other end of her string, logically it seemed improbable. However, Julie's job was to instill joy and every romantic notion into the heads of the circus attendees. She also didn't have the heart to tell the woman otherwise.

As the evening wore on, the line that formed outside Julie's tent slowly thinned out. Visitors left, satisfied with her readings and filled with thoughts of love and fate. A dull ache thrummed in Julie's head as the final guest ducked out of the tent. She supposed no gift came without a cost. Some days after using her Sight for hours on end and feeling the pain that came with it, Julie doubted her ability was a gift at all. Though, her father had felt differently. Her mind flickered momentarily to a fragmented conversation she had with him sixteen years ago.

'Can't everyone see the strings?' A six-year-old Julie asked with wide, questioning eyes.

'No, little one. You've been given a great gift, be sure to use it wisely.'

Julie didn't want to linger on the disappointment that would have lurked in her father's eyes if he knew what had become of her and Maggie. He never wanted them to be other people's entertainment instead of commanders of their own lives. But Julie was bound by more than the metal cuff around her ankle. She was bound by secret, whispered promises and a devotion to her sister so great that not even Pierre could deter her from seeing them through.

As if merely thinking his name had summoned the ringmaster, a tall, slender man slipped into the tent. His hardened brown gaze was cunning, sharp to the point that Julie imagined it could double as a weapon. Then his eyes flicked to Maggie and an invisible knife twisted in her gut. "Hello, my Doves." He cooed. "Did we have a pleasant evening?"

Julie stood from her table, ignoring the uncomfortable pins and needles sensation that vibrated through her chained foot as she shifted her weight onto it. "The crowd was in good spirits tonight." *Don't look into the coin cup, please don't look.*

Pierre rubbed his shadowed chin thoughtfully, but his attention lingered on Maggie who still stood at the tent's entrance. "Did one of my Doves try to leave her cage?" The candlelight caught on the silver strands peeking through his black hair. He angled his head towards Julie's sister.

"I was only assisting Julie." Maggie avoided Pierre's eyes, "You tell us to be useful, never idle."

A pleased smile crossed Pierre's features. "Such a good girl, I appreciate the ones who listen." His hand skimmed the curve of Maggie's beaded bodice. Disgust and hate roiled in Julie's stomach. The combination fueled her need to knock him away from Maggie, to shove him in the dirt like the pig he was. But, her sister's eyes locked onto Julie's, and she caught the silent plea in them. *Just let him, it's not worth it.*

"Are you frightened, little Dove?" Pierre asked Maggie, his knuckles dragging along the soft skin of her arm. The caress was a promise that could just as easily bruise. Julie's hands bunched into fists at her sides. *This was a part of her punishment, she just knew it. His way of pinning them underneath his thumb, like butterflies trapped under glass for their beauty to be admired yet never freed.*

"No, master." Maggie said quietly, lashes downcast in shame as Pierre tilted her chin closer to his. His gaze darkened as it swept across her mouth. *He was going to kiss her.*

"Don't!" Julie snarled, lunging forward but crashing to her knees mere inches away from them. The silver chain grew taut and yanked on her leg, sending a stinging pain through her calf. Pierre released Maggie like she was a toy he'd become bored with, his attention now settling on Julie. She thought she might buckle under the weight of it if not for the rage that poured through her veins.

He crouched down, the scent of his bitter boot polish assaulted Julie's nostrils as he pinched her chin and yanked her face up. "Never forget how fortunate you are to be here. Without me, you are *nothing*." His fingertips slipped down to her neck. With a swift but harsh tug, her jeweled necklace broke away, leaving an angry red line on the back of her neck. The stones crashed onto the wooden platform, shattering in every direction. Red glass, not rubies. An illusion, like everything else. "I know." Julie gritted out, knowing he would be satisfied with nothing less than her lie disguised as truth.

"You know, *what?*" He eyed her darkly.

Julie wouldn't say it. She refused to say it. "I know, *Pierre.*"

A growl rippled in the back of his throat, and he took Julie's hand, only to slam her palm down on top of the shattered glass. A sharp whimper escaped her as tears pricked at the corners of her eyes. Pierre wrapped her injured hand around the largest shard of glass before rising to his feet and hauling Maggie next to her. "Say it or carve my initial into her hand. Though, choose wisely. Her skin is *much* softer, I fear."

Maggie silently shook her head. She knew it would kill Julie to utter that word, and until today Julie had managed to refrain from ever speaking the two syllables. But Pierre had never threatened Maggie's pain at the hands of Julie before. He took hold of Julie's wrist and thrust it at Maggie's right hand. The abrupt jerking movement drew a thin line of blood from Maggie's golden-brown skin, the color a painful contrast.

"I understand, master." Julie blurted, the words aching like a physical blow. Pierre dropped her wrist, and the largest shard of scarlet glass fell from her clutches.

"That's a good Dove." Pierre nodded, pleased, as if he was aware of the bile scorching the back of Julie's throat. He strolled to the painted table and grasped the coin cup, emptying the nearly full container into the pouch at his hip. "I'm feeling generous, today." He tipped over the cup in front of them, and a singular aurum landed in the dirt with a small thud. Julie's mind was flooded with disbelief.

"Use it wisely." Pierre said in a sing-song tone. *If he only knew what a mockery his words were of the ones her father had once spoken.* Pierre exited the tent. As Julie glared at his retreating silhouette, something ignited within her spirit. Something that refused to yield even as the rest of her begged for a reprieve. They needed to find a way out, they *must.*

To escape the *Circle of lights*, they would have to embrace the shadows.

CHAPTER TWO

Julie

Every visitor flocked to the prized jewel of Pierre's domain, the grand tent. Aptly named *The House of Roses* for the gold painted flowers that audience members tossed into the center of the ring. Julie's hand gripped Maggie's a little tighter as they hung back in the wings. Pierre demanded all his Doves be brought into *The House of Roses* on the second Friday of every month. Oftentimes, the acts were as gruesome as they were enchanting, yet the macabre show delighted many on the benches. For instance, he was currently parading one of the girls around a ring of tigers. She had knife hilts strapped to her black ballet slippers which surely made walking difficult and painful. Maggie winced in sympathy when the girl wobbled on the weaponized stilts. Pierre swiftly caught her by the waist and dipped her like a well-trained dancer. The crowd swooned, believing it all a part of the act. Only Julie and Maggie saw the shadow that slipped over Pierre's mask as he glared at the girl with the threatening promise of a viper prepared to strike. The circus was a dream to the outsider, but a nightmare to all within. Pierre spun the girl outward, forcing her to pirouette into the throes of agitated tigers.

"Oh, no." Maggie whispered, pressing her hand to her lips. Julie's heart stuttered as she watched the largest tiger let out a growl that rippled through the audience before it lunged. The girl could barely scream before a heavy silk cloth dropped from the top of the tent and swallowed the scene in a sea of sapphire blue. Pierre withdrew a long, gleaming sword from the sheath at his hip. Turning on his heel, he looked every bit the valiant knight in shining armor come to save his love from the jaws of death. He plunged into the center of the silk, stabbing the distinctly tiger-shaped lump underneath. The audience gasped, on the edges of their seats. Julie's palms slickened as the silk swirled around the ring, masking Pierre and the poor girl from the audience's view. When the silk lifted not five heartbeats later, Pierre had hoisted the girl up into the air as she performed a handstand on Pierre's palms. She smiled triumphantly, not a drop of blood or sign of injury on her.

Because that wasn't the same girl. Julie swallowed past the tightness in her throat. He'd swapped them out before the audience noticed. They looked similar, but this was another one of Pierre's tricks. There was a reason the center of the ring and the benches where the audience sat were a carefully crafted distance away. Just far enough where it became difficult to make out someone's distinguishable features, yet close enough to see only what he wanted you to.

The crowd cheered, whooped and applauded, their golden roses raining down at Pierre's feet. *Murderer!* Julie wanted to scream. *Don't praise him, he's a killer!*

"I thank you, fine ladies and gentlemen. Tonight, we have a new act joining us. One that as soon as I heard of him, I *had* to welcome him into our magical, irresistible world of glamour." Pierre called out, calming the crowd while he twirled his sleek black cane between his fingers.

Who would willingly agree to a proposal from Pierre? Julie bit her inner cheek. They had, and look where it had gotten them. Stuck on the sidelines, terrified that they could be the next sacrifice in Pierre's all-too-real theatrics, and powerless to do anything about it.

The House of Roses darkened. One by one, small candles burst into flame. They dangled from above on invisible strings until the entire tent was filled with floating lights. It could have been considered beautiful if Julie didn't have the knowledge that somewhere within this tent was a girl's broken body, torn to shreds by a feral tiger. No amount of glamour could mask what occurred behind the surface of *The Circle of Lights.*

"I give you, the Dark Archer." Pierre sketched a grand bow, outstretching his arm to showcase a shadow slinking forward from an unseen place.

This man was taller than Pierre. Broad-shouldered and rigid like he was perpetually ready to strike. A dark emerald cloak concealed the rest of his features, flowing over his shoulders and reaching his knees. His boots were scuffed, worn from travel. If Julie squinted, she could make out untamed black hair peeking out from under his hood. The only bit of finery about him was the intricate golden stitching along the collar and hem of his cloak. She still couldn't see his face. Perhaps, Pierre had done that for a reason. He enjoyed making the audience wait. He claimed it added a sense of mystery and foreboding.

Julie's sense of apprehension had little to do with Pierre's tricks and everything to do with the way the man's grip flexed on a shining, onyx archer's bow.

"The Dark Archer's aim is as accurate as it is deadly." Pierre called from the rafters, his voice echoing into every crevice and corner. "Gifted with magical arrows that never stray from their target, he has ventured far and wide, honing his talent."

Julie rolled her eyes. She was tired of Pierre's false stories about his performers. The last time she and Maggie had the misfortune of being in the center of the ring, Pierre had loudly and brightly proclaimed that her gift was the product of a familial curse passed down from generation to generation. Pierre also announced that Julie was fated to never love, only to help others find love.

Some 'oohs,' and 'aahs' sparked through the audience. Their enchantment with this stranger seemed dangerous. He looked like the embodiment of midnight whispers, hidden secrets and the part of the sky the stars refused to touch.

And he was lighting an arrow on fire.

The Dark Archer raised his bow and loosed an arrow directly into the center of a hanging target, the flame extinguishing itself upon impact. Another target lowered from the tent's tapered ceiling, and his arrow struck the bullseye. Again and again, the stranger did this. Faster than lightning he fired the flaming arrows. He only stopped when a target descended behind him and he released an arrow over his shoulder without even turning around.

"Ladies and Gentlemen, joining the Dark Archer, our very own Princess of Doves!" Pierre grinned as the audience cheered louder. Julie's heart sank to the floor, weighed down like a circus elephant had stomped on it. *Maggie was the Princess of Doves.*

Maggie paled for a instant, and Julie's grip tightened on her arm. "You don't have to do this." Julie whispered, praying silently that Pierre would choose another girl, but he didn't. Pierre enjoyed the feeling of control that came with drawing his actors into a performance they hadn't been expecting. He was the marionettist, and they were his puppets wooden with fear.

"It's okay, Jules." Maggie squeezed Julie's shoulder affirmingly. She walked into the center of the ring as if they hadn't seen a woman murdered on that very floor a handful of moments ago. The silver and white beads on Maggie's costume caught the light like pearls being introduced to the sun. She raised her arms and called down flocks of white and gray birds from hidden trapdoors on either side of the great tent. The stage was alive in a fury of feathers and flames.

Flames. Julie's eyes darted to the arrow tipped with fire that the Dark Archer nocked, his bow raised like an extension of his body. Her hand drifted to the glass pendant around her neck, fingers curling around the heavy center stone. The necklace was unclasped before she could formulate a different plan. This was chance number three. Their final one.

She only hoped her aim proved true.

The Dark Archer sent his arrow flying, slicing the air towards one of the swooping birds. Julie cocked her wrist back and threw the necklace into its flight path. The glinting stone struck the arrow's shaft, diverting its trajectory as it plunged into the side of the tent. The canvas immediately ignited into an eruption of licking flames.

"Fire!" The crowd screamed, scrambling down from their seats as embers and smoke filled *The House of Roses*.

Julie vaguely registered Pierre's furious growl as her feet pounded into the sawdust of the center ring. Her hand latched around Maggie's arm, pulling her sister behind. The strings that once supported the small floating candles snapped and they dropped to the ground, igniting and consuming the sawdust. Julie shoved Maggie out of the tent's secondary exit, the one Pierre kept concealed for his acts to come and go unseen. *Who knew his trickery would one day be their saving grace.*

"Run." Julie commanded, coughing between her effort to draw breath into her aching, smoke-tinged lungs. Maggie's gray eyes were watery and panicked. They glanced back only to be met with the sight of *The House of Roses* buckling as plumes of dark smoke and ash rose into the air.

"You could have given me some warning that you planned on doing this today!" Maggie's curls whipped behind her, as wild as the feathers that flew from her costume.

"I didn't know until just now!" Julie yanked Maggie aside to the lineup of brightly decorated wagons belonging to *The Circle of Lights*. Horses were attached to each one, prepared to transport the circus when the night's show concluded.

"Get on." Julie searched over her shoulder, imagining the phantom sound of angry bootsteps but there was no one there. Maggie climbed up into the wagon's bench seat, grabbing Julie's forearms. When Julie's footing slipped into the spokes of the wheel, she drew in a sharp breath. The frightening sensation of plummeting seared through her body.

"I've got you." Maggie pulled her up the rest of the way. Julie didn't allow herself a solitary moment for the adrenaline to filter out of her blood before she gripped the reigns. "Hyah!" She spurred the midnight dark mare, Fiona, into action as the wheels of the cart rattled ferociously. Julie pictured that the billowing smoke pouring from the circus could reach out to snatch them back with long, gray claws. She wouldn't let that happen. *Capturing freedom oftentimes means one must burn the shackles that contained them.*

"Did that really just happen?" Maggie blinked, disbelief etched onto her delicate features.

Julie spared a final glance behind them, toward the night sky painted with the reflection of blazing orange and red. Already, they were further away than the last time they attempted to escape. "I think so..." The reality of the situation finally thrummed deep in her bones. She didn't know where they would go from here. But they had each other, their freedom, this wagon and mare. It would be enough, for now.

Still, she couldn't shake the feeling that they were not out of the woods yet.

CHAPTER THREE

Amor

Amor was fifty feet from death. The scent of ash and burnt trickery clung to his cloak like an inseparable shadow. He'd attempted to find her tonight, the Seer claiming to have that which he had lost. *The Sight*. Rumors about her had quickly slipped through the cracks, and Amor needed to know if there was any truth to her talent. He'd gained entry into the blatantly obvious money-grabbing spectacle called *The Circle of Lights* by agreeing to perform for one night only. Amor had been unable to seek the woman out before everything went up in flames, literally. He worked his jaw as his mind flicked to the fact his arrow had been knocked off target by some shining projectile. The girl in the crimson dress had thrown it.

The same one he'd seen running full force out of the tent like the devil was on her heels. *He would have to figure something else out, now. He had no choice.* Amor's thoughts faded into the background as he perched behind a brick arch. It was wide enough to obstruct most of his body from those he was watching. The cool, smooth bend of the bow in his hand was an anchor.

Wisps of black hair swept underneath his forest green hood. *Of all the places for these cretins to meet.* An empty Colosseum, the largest building in the city of Yral, didn't exactly scream discreet. Lucky for Amor, the many alcoves flanking the large wall provided ample cover for his mission.

Horse-drawn carts rolled over the brick-laid floor of the Colosseum, each sporting wooden wagons covered in dark tarps. Five of them entered and followed one another in a trail like ants returning to their hill. On the opposite side of the arena, two more concealed carts clattered in.

Amor's eyes narrowed as a different type of carriage arrived just behind the covered wagons. His fingers curled around his bow as the carriage pulled to a stop. Two broad-shouldered men dressed in coal-dark coats stalked to the last covered wagon. They wrestled with the tarp, revealing the contents underneath.

Amor scanned the scene intently as two prisoners both gagged and bound were hauled from the wagon bed.

"On your feet." One man in a long coat ordered.

Amor noted the captives' movements were slowed by exhaustion. As the cloth gags were pulled from their faces, it became evident that the prisoners were a set of twins. One of them looked at his captors darkly, as if his only thought was to choke the life from the well-dressed men. He probably would have tried if not for the inability to free his hands. Amor figured these men deserved it, but he wasn't here for a show. The exchange was missing one face, one body in which Amor longed to sink his arrow.

On the opposing side of the arena, a shadowy carriage door swung open on silent hinges and shining boots touched down upon stone. The new arrival strolled casually to the small group and smiled. "Gentlemen, fine evening wouldn't you say?"

One of the men folded his arms. "No need for pleasantries Elias. Are you pleased with them?"

"Short and to the point. I like it." Elias chuckled as he stepped around to face the prisoners. "That one looks a little weak." Elias's hand closed around the sickly looking twin's jaw and turned the man's head to his eye level. He scanned the prisoner's thin face and hollow gaze. "Did they not feed you during your travels?"

"It's the *brother* who you'll be most interested in." One of the sellers commented.

"Ah yes." Elias's eyes shifted to the other twin. "I'll buy them both."

The two "gentlemen" raised their eyebrows in surprise. "Both of them? In your correspondence you only showed interest in the one."

"Yes, well..." Elias reached into his jacket pocket and withdrew an envelope. "The Duke changed his mind."

Amor found it strange that neither twin was willing to fight for their freedom. They merely stood silently while their fate was decided for them. It made sense that the thin, gray-tinged twin wasn't attempting retribution. However, it surprised Amor that the brother didn't at least try. Then there was that name, *The Duke*. Was he the mystery man whose strings dangled above the heads of these lawless negotiators?

"They are yours." The man in the coat accepted the envelope with a pleased nod. "As long as you ensure *that* one lives, you can discard the other when you see fit."

Elias surveyed the twins once more. "Both will prove quite useful, I'm sure." He snapped his fingers, and guards left their posts to escort the twins back to the wagon. The other men climbed into their own cart and left the way they came.

Amor's focus trained on Elias and the golden key he briefly flipped in midair and caught with ease. He climbed into his carriage while the prisoners' chains were hooked behind the wagon. Their only choice was to walk behind it or be dragged along. Amor doubted the weak twin would survive the journey. He looked like he might collapse into a heap at any given moment. The driver made a clicking sound with his tongue and the horses steered the cart away.

"Where are you headed, Elias?" Amor questioned under his breath, straightening from his hiding place. He pulled his hood further over his face before following them at a distance. Most people travelled by daylight and on a path. Amor preferred the concealing bluish shadows provided by the moon and the rush that came from leaping from rooftop to rooftop. He would have opted for that method of the chase but Elias's carriage driver made the decision to take the road leading out of the city. Thunder rolled in overhead the instant Amor's boots touched the ground. He kept to the tree line, taking advantage of their gangly wooden limbs to stay out of view.

Yral became a haze of light in the distance the further they traveled. It was soon no longer visible as the wagon stopped in front of a dimly lit lodge. There were no other houses around, only forestry on all sides of the structure. The guards unhooked the chains and led the captive twins into the building, leaving Elias alone and unguarded. Elias pushed the door open and turned his gaze to the sky before a sharp and prolonged whistle filled the night air. Amor watched a black falcon swoop down from one of the trees before landing on Elias's outstretched arm. Elias slipped a square piece of paper into the metal cuff attached to the bird's leg before giving the signal for the falcon to depart.

Pity, Amor thought. *The bird's last assignment was in service to such a creature as Elias.* He didn't take pleasure in the killing of animals, but Amor needed to know what was written on that paper. After all, it was one of two things he'd come for tonight. Amor knelt and selected a jagged stone resting near his boot. He cocked his hand back and threw the rock directly at the falcon's skull. It struck the bird with a crack and its body fell limply to the earth.

Elias turned around. He had been moments away from walking towards the lodge when Amor stepped free of the shadows.

"What is the meaning of this?" Elias demanded.

"Have you ever played with dominoes, Elias?" Amor's voice was void of emotion.

"Excuse me? Who are you and-" Elias glanced at the heap of feathers not too far from them. "Why did you kill my bird?"

"When you tip one tile over," Amor nocked an arrow with a gleaming arrowhead into his bow, "the rest fall in a line right along with it. It's chaos, really."

Elias went still. "Are you going to shoot me with that?" A note of haughty disbelief entered his voice.

"I wouldn't if you had made a different choice." Amor raised his bow. "This is for her." He said under his breath, his green eyes darkening.

"Guards!" Elias shouted and tried to make a break for it.

He was too late. The second he pivoted on his heel, Amor loosed the arrow. It found its mark right between Elias's shoulder blades. Elias crumpled as blooming crimson stained his jacket. His guards burst through the door, swords drawn. When they scanned their surroundings, they realized there was no one in sight. Only the body of the man they were supposed to protect, a poisoned arrow through his heart.

One Year Ago

The Prince kept his prizes in cages. The more valuable the prize, the bigger the plan he had for them. However, these things were always terribly tricky. When they refused to accept their new calling, he stripped away that which made them human. The learning curve had taken decades, but the Prince wasn't alone in his endeavors. After all, a future King needs servants.

CHAPTER FOUR

Julie

The sky threatened to unleash its wrath upon their heads. The clopping of Fiona's hooves against the trail, coupled with the clacking of their wagon wheels, could not be drowned out by the rolling thunder.

"Should we stop until the storm passes?" Maggie craned her neck upwards. The wind whipped, tossing her shoulder-length curls in every direction.

Julie ducked as a swinging branch nearly collided with her face. She tightened her grip on the reigns and replied, "No, we need to try and beat it. Besides, it hasn't started raining yet and we are only fifteen miles from the nearest city." She jerked her thumb backward in the direction of a crudely painted sign.

Maggie stuffed her hands into her sleeves as a cold blast of wind lashed through the trail. "Fiona's nervous."

Julie studied the mare, observing her flicking ears and shallow breathing. *She could sense the storm.* "Come on, girl. Just a little farther." Julie coaxed.

Fiona tossed her mane and kept trudging forward. Five minutes later, beads of water pelted their skin one by one. Maggie pulled her hand out from under her sleeve, watching the rain collect on her palm. "I don't think we're going to outrun it, Jules."

"Well, at least the wagon will get a good wash." Julie shrugged as her gaze snagged on the darkening clouds ahead. *They were heading directly into the storm.*

Sheets of rain cascaded down from above. Julie's jaw set as the path in front of them turned thick and muddy.

"Hold her steady." Maggie warned, casting a glance over her shoulder to the wheels of their wagon. "We don't want to get stuck in the middle of nowhere."

Julie leant forward on the bench as raindrops dripped from her chin. Their surroundings were tinted with an unsettling gray-green hue. Fiona came to a halt... of her own volition.

"I said steady, not to stop entirely." Maggie's lips picked up at the corners and Julie gave her sister a brief look before snapping the reins. "Let's go, Fiona."

Fiona pawed at the mud and tossed her head, sending a spray of rainwater in the sisters' direction. Maggie spat out a wet curl that clung to her lips and said, "What's wrong with her?"

"I don't-" Julie started before a cracking snap reverberated through the air and they froze.

"Maybe a tree branch broke?" Maggie whispered.

Julie used the hand that held the reins to push back wet hair from her forehead. She squinted against the downpour and peered into the dark forestry surrounding them. They had to keep moving or the wheels would sink into the mud.

Another snap emanated from the woods to their right. The chill that crawled over Julie's spine had little to do with the rain-soaked fabric clinging to her body like a second skin.

Cloaked figures. Ten of them, and five were on horseback. They were going to be ambushed if they didn't get out now.

"Hold on." The reins snapped and Fiona broke into a run. The uneven and slippery ground made the wagon's wheels creak in protest. The entire structure rattled, jostling both Maggie and Julie in their seats. As Fiona pulled them along a sharp bend in the path, Julie nearly lurched off the bench. She would have, if Maggie hadn't thrown her arm out across Julie's stomach to pin her down.

Then the wagon veered, eliciting a near synchronized yelp from the sisters. Just as Julie feared, two wheels had been captured by squelching mud.

"What do we do?" Maggie turned to Julie with wide, alarmed eyes.

"Get down. We have to pull the wheels free." They couldn't just unhook Fiona and leave the wagon behind. It was all they had, and they could not afford to lose it.

Maggie and Julie hurried to the side of the wagon. *If they could just push it back up then Fiona might be able to pull it out the rest of the way.*

"Afraid that's not going to help you very much." A deep rumbling voice matched the thunder overhead. Julie's breath caught in her throat and Maggie's lips pursed into a thin line.

The cloaked men from the woods had caught up to them. Past the rain that stung her eyes she realized they were surrounded.

"Come on boys. Let's give these ladies a hand." The stranger's lips curled into a grin.

CHAPTER FIVE

Julie

Julie crept backward as the strangers drew near, shielding her sister with her own body. "We don't want trouble." She said firmly.

One of the men on horseback dismounted. "And we're not looking to give you any." He flicked his wrist, and three other men also left their horses. "On three, we're going to push the wheels free."

Maggie looked as confused as Julie felt. She raised her eyebrows as they were both pushed out of the way for the supposed "outlaws" to get into position.

"One. Two. Three." With that, the men grunted from exertion and heaved the girls' wagon out of the mud.

The rain was beginning to lighten. Maggie and Julie exchanged a glance as Julie said, "Thank you. We appreciate the help."

The first man pulled his riding glove off with his teeth and offered his hand in greeting. "Don't mention it. We didn't mean to frighten you."

"We weren't expecting to see such a large group lurking in the woods." *The group didn't seem to have malintent towards them but what could they possibly give in return? It was awful to think that way, but Julie learned early on everyone wants something in return for the good they do. She'd yet to be proven wrong.*

The man laughed. "We're travelers as well. We're coming from Yral. Our next stop is Seltor."

Maggie stepped forward. "We're on our way to Seltor too." Her soft gray eyes locked with Julie's. She could practically hear her sister's silent question. *Can we ask to join them, so we won't have to travel alone?*

Julie weighed her options. On one hand, it would be safer to travel in a group. However, they had no means of payment for shelter and food until she could earn more aurums in the next city.

Then again, if they were robbed because they chose to go alone, they would have nothing left anyway.

"Is there room in your caravan for two more?" Julie asked, sweeping the wet hair from her shoulders to her back.

"Always." He smiled. "I'm Trace and these are my merry men." More of his group slowly came out of the woods and Julie realized half of them were not merry men but women as well. One of whom walked right up to them and gave the girls the warmest smile. "My name is Lyric." The woman tugged her hood free from her wild, red hair. "Come with me. I'll get you some warm cloaks and the boys can bring your horse and wagon."

Julie took Maggie's hand and cast a glance back to their wagon. The warmth radiating from the gypsy woman helped to chase away Julie's wariness. But, would she ever truly be able to put her trust in a stranger's hands? Pierre had robbed her of blind faith.

"We have family in Seltor." Lyric chattered on as she handed both Maggie and Julie a pair of cloaks to warm them from their rain-drenched cotton clothes. "We'll be meeting them tonight and you will eat with us." She nodded her head as if everything was now settled.

"Thank you for your kindness." Julie gave the woman a smile of her own. Before she could say anything further, Lyric clapped her hands to get Trace's attention. The men worked to readjust the saddlebags on their horses, and she left the girls to have a word with him. As the wind picked up, Julie tied her hair back with a faded red ribbon she wore on her wrist. The cluster of travelers were eager to get a move on before the storm unkindly visited them for the second time that day.

The sun crawled from their grasp by the time they made it to the campground. Laughter and conversation rippled through the air as their new companions set up camp for the night. The energy that surrounded them felt as electric as the static lingering from the storm. As they started walking, Lyric bounded over.

"Where do you two think you're going? You haven't eaten yet." She pointed in the direction of the large bonfire sending amber sparks into the navy sky.

"We didn't want to impose, especially since this is your family's reunion. You've already been kind enough to two strangers." Julie smiled politely.

Lyric laughed, "Strangers? Girl, we were all strangers at one point. That was until we became family."

Julie's gaze flit to the sizable number of gypsies, all dancing and singing. "If you're sure we aren't intruding."

Lyric's smile mirrored the brightness exuding from the fire. "Not at all, as long as you girls can handle some kick to your stew."

Maggie raised her eyebrow, amused. Julie bet she knew what memory floated through Maggie's head at that moment. Thinking back, Mama's cooking only had two levels of heat. Warm, and impossibly warm.

"We can handle it." The sisters said in unison. With that, Lyric snatched both of their free arms. Soon they were seated on wide logs and surrounded by unknown but happy faces.

"One for you and one for you." Lyric handed them their plates and sighed with exasperation when her eyes shot to Trace. He was helping himself to another plate from the large pot on the makeshift table. "Leave some for the rest of us, will you?"

Trace gave her an easy grin, but he only took a bite off his spoon as he stepped away from the pot. "Yes, dear."

"Dear?" Julie blurted, surprised by the statement. Maggie, on the other hand, cackled, "How did you not see it?" Her gray eyes crinkled in amusement. Of course, being the more hopeless romantic of the two, she would have deduced what Julie missed.

Lyric rolled her eyes at Trace but ultimately she laughed too. "Five years and counting." She told the sisters.

"Seven, if you count the two years you ignored me." Trace stated very matter-of-factly.

Julie peered at their hands. *How she hadn't noticed before was beyond her, but there was the string. Strong, bright, and scarlet.*

"I ignored you because you were a brute in your youth." Lyric nudged Trace in the ribs as she sat down.

"Oh, don't say that. You'll make me feel old." Trace groaned. A little girl with beads in her dark braids tumbled into his legs and he swept her up as she squealed in delight.

"Twenty-seven is hardly ancient." Lyric shook her head, as Trace dropped the child into her lap.

Maggie leant her head closer to Julie as Lyric and Trace continued their playful argument of determining exactly who was more stubborn in their younger years. "That's what I want." She whispered.

"Bickering?" Julie mused.

"No." Maggie rolled her eyes. "That undeniable con-nection."

Julie draped her arm around her sister's thin shoulders. "You'll find it. It's only a matter of time." She murmured. Julie would do whatever it took to give her sister the life she so desperately desired and so purely deserved. Fate wasn't in her power to control but at least she could see its strings. Perhaps there was another soul wandering the land, missing his own string, with a heart that would love Maggie unequivocally.

Julie was dragged from her tangled thoughts as Lyric clapped, a sound that summoned all the chattering gypsies to gather around the fire. "We have two lovely guests in our company tonight. I believe it's only right that we share our special tradition with them."

A chorus of agreeing smiles and some scattered cheers turned the energy of the circle into near palpable glee. Julie was almost convinced that if she reached out, their excitement could reverberate through her skin.

"What's the special tradition?" Maggie posed, leaning forward on her elbows as not to miss a word.

"The telling of legends, of course." Trace said, a mysterious air hovering around his words. Every man, woman, and child fell silent in preparation for the promised legends. Trace turned a stick over in his hands as he spoke, "The woods come alive at night..." The twig twirled between his fingers as their ears perked up intently. "But you'd never know it, if you had no warning. The further you go into the forest, the more the claws of silence slink up to deafen you."

The smaller children looked a mixture of intrigued and fearful. Trace was silent for a long moment, before a loud snap echoed through the quiet and several bodies jolted.

Trace smirked and tossed the now broken branch into the fire, fueling its light. "Most refrain from visiting the woods when the shadows of night command its floor, but not everyone." His eyes flicked to each individual around the circle. "Two children fled into the forest one evening, the brambles and thorns at their heels... but those were the least of their worries."

Trace turned his gaze skyward, where the clouds had just begun to part to make way for a few winking stars. "The deeper they went, the more lost they became. And then," he paused, ensuring he still had everyone's attention, "they heard the voices."

Maggie propped her chin up with her hand, enraptured by the tale. "Voices?" She questioned softly.

"Yes, voices." Trace nodded gravely and Julie wondered if he truly believed this story or if it was all an act to scare the little ones. "The children thought perhaps they were saved. That they were not lost." Trace tilted his head. "The voices coaxed them to come closer, further into the trees. The voices said the children would be alright, just to hold on for a little longer."

"Did they get free?" A girl who Julie hadn't noticed yet spoke up.

"They were never seen again." Trace rubbed his jaw thoughtfully. "It is said that anyone who crosses the tree line on the edge of freedom and captivity, will be drawn in by unseen hands. Urging them, no, *luring* them into the woods."

Maggie looked dissatisfied with such an ending. Julie knew Maggie much preferred happy endings. The ones where everything works out, no one gets hurt, and the prince marries the princess. But sometimes the real world wasn't like that. Things didn't always work out. People did get hurt. And the princess just might be missing her soulmate string.

A more burly-looking man interlocked his fingers behind his head. "If everyone who comes close gets sucked in like a dust devil, how did you come to know about it?"

The adults laughed and Trace's lips curled in a smirk. "Are you willing to prove me wrong?"

The man raised his eyebrow before raising his cup halfway into the air. "I know better than to question a bonfire tale." With that, the group applauded the end of the story and Trace sketched a slight bow.

"You all don't actually think that story is real, do you?" Julie asked.

Trace shrugged as he sat cross-legged on the grass. "It's quite a well-known fable in this region. All stories stem from truth at one point in time or another. That's what makes them fun."

Lyric chuckled, "Just be glad he didn't tell the one about the Rogues."

"Oh, that will be perfect for tomorrow." Trace's eyes glimmered.

"Are those the woods the story comes from?" Julie's gaze tracked to the shadowed tree line in the distance, past the hills.

"Yes ma'am." Trace nodded once. "Even if the legend is utterly false, that forest does look eerie at night."

Maggie shivered, "It sure does."

Trace's tale lingered in the corners of Julie's mind as she pulled down a rolled-up blanket from the back of their wagon. Bits of grass and fragments of crunchy leaves still clung to the material from the night before. Julie snapped the fabric out and it fluttered down atop the grass. She settled on the left side of the blanket which was wide enough to fit both sisters.

Julie folded her hands over her stomach as Maggie laid beside her. "We'll have more than this one day. I'll make sure of it."

Maggie rolled over onto her side and propped her head up with her elbow. "What do you mean?"

"I mean there will be a time when you can sleep on a real mattress again, and you'll eat so much you'll pop."

Maggie laughed. A clear and melodic sound. "No one should eat that much. They'll be sick! Besides, we have something people with feather-down mattresses will never get to enjoy."

Julie's gaze shifted to Maggie. "And what is that?"

Maggie lifted her hand skyward and waved her fingers. "A clear view of lights from heaven. All they get to see is some boring old ceiling. We have diamonds that shine just for us."

Julie's hand wrapped around Maggie's. When her sister talked like that, she reminded Julie so much of their mother with her dreamer-like spirit. "You're right, it is quite beautiful."

"Now, let's get some sleep, we have a long journey ahead of us." Maggie rolled flat on her back and shut her eyes. "Love you whole, Jules."

"Love you whole, too." Julie smiled at the familiar saying. Their father started that tradition when they were young. *He'd told them it was easy to love someone to pieces but loving them whole meant that you take them as they are, broken pieces and all.*

CHAPTER SIX

Amor

"The mighty hunter has returned." Silver applauded with mock sarcasm as Amor stalked to the crackling fire.

"I intercepted the message," Amor tossed the bird's limp body into Silver's waiting hand, "and caught dinner."

"Killing two birds with one stone." Silver glanced at the feathery corpse and the matted feathers around the crown of its skull. "Judging by the looks of it, quite literally." He set the falcon on a moss-covered rock. "What of the note?"

"Another place. A meeting, I assume." Amor unfolded the scrap of paper and read aloud, "Ember District. Lodge. Seltor."

Silver scratched the side of his head in thought, "Seltor… that's about thirty miles from here. It's a market village mainly for tradesmen and vagabonds."

"Of course it is." Amor leant against the rough bark of a tree, staring into the weaving smoke of the campfire.

Silver's gaze flicked over to Amor. "You're thinking there's more to this aren't you."

"I'm thinking I'm going to need more arrows." Amor drummed his fingers on his arm. His quiver felt light, especially after wasting so many on that wretched circus.

"I'll have them ready for you by morning." He jerked his thumb backward to the basket filled with fletching tools.

"Thanks, Token." The ghost of a smirk flit across Amor's lips from the familiar nickname. When they'd met, Amor saved Silver's life. He asked if he could somehow offer Amor a token of his appreciation. Amor refused, but Silver's wording had been so amusing to him that the nickname stuck. Their friendship stood the test of time, their routine as natural as breathing. In a world where no one knew you existed nor did they care, it was a refreshing balm to find another like you. Created to be something you weren't born into, subjected to a role you weren't fit for.

"Did you find her?" Silver asked suddenly as he stoked the fire.

"No. But I will find another way."

There was a fleeting, somber look in Silver's piercing blue eyes, but Amor didn't linger on the reason. "Get some sleep, Am. You'll need it."

Amor dipped his chin once in acknowledgment but did not settle down onto the cot by the fire. Instead, he hoisted himself up on the wide and welcoming branches of a sturdy oak. Amor seldom rested well, but his chances of a semi-relaxed state were greater at a higher altitude. On the ground one was too exposed, too easily targeted. From a vantage point like this he could take notice of any threats as they appeared. He learned the mistake of letting his guard down in his youth, but never again. Amor plucked a rough sprig from the bark of the tree his back pressed against, twirling it between his thumb and forefinger.

Elias was dead but he still saw the faces of the four others from that horrible night.

He could still hear her scream. The echoing horror plagued his every waking moment, but not his nightmares. Amor hadn't experienced a nightmare in years. A side effect of feeling numb, he supposed.

Amor wrenched his eyes shut and turned his head to the side as the memory darted behind his eyelids. It wasn't enough to simply shoot a poisoned arrow into their hearts. He would make each one of them grieve until they broke under the weight of their own pain. He wanted the last thing they heard to be their name on the lips of the one they loved more than anything.

Because that is what they had done to him.

Tomorrow would determine exactly what a man with a heart so black could still hold dear.

CHAPTER SEVEN

Julie

The people of Seltor, both residents and travelers, were distracted far too easily for Julie's liking. The sun was reaching its highest peak, bearing down upon them with unforgiving rays. Yet, no visitors came to seek a shadowed reprieve underneath the canvas of their wagon. Julie dipped her fingers into the designated coin cup. She was met with only two aurums, one more than what Pierre used to let them keep. Being a "Seer," as Maggie called her, was both a blessing and a curse. It was a blessing to have the power to bring soulmates together, but a curse to know that some people's strings connect to nothing.

Some people like her sister.

Of course, she could never tell Maggie. One day when the timing was right, Julie would find someone her sister could love. For now, she would make sure Maggie believed a beautiful red thread adorned her hand instead of one ending in tatters.

Julie swallowed and forced her feet forward. Perhaps both sisters were cursed in a way, like Pierre had said. Most days, Julie tried not to pay attention to the abnormality that was her own soul-thread. It wasn't torn and damaged like Maggie's or bright and strong like an inseverable rope.

It was just... black.

When Julie was younger it had been a beautiful color but as the years went on, the thread got a little bit darker until it was completely void of crimson. She tried not to dwell on it, but it was hard when her every waking moment revolved around bringing soulmates together. Only she knew that hers was dead.

Maggie swept her curls back into a cloth headwrap one of the gypsy women had gifted her.

"I don't think anyone's in the mood for a reading today, Jules."

Julie set the cup back down, surveying the bobbing crowd just underneath the cresting hill they were stationed upon. "Or maybe, they don't know what they're miss-ing." Julie wagged her finger pointedly as an idea formed in her mind. "Miss!" Julie donned a welcoming smile as she strode across the grass to a wandering young woman. Judging by the basket in her arm filled with miscellaneous oddities, this woman held an appreciation for the unique.

"Can I help you?" She tucked a hazel-brown curl behind her ear, clearly confused by Julie's reason for approaching.

"Do you fancy yourself a romantic?" Julie questioned, waving a hand toward their wagon and the sign that swung forward and backward in the breeze.

"Oh, um... I suppose?"

"Allow me to give you a reading. I can see where your soulmate string leads."

The brunette looked puzzled. "My soulmate... string? That's actually real?"

Julie blinked. Any time someone denied the existence of their scarlet cord, it came as a surprise. Its existence proved a shred of magic still lingered in their world. "Yes, yes!" She assured the woman. "It's as real as you and I. I'll even give you a deal on the reveal. Two aurums instead of three."

The woman shifted her basket from hand to hand before ultimately nodding and following behind Julie.

"So, what do I do?" The woman took a seat on the rounded stool in front of the table and slid two coins over the tablecloth.

"Let me see your left hand." Julie smiled. When the other female complied, Julie cocked her head, brass earrings clinking. "Oh, a long-distance love I see?"

The woman's shoulders sank almost imperceptibly.

"That cannot be. My husband is from this town."

Maggie's glance switched to Julie, something akin to sympathy in that look.

"Perhaps he's away on business, or traveling?" Julie reasoned, letting go of the brunette's hand.

The woman shook her head, "He's-"

"I've been looking all over for you, Amy." A tall, burly man with a sandy-colored beard stalked up to the wagon. His hands curled around her shoulders. "What's all this?"

"She's a fate-teller, Peter. An entertainer." Amy's body language clearly conveyed her unease. She was comprised fully of stiff shoulders and a clenched jaw.

Peter sneered at the sisters. "A gimmick is what it is." He frowned as he took in the colorful wagon and inviting shadowed sitting area amongst the plush blanket of grass. "Con artists, touting special make-believe gifts for coin."

Maggie's lips pursed in a thin line, slamming her hand down on the table. A jolt of surprise ran through Julie. Her sister usually had the demeanor of a lamb. The outburst reminded Julie more of a ruffled hawk.

"Do *not* accuse my sister of lying. Her gift is real."

The man ignored her. "Did you pay this wench?" His eyes turned to Amy. Julie internally recoiled at the darkness lurking in his bluish-gray gaze.

"She did." Julie stood from her seat, pinning Peter with her stare. "It was a fair business exchange. I provided her with the information that I promised, and she awarded me the compensation the reading required." Julie's hand snaked to the tablecloth, pocketing the two aurums before Peter could swipe them.

The man grumbled. "What was this information that you conjured up? That she's got a strong lifeline and will bear me four sons?" His voice was flat, but Julie noted annoyance simmering underneath his brash exterior.

"If you can read," Julie pointed to the sign above the wagon, "it clearly says I offer revelations regarding the state of a person's soulmate string. Now, I would appreciate it if you would clear this space for the next customer."

"Yes, Peter, can we go?" Amy moved from the stool and Peter's hand slid from her shoulder to her forearm.

"Look what you've done. You've upset her. What did you tell my wife?" Peter sized up Julie with a sort of condescension that either stemmed from pure unbelief or simple aggravation.

"Well, I think it's pretty obvious what the girl told her." Trace and several of his men happened upon the hill at that moment, each with a limp and bleeding deer slung around their shoulders. "You aren't her soulmate and Miss Julie has kindly asked you to vacate the area."

Peter looked between them. His hand flexed on Amy's shoulder once, then twice before deciding it wasn't worth starting a fight he might not win. "This is bull, the lot of it. No one else will be coming to this swindlers cart, I assure you." Peter stated. He and Amy left and soon blended into the crowd along the outskirts of the town.

"You girls alright?" Trace asked, looking between Julie and Maggie.

"We're alright." Julie dipped her chin. "Thank you for your help."

"Don't mention it. People like that make it difficult for people like you, who are trying to make a difference."

"We're just trying to make a living." Julie sighed, tilting her head skyward. "A difference, I can worry about later."

Trace made a thoughtful noise in the back of his throat. "You might as well take the rest of today off and see the city."

"He has a point." Maggie said, bending to pluck a half-crumpled dandelion from the ground. "Maybe a break will do us some good." Julie's sister smiled brightly and pressed the flower into Julie's hand.

Julie tucked the dandelion into her braid. "I guess an hour to explore wouldn't do any harm."

Maggie clapped, filled with a newfound sense of energy. "I want to see the window shops. Lyric was telling me earlier how beautifully decorated they are this time of year."

Julie added the aurums from today to the satchel at her hip. "Then window shopping it is." She linked her arm through Maggie's, who nearly dragged Julie behind her in excitement.

The grass underneath their feet shifted from dirt and gravel to paved cobblestone and wooded boardwalks. The town was a beautiful mess but there was something oddly coherent in the way every shop lined up, one against the other. A sense of symmetry amongst a sprinkle of chaos. Maggie's near skip came to a pause in front of one particular window. "Oh, well isn't that a lovely thing." She breathed, placing her palm against the pane.

Julie took in the object in question. It was a dress made of gray silk and white lace. The sunlight reflecting from the window bounced off the material, making it shimmer. "It's beautiful." Julie's gaze slipped from the gown to her sister's enraptured features. She wished she could get it for her. But even if Julie were to sell everything she had including the clothes on her back, it wouldn't be enough.

"I bet the girl who ends up buying it will go to a ball." Maggie allowed herself one last moment to stare at the garment before she re-hooked her elbow through Julie's.

"A ball sounds awfully stuffy." Julie leant her head against Maggie's shoulder as they walked.

"Stuffy, possibly. Enchanting, most definitely." Maggie laughed and Julie arrived at a silent conclusion in that moment. This way of life, this struggle to make ends meet was not the life she wanted for her sister. Something needed to change, something... *had* to change. Julie wanted Maggie to attend the most lavish of balls and dance with whomever her heart desired.

Julie needed a miracle.

She needed to fulfill the promises she'd made... even the ones Maggie never knew were uttered.

She needed to ensure her sister was well taken care of and eternally happy.

Julie stopped in her tracks. Her breath escaped her like someone wrapped their hands around her lungs and squeezed.

She also needed to know why she was pinned to the cobblestone by a pair of the most startlingly green eyes she'd ever seen.

CHAPTER EIGHT

Amor

Amor hated crowds. On the ground, it was increasingly difficult to track a target in a sea of swarming bodies. This was why he preferred traveling by rooftop. He was partial to the rush of adrenaline which followed leaps across buildings and the satisfaction of a successful landing. From a high-enough vantage point on a particular roof, the entire layout of the city stretched below him. Directions were unnecessary when the map was painted under one's feet.

The Ember district resided in the west side of Seltor. The further Amor traveled, the more apparent it became that the buildings stood in varying degrees of disrepair. Paint was peeling, stones were overturned, shingles were missing from every second roof and most doors were boarded shut. It made sense for them to meet in such a dismal location. They destroyed everything they touched. It was only fitting that their meeting places would be falling to ashes as well.

A few people shuffled on the ground with their heads down. Some were covered in dark cloaks much like his own, but no one spoke. There was little life in this part of the city. Day seemingly ended when one left the marketplace, and night began upon entry into this particular district.

Amor crouched behind one of the roof ledges. The chalky powder from the stone came away on his palm as his hand pressed up against it. The Ember district was for the most part, abandoned. So, why were men slipping into the one tavern whose doors were still open?

Amor jumped down onto the cobblestone street with not a soul aware of his presence. He adjusted the clasp of his cloak, pulling the small square of fabric sewn into the hood up over his nose. The floorboards creaked underneath his boots as he crossed the threshold of the establishment. Only a handful of wary gazes flicked in his direction. He didn't look out of place amongst their dark cloaks, lowered heads and stiffened shoulders. It was not a shock to be greeted with the lingering scent of malintent and trickery in the room. Perhaps it should have frightened him that he had become used to the feeling… that a similar darkness clung to his person.

It didn't frighten him, though. Because when his gaze landed on a face he remembered all too well, it was not regret in his heart. It was hatred. It was the memory of feeling terrified, screaming for them not to take her. The stitches that never healed over his invisible, yet raw wounds reopened as it all came flooding back.

"Is this seat taken?" Amor's voice was slightly muffled by his mask.

The man in question tucked an envelope into his cloak.

"I'm waiting for someone, actually."

"Yes, he won't be able to attend this meeting, unfortunately." Amor cocked his head, one hand curling around the top of the chair.

His eyes darted to Amor. "Keeled over dead on the journey, perhaps?"

"Something like that."

"Well then." The man folded his hands and set them on the table. "Has he sent you in his stead?"

"No." Amor's fingers itched to pull his bowstring back and plunge an arrow into the man's throat. Though, that would only be momentary pain before the relief of death. It wasn't the agony he deserved. His eyes flicked to the pewter band on the man's left ring finger. "That's a new accessory since the last time we crossed paths." Amor commented, his voice taut like a string about to snap.

The man clenched his hand into a fist. "So, we have met before? Did we conduct business in the past that did not meet your expectations? If so, you should get in line." He stood from the table, but Amor firmly locked his hand around the other man's shoulder, pressing him back down.

"I don't think you understand." Amor's voice was devoid of all feeling. "You aren't leaving this place with all the blood you came in with."

The man swallowed thickly. "What do you want? Money? The Seruvian gears for yourself? I'm not in charge of their distribution."

Amor's grip tightened with enough pressure to dislodge a bone from its socket. "I want my sister back."

"Your sister?" The man sputtered, a gasp of pain wheezing past his lips. "I don't even know you, much less your sister!"

"I should kill you right here so that your pitiful soul is forced to stay in such a miserable place. But, I believe you possess the information I am after."

"I don't know anything!" His voice turned frantic, but no other patrons turned their attention to Amor's threats.

"There's nothing you have against me that could possibly coerce me into telling you anything."

"We'll see about that." Amor's jaw tightened. In one smooth motion he withdrew an arrow, broke it in half and plunged the jagged weapon into the man's leg. A grunt left him, blood burbling through the fabric of his pants. Amor's gaze dropped to the man's finger where for a fleeting second, his soulmate string appeared.

Then it was gone. Amor yanked the arrow from the man's thigh, making him double over in his chair from searing pain. The laced arrowhead paralyzed the man, his heartrate slowing to unsteady and struggling beats. "If you even think of leaving this city, I will personally deliver the same fate to your wife." Amor raised the bloodied weapon in front of the man's horrified face.

"You're insane." The man wheezed as he gritted out the words.

Amor did not respond.

The broken arrow lay heavy in Amor's grasp as he stalked out of the tavern. He knew he'd been losing his powers for a while now but usually he could see the strings for longer than the blink of an eye.

He couldn't even see his own anymore.

A voice in the back of his mind couldn't help but question what he was becoming. He didn't care. He sought revenge even more than he craved air to fill his lungs.

It seemed impossible that men utterly blinded by greed could love. But they must, as evidenced by the man's wedding ring. Amor scoffed to himself.

Who could possibly fall in love with such a killer.

The sunlight crept out from behind the canopy of clouds as Amor left the Ember district. To his slight annoyance, he stumbled across a small gathering of passersby. They all crowded around a fountain where a very frustrated man vehemently protested some traveling sideshow. *People allow themselves to be entertained by anything these days.* Amor pushed his way silently through the barrier of bodies. He was almost through the crowd when the words, 'Fate teller' and 'Soul string' floated to his ears.

Amor stopped, turning his attention to the man with a sandy-blonde beard and a gleam in his eyes.

"They're con artists, those girls." He spat. "Nothing more than pretty faces to lure you in and trick you."

"To think, I almost went to their wagon." One person sounded shocked, as if they'd already been swindled by these so-called fate tellers.

Something nagged at the back of Amor's mind. *It couldn't be the same woman, could it? The one he'd searched for in The Circle of Lights?*

The crowd dispersed and the bearded man looked satisfied at driving away any potential customers these mysterious fortune tellers may have procured.

"Where could one find their wagon?" Amor asked the man. When he didn't respond, Amor waved a casual hand and lied. "I have family coming into town. I'd hate for them to be blindsided."

The man thrust his thumb over his shoulder. "On the edge of town." His eyes then tracked to the street across from the fountain. "Well, looks like they've left their cart. The swindlers are over there."

Amor followed the man's gaze to two women walking arm in arm along the sidewalk. One of them pointed excitedly to every window they passed before stopping in front of one particular shop.

"A ball sounds awfully stuffy." The taller of the pair commented as they peeled away from what Amor now realized was a dress shop.

"Stuffy, possibly. Enchanting, most definitely." The younger girl sighed dreamily, leaning her head on the other woman's shoulder.

It was her. The girl in the scarlet dress who'd thrown something into the path of his arrow, setting the circus aflame. She didn't look like your typical deceiver, but appearances could tell a thousand lies. Perhaps the heat of his stare caused her to lift hazel eyes in his direction and she stopped in her tracks.

He had her within his sights once. This time he wouldn't let her slip through his grasp.

CHAPTER NINE

Julie

"It's you." Julie's eyes swept over the broad-shouldered man in front of her, recognition sparking in her mind. The onyx bow, the emerald cloak kissed with shadow, the black hair falling into glittering green eyes... he was the Dark Archer from *The House of Roses*.

"You're the fate-teller people are talking about?" He questioned.

"Yes...?" Julie replied, hesitancy woven into her voice. *How had he found them? Was he working with Pierre? What if he was here to drag them back to The Circle of Lights?*

"Prove it." The man's emerald-green eyes flicked between Julie and Maggie.

Julie blinked at him. "If you want a reading, you're welcome to visit our wagon-"

The man reached inside his cloak and Julie pulled Maggie behind her protectively. However, he only withdrew a small satchel of clinking coins and handed it to her.

"This should cover your going rate."

"I..." Julie fumbled for her words. This was an odd exchange. In her grasp, lay more money than they'd been able to save in the two years with *The Circle of Lights*. "If I can see your left hand?" Julie handed Maggie the pouch and outstretched her hands palms-up toward the green-eyed man.

"Not me." He took one step backward and swiped his hand over his slightly shadowed jaw. Julie glanced at his hand and to her absolute shock she realized that he had no string at all.

He looked around the square, ultimately selecting a young couple who smiled as they walked, hands entwined with one another's. "What about them?"

Maggie shrugged in her confusion but nodded for Julie to go ahead. Julie stepped out onto the street, approaching the couple in question. "You both are a lovely couple. Would you like to know if you're soulmates, at no cost?" Julie adopted her sparkling smile and warm tone. "I can see your soulmate strings if you're interested."

The girl laughed. "Why not? Although I think I might be able to answer that myself." She looked adoringly at the young man whose eyes watched her with the same level of affection. That look of overly brimming love pulled at something in Julie's heart. Someone would look at Maggie that way, one day.

Julie eased the girl's soft hand into her own, noting how short her soulmate string was. It was wrapped completely around the young man's wrist, not just his finger.

"You are so fortunate to have found each other. Treasure this happiness." Julie squeezed the girl's hand before leaving them to return to the slightly unnerving gaze of her unexpected customer. "They're soulmates."

"Mmhmm." He nodded thoughtfully and Julie would have expected anything other than what he did next. He had a smooth black bow in his grip, the string pulled back, with an arrow nocked.

"Wait!" She cried, but her words were synonymous with the snap of the bowstring as the arrow pierced the air. It plunged its razor-sharp tip into the back of the young man who'd looked upon his girl with such love. Everything happened in slow motion. The Dark Archer squinted, struggling to see something lost on Julie but then the arrow... vanished? There was no gushing, open wound.

The young man merely turned around as if looking for whomever tapped his shoulder before shrugging it off.

The jaws of both sisters fell open in sync, trying to desperately piece together what was happening before their eyes.

"Interesting." He tucked his bow back behind him and turned his gaze to the girls. "You were telling the truth."

Julie's head was swimming. "What... what did you just do? What *are* you?" Maggie seemed to be just as dumbfounded, but she was quieter in her surprise.

"I was testing the validity of your claimed gift." He said simply. "As for what I am, I could ask you the very same thing." Julie noticed he refused to lean against the façade of the building. Maybe the tension he clearly held in his shoulders wouldn't let him.

"We're just trying to make an honest living." Julie explained, biting back her retort.

"Yes, and tell me..." His words trailed off, awaiting her name.

"Julie." She watched him warily, waiting for the moment he might decide to redraw that bow and shoot them both for his personal target practice.

"Julie." He repeated, testing out the name on his tongue. "Tell me, Julie. What is your price to have your... gifting at my disposal?"

"Can I talk to you for a moment?" Maggie interrupted, speaking out for the first time since they'd met the archer. She pulled Julie away by the arm until they ducked underneath a boutique's blue and green striped awning. "What is happening right now?" She whispered.

"I don't know." Julie pinched the bridge of her nose. "How much did he give us in that pouch?"

Maggie turned the velveteen bag over, spilling its contents into her hands. "There are at least thirty aurums here." She breathed in awe.

"So money's not an object for him." Julie thought aloud. *How much more could they earn if she accepted his offer*? She might be able to actually save some of it and put it toward a better future for Maggie.

Then again, did she really want to agree to a deal with someone who just shot a man without a flicker of emotion?

"What do you think we should do?" Julie's gaze fell into her sister's soft gray eyes.

Maggie exhaled slowly. "I don't know anything about him..."

"But you think we should agree." Julie finished for her.

"Yes. Though you should inform him you want the right to back out of this agreement if it explicitly puts you in danger."

"Or you." Julie added firmly.

Maggie stuffed the coins back into the pouch and tucked it into her belt. "Well, I'm thinking you would be the one in harm's way, not me." She shook her head in amusement.

"And I'm thinking, you're my only priority."

Maggie pulled Julie in for a quick hug and told her, "Who knows? This might be what we've been hoping for."

Julie nodded as they stepped out from under the alcove. She had wished for a miracle... but she wasn't sure a miracle should come armed with arrows.

Julie was unsurprised to see the man had not moved. He was staring toward the west of Seltor with his spine rigid, boots firmly planted and jaw set.

"Each time you are in need of my gift, I require thirty aurums like the amount you gave for the initial reading." Julie stated.

He shifted his piercing gaze to her, "Of course-"

"And if this agreement puts me or my sister in danger, I reserve the right to back out." Julie gestured to Maggie, interrupting him before he could finish his sentence.

"Naturally." The word flowed over his lips so easily that Julie couldn't help but wonder if he was a trained liar. His tone did not hold the weight of truth it should have, and that unnerved her.

"Also, the side of my wagon needs to be painted." The emblem for *The Circle of Lights* was still emblazoned on their stolen cart. Julie didn't want the design to draw unwanted attention.

A slight look of confusion darted over his features and Julie found satisfaction in it. "Okay? I'm sure there's someone in this bleeding city that can paint it."

"No. I'm adding that to my terms." Julie planted her hands on her hips.

The man's full lips flattened. The frustration simmering underneath his cloaked surface was nearly tangible.

"Fine."

A real conversationalist, that one. "Good."

"Let's go." With no further instruction he started to leave, just *expecting* Julie to follow blindly.

"Wha-" Julie sputtered. "Right now?"

He sighed, turning back around. "Yes, right now." Annoyance bled into his voice.

Julie rolled her eyes. "At least let me get my sister back to our hosts."

"I don't have much time to lose." He said flatly.

"I can get back on my own, Jules." Maggie pressed her hand to Julie's shoulder comfortingly. "Be careful."

Julie paused. "Are you sure?"

"Yes, she's sure. Look, she's already leaving." The Dark Archer waved his hand toward Maggie who nodded and started to slip away from them. Julie resisted the temptation to glare in his direction.

"Are you on the run or something?" She quipped, having to quicken her pace to keep up with his long strides.

"No." He didn't even spare her a passing glance.

"Then why are you so pressed for time?"

"Because I am. Now, be quiet." Finally, he slid his green gaze to her.

Julie's eyebrows narrowed and she planted her sandals directly in front of his path, blocking him. "Look, I'm doing this because I need the money to take care of my sister. But do not dare tell me to be quiet again." She stabbed her finger into his chest.

His dark eyebrows barely flicked up. "I was telling you to stop talking so we blend in, look." He placed firm hands on Julie's shoulders, effectively turning her to see their entrance into a dismal district of Seltor.

The people on the streets barely made noise other than the shuffling of their own feet.

"I don't like being on the ground, and your dress is startlingly red. It's better not to draw added attention to yourself." His hands fell away from her shoulders and his steps resumed.

Julie sighed through her nose. *This was coming from the man who loosed an arrow in the middle of town square.*

"Alright."

"Hold on." He abruptly stopped and unhooked his cloak, removing it from his frame. Without the dark fabric, Julie's eyes were immediately drawn to the bow and the quiver of arrows strapped to his back. He wore a deep green vest, with a white shirt tucked into fitted black pants. Wide leather bracelets took up both of his wrists. Now that his head was not concealed by the hood, she also saw that his hair was messy in the way it carelessly fell into his eyes.

"Put this on." He thrust the material into her arms.

This was probably to cover her 'startlingly' red dress. Julie grumbled in her mind as she pulled the cloak on. It smelled like it had been laid out to dry in the sun, and a little like pine and burning embers. He tugged the hood of the cloak over Julie's hair and stalked towards one building in particular.

Julie had to hold the bottom hem of the cloak up, so she didn't trip on it. She briefly glared at the retreating back of the Dark Archer. With each step she took to follow him, one thought would simply not leave her alone.

Whatever she was getting herself into might not be worth thirty aurums.

CHAPTER TEN

Julie

"Use your Sight on him." The man turned to Julie as he brought her in front of one specific chair barely propping up a slumped over man. Something dark and sticky stained the unconscious man's leg and Julie feared his slumber was not from drunkenness.

"Is he dead?" Julie's eyes darted to the other patrons.

The Dark Archer tapped something at his hip slowly. "No."

"That's reassuring." Julie rolled her shoulders and eased the man's limp hand into her own for a better angle.

Her new employer sighed. "I thought this reading thing was quick work."

Julie narrowed her eyes. "Calm down, your impatient-ness. I can see it."

"Fantastic. Where does it lead?"

The bleeding man's string limply strung itself over the table and out the door. Julie focused her vision on it as she followed the cord into the street. Unfortunately, this also meant her grumpy partner was at her heels as well. Julie craned her neck back as the string roped up and around what looked like a dilapidated hotel before vanishing into one of its dingy windows. "His string leads there." She pointed.

The Dark Archer gave a curt nod and started to walk away in the direction she gestured.

"Is that it?" Julie's eyebrow flicked up.

He turned on his heel, a momentary look of confusion passing over his shadowed features. "That's all I needed today."

That was the easiest thirty aurums she'd ever earned. It was also the first time she'd earned such a sum in one day. "Alright, but don't forget about my wagon."

"Your wagon...?"

Of course, he'd already forgotten.

"You said you'd paint it." Julie raised her chin.

He adjusted the strap of his quiver over his chest and just looked at the sky. "Right." With that sorry excuse for a reply he started to leave yet again.

Julie pinched the bridge of her nose and started after him, hiking up the length of his cloak around her ankles.

"Did you not hear me say we're done for today?" His emerald eyes shifted over to her in the same instant that she unhooked the clasp and pulled the garment off her shoulders.

"My ears work fine, thank you very much." She pushed the cloak into his arms. He must not have been expecting it because the gesture actually pushed him backward a step.

"One more thing." Julie grabbed his sleeve before he could take off, because heaven knows she wouldn't chase him.

"Yes?" His impatience was thinly veiled.

"You've not told me your name. If we're going to work together, I would like to call you something other than the Dark Archer."

His eyebrows furrowed briefly. "Is this really necessary?"

Julie's mouth set, unbudging. He shook his head and redonned his cloak, covering the weapons that lay strapped to his frame. "It's Amor."

If that wasn't the most ironic thing. The most prickly man she'd ever met was named after love. The 'Dark Archer' suited him better. "That wasn't so hard, was it?" She thrust her hand out to him.

Amor looked down at it. "I don't care for those kinds of frivolities."

How could someone exhaust you so after only being in their company for less than a day? "I'd say goodnight but that's a frivolity too, isn't it?"

"Yes." He didn't spare her another moment before he vanished behind the hotel's creaking doors, leaving Julie alone on the edge of the dusty street.

She hugged the sides of the path as she walked out of the district. The off-putting looks she received were rare, but they all conveyed one message. *'You don't look like you're supposed to be here.'* Perhaps she should have kept Amor's cloak on and left. After all he couldn't have much of a sentimental attachment to the garment if she had to practically flag him down to return it.

The stars made their debut for the night by the time Julie returned to camp. She climbed into the wagon, lighting the small lantern hanging from a hook on its arched ceiling. She sat cross-legged in front of the small, chipped mirror nailed into the interior. The reflective surface was dingy, but she could see well enough to remove her glass jewelry.

"I thought you were one of the kids playing hide and seek." Maggie popped her head in, peering through the open back door. Her curls were tied back in a braid, dotted with field flowers.

"It looks like they got to you first." The corners of Julie's lips lifted as she settled her earrings into a bit of cloth to keep them from scratches.

Maggie's hand drifted to the braid, laughing. "I was swarmed and one can never turn down the chance to be pampered."

"The more coins that man gives us, the quicker you get your chance for a real pampering." Julie stretched her arms behind her.

Maggie climbed into the wagon, perching atop the trunk that housed their few clothes. "That was a real pampering. The little ones were so gentle when my curls got tangled. It reminded me of how mother used to brush it." Maggie plucked one of the daisies from the middle of the woven hairstyle.

"You know what I mean." Julie took her sister's forearms and tugged her over so Maggie could curl into her side. They had to scrunch up their legs in order to fit in the wagon. If they had each been a bit shorter, they could have fit nicely instead of having to sleep outside.

"I wish I remembered more about her, but her face has started to blur in my memory."

Julie leant her head back, watching the swaying lantern cast shadows across the objects in front of them. "You got your eyes from her." Julie's hand softly traced Maggie's arm. "And the way you talk."

Maggie turned soft, gray eyes to her sister. "You got yours from father, didn't you?"

Julie rested her cheek against the top of Maggie's head. "I think so." Maggie had been so young when they'd been taken from them. While Julie wished she'd inherited her father's strength... there were times she felt so weak that she questioned if he'd passed it down to her at all.

"Tell me one of his stories?" Maggie asked quietly. She sounded like she had when she was merely ten years old, instead of the 19-year-old woman she was now.

"Well, one that he favored over all the others was his tale of the siren and the sailor." Julie recalled being no more than seven when she'd sat on his knee, eagerly awaiting all the twists and turns that would form with his words.

"Once upon a time, there was a weary sailor, lost amongst the tumultuous waves and the starry nights." Julie began. "He'd traveled a great distance in his search for the Onyx Pearl, the rarest gem of the ocean. Whoever captured it would become immensely wealthy and attain a position of high power. Seeing as the sailor didn't come from much, he saw the Pearl as his ticket to a better life."

"Did he find it?" Maggie interrupted, already enraptured in the tale.

Julie shook her head. "His ship was pulled to the depths of the sea by monsters but at the very last moment he was rescued by a siren. A beautiful, ethereal creature with hair like a raven's feather and skin like snow. She took him and swam to safety. To a cove never before discovered by any man. She could only speak his language partially, but she cared for him nonetheless."

"Did they fall in love?" Maggie waggled her eyebrows playfully.

Julie tapped her nose. "Not all fairytales end with love."

Maggie huffed. "They should. You can't seriously tell me they didn't."

Julie paused for a long moment to keep her sister in suspense before she conceded with a dramatic sigh. "Okay, okay. They fell in love." *That's not how her father told the story, but it was the story Maggie needed.*

Maggie made a contented noise. "I knew it."

"It was more important than ever that he locate the Onyx Pearl. Because, now his ship lay at the bottom of the sea with every belonging he had."

"Why didn't he ask the siren? Wouldn't she know the ocean better than anyone?"

"That's exactly what he did." Julie hummed. "Since her heart was so filled with love for the sailor, she agreed to give up the location of the Pearl."

"But," Julie interrupted her own story, "when the siren brought the sailor to shore instead of taking him to the Pearl, he was confused."

Maggie snapped her fingers. "Maybe it was her way of not letting him go? Because if he had the Pearl then he would live on land, and they would be apart."

"No, it was much more of a sacrifice than that. You see, the siren *was* the Onyx Pearl. She was willing to give herself up so that he could have the life he always wanted."

Maggie wiggled away from Julie's side and gave her sister a stern look. "Julie Camila Seir, tell me he made the right choice."

"What would be the right choice?" Julie tried to keep her laugh from bubbling to the surface. She always found it so amusing how attached her sister got to fictional characters.

"Forgetting about that wealth and glory nonsense to be with the girl he loves." Maggie stated very matter-of-factly.

"They were from two different worlds, Mags." Julie reminded her sister.

"Worlds, schmorlds." Maggie waved her hand flippantly. "They love each other, they're going to have to figure something out."

A laugh escaped Julie. "Alright, I'm done teasing you. The sailor decided that to turn her in for the reward would be the equivalent of ripping his own heart out. So, he left the world he once knew in order to be with the rarest gem of the ocean, and the gem of his heart."

Maggie gave Julie a sparkling smile. "Who knew father was so sappy with his stories."

"Who knew?" Julie echoed, knowing very well the original tale took a much darker turn. Julie had to admit she liked the thought of a happy ending for the sailor and his siren. Maggie settled back to rest against her. After a few comfortably quiet moments she asked, "What happened today with the Dark Archer?"

Julie loosed a breath. "Oh, Amor."

Maggie raised her brow. "Giving him nicknames already are we?"

Julie sputtered for a second. "Oh Fates, no. That's actually his name, odd isn't it?"

Maggie shrugged from her half-slumped position. "Less odd and more interesting. Although, I have to say it doesn't fit him well. He seemed very... stoic."

"He's up to something but I think the less questions we ask, the better. Hopefully, soon we'll have enough money saved to leave and start fresh somewhere beautiful."

"I wonder what it would take to get him to laugh." Maggie smirked, "That would be a sight."

"If you can get a laugh out of that man I will be amazed."

Maggie nodded. "Challenge accepted."

Julie hugged her sister tight. That was her Maggie, always ready to bring joy into someone's life.

Although, Julie couldn't help but wonder if Amor thought joy itself was a 'frivolity.'

CHAPTER ELEVEN

Amor

The sound of the woman's hiccupping sobs was giving Amor a headache. The scuffle of wooden chair legs against stone scratched dust into the air as she tried to pry her body free. Particles rained down, highlighted by the thin shred of moonlight pouring through the tattered roof. "Be quiet." Amor said, his annoyance palpable.

To his distaste, this only made the woman wail more. Her screams were muffled by the gag in her mouth. The shrieking roused the previously unconscious man from his state with a groan of discomfort. When his eyes landed on his wife, bound to a rickety old chair in the middle of an abandoned warehouse, he swore. "Sara!" Then he saw

Amor and yelled with every ounce of strength he could muster. "Don't hurt her! Let her go!"

Amor deliberately circled the chair as the woman attempted to shake her way free. "Are you now wishing you had been more forthcoming with your information?"

The man tried to lunge for Amor, but the poison in his veins coupled with his restraints worked against him. "I told you. I don't know what you're after!"

Amor's eyes narrowed. "Perhaps, you require some motivation." Amor reached into his cloak and withdrew a blade. The handle was foreign in his grip, but his intent was clear. The man's eyes locked onto the serrated edges of the knife and a growl sounded in his throat as Amor brought the gleaming silver just underneath the woman's jaw. "Do *not* touch her!"

The man's wife stared at Amor with wide, terror-filled eyes and her chest rose and fell in panic. She whimpered jumbled pleas, but Amor pushed them from his mind. "It's simple. Offer me the location of your associates or she dies."

The bound man gritted his teeth before spitting in the direction of Amor's feet. "I call your bluff."

Amor's eyebrows flicked up slightly. "Pity." The point of the knife pressed into the delicate underside of the woman's rapidly paling chin. A thin stream of blood dripped from the puncture.

"Stop! Stop." Fear finally sunk its dark claws into the man. "I'll give you what you want!"

Amor didn't pull the blade away. "You have ten seconds."

"I only know where Pascale and Varian are. I swear on my life I don't know where the Duke is."

There was that name again. *'The Duke.'* "Locations. You have five seconds left."

The man swallowed thickly. "They're both in Seruvia."

A flicker of recognition flashed in Amor's mind as the syllables of that city echoed across the musty space.

"And what of this, *Duke*?" Amor shifted his grip on the dagger's hilt, eliciting a gasping cry of pain from the woman.

The man panted in his struggle to free himself but to no avail. "He gives the orders, and we carry them out, that's all I know!"

Amor slowly withdrew the tip of the blade and the man's shoulders slumped in relief. "I gave you what you want, now release us."

Amor's eyes flit over to him. "Don't worry, you will live to see another day." The words were empty as Amor turned to the trembling wife.

Tear-rimmed, bloodshot eyes locked with Amor's as the knife slashed her throat. Blood sprayed onto Amor's hands and cloak as her husband, now a widower, cried out.

"What have you done?!" Fury and shock lashed through his voice while he choked on a garbled sob.

Amor stepped away from the body, discarding the knife into the corner of the dusty warehouse. "You shouldn't have brought her into your twisted world. She was bound to get hurt."

"You..." Hatred and pain dripped from the man's voice. "I'm going to rip your heart out!"

Amor crouched down to the man's level, swiping the unsettling sensation of an innocent's blood from his cheek. He held the man's gaze, burning with venom.

"You already did."

In the pale wash of the moon, Amor could still see the stains on his hands no matter how vigorously he tried to scrub them. They seemed to settle into every line of his palm, every crevice. *He could wash his hands until they bled, until the skin was utterly raw, but he could never be cleansed of his actions.*

"Long day?" A gentle voice met Amor's ears. Silver eased down on the riverbank beside him, flicking stones and pieces of twigs into the water.

Amor shifted his gaze to Silver for a moment, but the right words perished on his tongue.

"That's a yes." Silver locked his fingers around one of his knees and drew it to his chest. He was quiet for a few moments before he spoke again. "Do you feel different?"

Amor shook the droplets of water from his hands. He knew what Silver was truly asking... whether or not he felt better. "No."

Silver nodded once, slowly. "Do you ever think you will?"

Amor tilted his face to the sky, seeking answers in the constellations but the stars mocked him. Perhaps they were mute for the stains on his hands, or sorrowful for the destruction he carried with him like a shadow. Either way, they granted him no relief.

"I don't think peace will find me until I've avenged her." Amor turned his eyes from the stars only to find Silver staring at them himself with silent longing.

"Do you wonder if they think of us?" He questioned. It was so quiet Amor wondered if Silver meant to voice that aloud.

"Maybe." His fingertips slowly reached up, hovering in the air to trace the outline of a constellation. Amor didn't know if the stars thought of them. He hoped they couldn't see what became of the ones they left behind.

Silver dragged a hand through his hair and stood to his feet. He brushed the dirt from his pants, angling his head towards camp. "Come on, let's move toward the fire before it turns colder."

Amor unhooked his cloak from the tree branches above him before he followed Silver deeper into the forest. The embers braiding through the curling smoke welcomed them.

Amor sat on the wooden stump in front of the flames, draping the forest-green fabric over his knee. His hand ghosted atop the crimson splatters now adorning it. When he turned the material over, his fingers caught on a single strand of red thread. He pinched it between his forefinger and thumb, holding it in front of his face. Silver bent and placed a wooden bowl of stew on the log beside Amor, his eyes catching on the string. "So, when are you going to tell me what happened today?" The blue-eyed man settled down amongst the grass with his own bowl in hand.

Amor let the thread dangle in front of the fire, yet to toss it in. "I found the woman, from the circus. We've made a deal, thirty aurums for her abilities."

Silver's eyebrow quirked. "I thought the circus was destroyed?"

Amor's gaze settled on the burning charcoal at the base of the fire. "She escaped with her sister."

"Ah." Silver dipped his chin in acknowledgment. "What's her name?"

Amor twined the crimson thread around his finger. Although it was the same color as the stains along his palms, something about it was different. "Julie."

"Sounds like a sweet girl." Silver chewed a bite of his stew thoughtfully.

A slight scoff traveled over Amor's lips. "I've seen sweeter wolves, Token. She's exasperating and relentless."

Silver stirred the broth in his bowl. "And yet, you let her wear your cloak." His eyes flicked to Amor whose jaw promptly set as the thread around his finger was discarded into the fire.

"She stood out like a burning flare in the Ember District. I was forced to."

The ghost of a smile crossed Silver's features, gone as rapidly as it came. If Amor hadn't been watching, he might not have even caught it. "I see."

Amor turned his attention to his stew, noting the way the broth darkened the bowl. "I need to find paint." He muttered.

Silver sputtered a surprised laugh, blue eyes twinkling with mirth. "Excuse me?"

"She's making me paint the side of her wagon." Amor shook his head. "I don't have time for such things."

Silver tossed a few more sticks into the flames, watching them lick up the wood greedily. He chuckled, "I like her. It sounds like she gives you a run for your money... literally."

Amor cut him a look. "At least it's not my money." He shrugged. He would have to leave early in the morning to pickpocket thirty more aurums for her payment.

After he had eaten, Amor folded his cloak over his arm and turned on his heel towards his favored tree. Before he took more than two steps, Silver spoke quietly, "Am, are you sure this is a good decision? Bringing her into this?"

Amor glanced over his shoulder, "It's a good decision when you have nothing to lose."

He could tell that Silver wanted to speak further but held his tongue. "Alright then, get some rest. You have a big art project to tackle tomorrow."

Amor sighed and shook his head, hoisting himself up into the branches for a sliver of solace. His gaze scanned the forest before dropping to the campfire below.

He was glad he'd thrown away that thread from her dress. It wasn't as if he would have held onto it, because that was ridiculous. The more he thought about it, the more he realized the color wasn't that different from the shade on an abandoned dagger in a lonely warehouse.

CHAPTER TWELVE

Julie

Julie was unable to bite back her smile as she gingerly wrapped the necklace and the small vial of fragrance in a bit of blue cloth. *Maggie would love these.* Her sister's birthday was tomorrow, and Julie rushed to town while Maggie slept to purchase the gifts. Julie had been nearly giddy when the shopkeepers told her the price of both items and she had *just* enough to buy them. They would start saving the aurums that Amor paid them from now on, but Maggie deserved a proper birthday. It was her twentieth, after all.

The limp brown string she had didn't quite match the velvet of the cloth nor the presents inside. But, she arranged the bow in a way that daintily draped over the cloth. On a small slip of paper that Julie used as a tag she wrote: ***Happy 20th birthday to the best sister ever. I love you whole, Mags.***

As soon as she finished writing, a thud and a clang reverberated into the wagon that sounded incredibly close. Julie jerked, pressing the objects to her chest in an effort to hide them. *Maggie was outside.* Julie stashed the presents underneath a pillow in one fluid motion. She flung open the back window, only to be met with a piercing pair of emerald eyes.

"Oh, it's you." Julie swiped her hand over her face.

"Good to see you too." Amor said flatly. Julie had to fight the urge to roll her eyes at the amount of masked sarcasm in his tone. "Where do you want the paint?" He lifted the can halfway in midair and Julie noticed he was without his cloak.

And his quiver.

And his bow.

Julie leant into the window's small ledge. She pointed at the opposing face of the wagon with *The Circle of Light's* logo scrawled across its exterior. "That entire side will do."

Amor didn't spare her another glance before moving to the side as instructed.

"Where's your stuff?"

"My stuff?" Amor glanced up at her from his knelt position to undo the lid from the paint container.

"Your archery things."

"Not far." He replied, standing and rolling his sleeves a quarter of the way up to reveal tanned and muscular forearms. If his arms were any indication, then perhaps the reason he appeared at ease without his weapons was because he embodied one.

"I didn't think you were going to show up." Julie set her hand on her hip, watching him closely in an attempt to decipher his expressionless exterior.

"The sooner I get this over with, the better." Amor dipped the bristled brush into the bucket.

"Speaking of, when will I get paid next?"

Amor's brows furrowed briefly. Yet, he didn't shift his attention from his task at hand. "I paid you yesterday. Surely you didn't spend it all in one day."

When Julie didn't offer up a response, Amor turned to her with a baffled look. "Don't tell me you did exactly that."

"It's my money and I will do with it what I please." Julie raised her chin. "Not that you deserve an explanation, but it's my sister's birthday tomorrow."

"Oh." Amor said abruptly, and Julie noted that his grip on the wooden paintbrush tightened.

"I don't expect you to understand. You probably classify birthdays as frivolities." Julie gathered her hair away from her neck as the sun beat down, tying it up with her faded red ribbon.

To Julie's absolute befuddlement he asked, "What did you get her?"

Julie looked up and squinted in the sun's general direction. "A necklace... and rose water." She said slowly, trying to get a read on him, but he was about as easy to decipher as one of the lost languages of old.

Amor dipped the brush back into the paint and fell silent when Maggie came bounding over like a fawn in a meadow. "He actually showed up?" Maggie leant in, whispering to Julie.

"I'm as surprised as you are."

"Lyric wanted me to ask you if we could help with lunch. She has her hands full with the kids."

Julie nodded, casting her gaze to the bottom of the hill where the gypsy camp was located. "Of course. What's wrong with the kids?"

Maggie scratched the side of her head. "The little ones seem to be coming down with something. So far, it's only the youngest that are affected."

"Tell her I'll be right there." Julie patted Maggie's arm as her sister nodded and whisked herself down the hill.

"I have to help a friend so-"

"I'll make sure the wagon is finished before I leave." His green eyes sharpened as the sunlight struck them.

"Good." Julie took a quick survey of his progress, deeming it decent work before she followed her sister.

The sun was no longer at its highest peak and the breeze roaming freely through the camp was a welcome sensation on Julie's skin. She pushed back damp pieces of hair from her face and neck as her eyes traveled upwards. Julie made out Amor's silhouette, still working diligently in the heat.

She sighed. Just because she found his company frustrating, didn't mean that he should go thirsty. She found a cup and filled it with water before ascending the grassy rise.

Somewhere between the time she'd left him to continue working and now, he had abandoned his vest and shirt. The slowly settling sun cast both shadows and light in hues of shifting gold over his chest. The rays highlighted every particularly defined muscle and vein. She knew archers possessed a certain amount of strength, but seeing him now, it was obvious that Amor was a weapon in his own right.

He looked like he'd been painstakingly crafted by the stars themselves.

Julie wanted to splash the cup of water in her face as a scolding for thinking such a thing, but she determined that it would be of better use if he drank it instead. "Here."

Amor jolted slightly, perhaps lost in his own thoughts to the point he was unaware of her presence. She could only hope that was the case.

"What's this?" His eyes flicked to the cup, the brush hovering from his hand in midair.

"Vinegar." Julie said flatly and at Amor's uncertain look she continued, "It's water. I figured it wouldn't be conducive if you died of heatstroke."

Amor studied the cup that was still in her hand before he set the brush down and reached out to take it.

Julie hadn't expected his fingertips to graze her knuckles during the exchange, nor was she exactly appreciative of the lingering tingle it left in her hand. *Maybe she was allergic to him.*

"Thank you." Amor said nothing about the accidental touch, and it was unlikely he even noticed with how he gulped the water down like a drowning man needed air.

Julie hummed a response and stepped around him to garner a better look at the side of her wagon. It was an excellent alternative to the much more awkward option of looking everywhere but his bare chest.

"You did well." She said over her shoulder. He hadn't missed a singular crevice or notch in the paneling. Not even a sliver of the previous design was left. A clean slate. This type of quality paint job would have cost her dearly had she been paying for it.

The soft sound of rustling cloth met her ears and when she turned back around, Amor had redonned his shirt and vest. "How long will it take you to pack?"

"What do you mean?"

"We are going to travel to Seruvia day after tomorrow. You and your sister need to pack whatever you deem necessary, and I will take you to your new camp."

Julie's stomach dropped and her gaze flit to the glowing fire underneath the hill that the gypsies circled around. "Oh..." They were safe here. *Maggie* was safe here.

But if she didn't go with him, then she couldn't afford to build the type of life for her sister that would allow her to thrive.

Determination steeled her resolve. "Alright. I'll tell her, and we'll pack up the wagon."

Amor's eyes darted between her and the structure he'd freshly painted. "No, we can't bring the wagon."

Julie tried not to balk but it was difficult. "Yes, we're bringing the wagon."

Amor dragged a hand through his hair. Whether from agitation or exhaustion, Julie couldn't tell. He was silent for the longest moment, and she found herself holding her breath for his response.

Had she gone too far? Did she just blow their only chance of earning a decent living?

Finally he expelled a long, slow breath. "Fine."

Julie almost melted with relief, but she squared her shoulders instead. "Stay here. I'll fetch Maggie."

"We're leaving?" Maggie ducked from underneath one of the tent flaps to follow Julie outside.

"Yes, to Seruvia. We'll be making camp somewhere else tonight." Although, she didn't see why Amor couldn't just come for them tomorrow to give Maggie time for a birthday celebration amongst friends.

Maggie took in their surroundings, engraining them into her memory because she knew they wouldn't be returning. "Do I have time to say goodbye to everyone?"

Julie hesitated, her eyes roving up to their wagon. "We might only have time to say goodbye to Travis and Lyric. The wagon still needs to be packed."

Maggie gave Julie a smile, disappointment masked behind the softness in her expression. "Then let's hurry." Maggie's hand latched around Julie's, and they ran to locate their hosts.

"Lyric, can we talk to you for a minute?" Both girls found the red-haired woman folding a blanket over a clothesline.

"Of course, what is it?" She gave them a smile, but Julie noted the dark purple tinge underneath her eyes. Lyric's skin had paled from its usual rosy hue.

"We have to head out tonight. We wanted to say goodbye." Julie squeezed Lyric's hands.

"You know you two are welcome to stay with us for as long as you need." Lyric looked between the sisters. "Though, I do understand."

"We thank you for your kindness. We'll never forget you." Maggie pulled the other woman into a tight hug. As soon as Lyric pulled from Maggie, she gathered Julie into her arms as well. "You two be safe, you hear me? If you find us again you will always have a spot around our fire."

"I hope we will cross paths in the future." Julie said, and she meant it. Initially, she had been wary of their unexpected kindness but there was something comforting about knowing they had a group of welcoming faces to come back to. She was trading that for a stranger with emerald eyes and a perpetually set jaw.

The women exchanged one more series of hugs. Travis still hadn't made his way back to camp and Julie doubted Amor would be appreciative if they spent time waiting on him. He was already grumpy enough. She didn't want to know how his mood might sour within a time constraint.

The girls worked quickly to hitch Fiona to the wagon. Amor stood off to the side, his gaze scanning the dark forestry that flanked them. Julie was unable to make out anything besides shadows and dark tree limbs, even if she were to squint. But, maybe he could see what the rest of them couldn't.

Night's shadows coated everything the moon refused to kiss, including their traveling partner. When he finally turned away from the direction of the forest, his eyes locked onto hers.

And for two heartbeats, Julie couldn't move.

If emeralds caught the light in order to shine, his eyes caught the darkness, somehow glowing through it all. To look at him was the equivalent of being pierced with a blade. Sharp, cold, and unwavering.

Then he looked away and the spell was broken.

"Let's go." Amor angled his head briefly towards the tree line before he started walking.

Maggie leant in closer to Julie, the sound of Fiona's hooves masking her whisper, "What was that?"

"What was what?" Julie rolled her shoulders, maneuvering Fiona around a bend in the road.

"You two were staring at each other for five minutes."

"It was not five minutes, it was two seconds. And not intentional, may I add." Julie's lips pressed into a displeased line.

"I thought perhaps you irked him." Maggie smiled with mischief.

Julie muttered something under her breath as she looked up to the sky. "He's very easily irked, so who knows? I might have."

Maggie unfolded their blanket from the spot beside her and draped it over both their legs. "Do you think he's cold?"

Julie shrugged before a smile crossed her features. "I think he warms himself with sheer agitation."

A giggle left her sister, along with a soft elbow jab to the ribs. "Shh, he might hear you."

"Let him hear me. Perhaps it'll encourage him to un-clench that jaw of his once in a while." Julie mused, sat-isfaction washing over her when she caught the tensing of Amor's shoulders. He reminded her a lot of the bow he always carried. Or rather, the string attached to it. He seemed to be a breath away from snapping if pulled back too far.

The scenery around them began to shift from open skies to a canopy of shadowed leaves. Julie could barely make out more than six stars from the gaps in the foliage when she searched for their familiarity. There was no longer a pebble dusted path underneath the wheels of their wagon but the dip of soft dirt and grass.

Fiona nickered nervously the deeper they traveled into the forest. Julie couldn't blame the mare. Dead, gang-ly branches cast claw-like markings over the forest floor, while an unsettling chill crept over Julie's spine.

"How much further?" Julie leant forward in the seat to get Amor's attention, who'd put distance between himself and the wagon.

Amor didn't respond but his gait slowed. *Maybe this was it? Were they supposed to stop here?*

"Amor." Julie reached up and broke off a twig from a low-hanging branch to poke him. He abruptly halted. His hand wrapped around the stick without sparing a glance in her direction.

The annoyance surging in Julie's chest fizzled out like steam as the hair on the back of her neck rose. Beside her, Maggie stiffened. *Something wasn't right.*

Amor's eyes locked onto the darkest part of the woods, slowly and fluidly nocking an arrow into his bow. The forest itself seemed to kneel in silence as he raised it. Amor was so still that Julie wasn't sure he was breathing.

She knew she wasn't.

Because she could finally see what he did. Gleaming, golden eyes shone out from the shadows, prowling into the pale moonlight on claws made to tear flesh from bone.

Wolves.

CHAPTER THIRTEEN

Amor

This was going to be a waste of arrows. The beast slinked closer, saliva dripping from its maw. A low growl vibrated through the air and with each passing step, the moon highlighted the sunken sides of the creature. *It's hungry. That means it's desperate.*

The wolf leapt with every intention of sinking its sharp fangs into Amor's throat. His arrow flew directly into the soft underside of its belly. The wolf collapsed with a heavy thud, blood leaking from its mouth.

Good. That's over with. Now they could-

Twigs snapped to his left. Shattered starlight cast onto bristling gray fur, boasting more sets of incisors than

Amor cared to count. Four beasts gradually made their presence known in an array of growling and bared teeth.

Amor gripped the familiar curve of his bow. If he moved too rapidly, they would all lunge. Amor took one, then two slow steps backward, hoping to prolong the precious moments before their attack. Before he could think, two of the wolves paused their stalk. They briefly scented the air before their attention diverted away from Amor. *They found the girls.* His gaze flew to Julie, who protectively shielded her sister as the creatures approached. He wouldn't let them hurt her. He needed her alive for her gift.

Amor slammed the side of his bow against a tree trunk. The clatter demanded the attention of the silent forest, and the wolves in it. "You want me?" Amor's voice was as sharp as the arrows in his quiver. "Come and get me."

The wolves snarled and changed course, plunging after him as he tore through the forest. Amor slung his bow over his shoulder and pulled himself up into a tree with branches of questionable strength. He ignored the creaking of the tree underneath his weight as he nocked an arrow and let it fly into the necks of two wolves below. High-pitched whines of pain left the animals. The poison seeping into their bloodstreams was stronger than their desire to relieve Amor of a few limbs. They swayed before their massive frames hit the dirt, one atop the other. The wood groaned and split, allowing Amor mere seconds to jump down before it splintered completely.

The instant his boots connected with the earth, he was knocked forward with vicious force. An uncomfortable pressure dug into his chest and shoulder as the wolf yanked backward on Amor's quiver, practically dragging him along with it. Amor gritted his teeth and twisted his body away, spurring the wolf's anger. Its jaw latched further onto Amor's quiver, shaking his arrows loose of their confinement. Amor managed to grab hold of the knife at his hip and thrust his arm back blindly. The point of the blade sunk deeply past fur and skin, but Amor couldn't tell what part of the wolf he'd injured. For a single breath, Amor allowed himself a moment of victory. The wolf relented its brutish grip long enough for Amor to pull himself to his feet. His eyes darted across the scattered arrows. He didn't have any left in his quiver. If he knelt to gather them, it would be the equivalent of signing his own death warrant.

When he glanced back to where the wounded wolf had stood, the hair on the back of his neck rose.

The wolf was gone.

It was eerily quiet.

Then a scream split the night air and Amor was forced to the ground.

CHAPTER FOURTEEN

Julie

*F*ates above, he was using himself as bait.

"You want me? Come and get me." Amor snarled. The heartbeat that followed gathered the wolves' attention, raptured by hunger and hunt. They broke into a run, chasing him into the pitch-dark woods.

Now was their chance. "Come on. Come on, hurry." Julie gripped Maggie's wrist, pulling her from the wagon seat. Her pulse pounded in her ears as she stuffed Maggie in the back of the wagon. Before she could shut the door and lock her sister inside, Maggie planted her arm in the way. "No, you're coming in here with me."

"Don't argue." Julie said firmly. *Amor had diverted some of the wolves but if more lurked around them, they would be blind to it until it was too late.* "I need to help him."

"He can take care of himself. Please, Julie-"

A howl. If they saw Maggie in the wagon they would rip it to shreds to get to her.

"Margret." Julie pleaded. "Hide." She looked into her sister's worry-filled gray eyes for one more second before she shut the door. Julie hurtled herself to the ground, putting distance between her and the wagon. Sticks and brittle leaves clung to her pants as she ducked behind one of the trees. Julie held her breath and pressed her back against the rough bark, the sound of footsteps littering the forest. It was dark now that the clouds concealed the moon. If she squinted, she could barely make out the form of one of the fanged beasts, stalking around the wagon. Julie's heart was in her throat. *Don't make any noise, Maggie.* Julie begged in her mind as if by sheer force of will, the wolf would depart.

A loud crack ruptured the air in the woods beyond. The wolf bounded in that direction, leaving her sister alone. Julie leant her head against the tree before she pushed herself away and tore through the bramble ridden path. Sharp branches reached out for her neck, but she kept on. She didn't even have a plan. For all she knew, Amor could already be down, torn to ribbons by the number of wolves he distracted to keep them safe.

No. He was too stubborn to let an overgrown dog be the death of him. Or, he better be. She needed him alive so she could take care of Maggie.

The nearly worn-through sole of Julie's boot connected with a gleaming arrowhead. Julie's eyes fell to the scattered arrows just in front of her, shining in the moonlight like fallen stones. Her gaze dragged forward to a shadowed silhouette pulling himself from the ground.

The confusing little surge of relief was quickly drowned by adrenaline. Her body moved of its own accord before her mind could fully comprehend her movements.

Julie saw the wolf prowling from the darkness, prepared to launch itself onto Amor's back. He was turned away and wouldn't see it until it was too late.

Julie forced her lungs to fill with air and she screamed, summoning the wolf's attention. She dropped to swipe one of the arrows before she threw herself into Amor. The wolf lunged for her head in the same breath. As their bodies connected with the dirt, Julie plunged the jagged arrow into the wolf's neck, ripping the skin and fur from collar to sternum. Hot blood sprayed onto her hand and down her arm. The creature landed just inches from their heads, a pool of crimson spreading underneath it.

Julie's breathing shuddered and she lowered her head against something warm and solid. After a few moments, she lifted it only to realize she'd collapsed against Amor's shoulder. His body had broken her landing. The warmth from his palms seeped into her thin cotton shirt, strong hands bracing her waist until Julie was all too aware of their situation.

The wolves were gone. The threat was lifted.

Yet, Amor's protective grasp hadn't relented. Her hands were planted on either side of his head, her body's instinctual attempt to catch herself.

"What are you doing here?" Emerald eyes collided with hers, blinking as if clearing from a haze. Julie swallowed in an attempt to erase the dryness in her throat, but was unsuccessful.

"Preventing you from becoming a midnight snack." Julie's gaze lifted from him to the dead wolf within arm's reach.

"You're bleeding." Amor said, a furrow to his brow that was there and gone so quickly she was certain it was a trick of the moonlight and its shadows. Amor's hand shifted away from her waist to brush aside her hair that settled around them like a curtain. His fingertips grazed her neck, surveying the damage the stray branches wrought.

Julie held her breath. The stinging sensation only drew several pinpricks of blood, nothing to warrant concern. "I'll take care of it when we get to camp." She rose to her feet, dusting the debris from her meager, slightly torn attire.

Amor shut his eyes for a second, yet to move from the ground. Then he reopened them and pulled himself up. "We shouldn't be far now." Amor bent to retrieve his arrows and quiver before leading the way back to Maggie and the wagon in silence.

CHAPTER FIFTEEN

Julie

Amor hadn't spoken a word since their little debacle. Julie wasn't necessarily surprised. Grim silence seemed to be the Dark Archer's favorite pastime. Whatever glimpse of something *else* she'd imagined was now replaced by an unwavering mask. They stopped just outside a portion of the forest concealed by draping vines. His arm swept aside the leafy curtain, ducking inside. Maggie's hand curled around Julie's arm before they followed suit.

"I thought you got lost." A richly amused voice rolled through the enclosure. A young man with hair of silver and eyes like ice stood from his seat by the crackling fire.

"Wolves." Amor rested his quiver against one of the logs that had been converted into a fireside bench.

The other man grimaced, "Are you okay?"

"Yes." Maggie said so quietly, drawing Julie's surprise in her sister's direction. It was unlike Maggie to answer a question that wasn't meant for her. But... Julie wasn't entirely certain her little sister was paying full attention. She seemed enraptured by this silver-haired young man.

The man turned around, his lips parting slightly at the sight of Maggie. He was rendered utterly still and quiet. As if she was a diamond he'd spent his entire life searching for. Something new and sparkling rolled through the air as their eyes locked.

The fire provided ample light for Julie to subtly slide a glance to this young man's hand. *It wasn't that their strings didn't connect... he didn't have a string at all. Like Amor.*

"Hello." The young man slowly approached. The softness of his steps reminded Julie of how one would approach a bunny in a meadow.

"Hi." Maggie said, lowering her chin shyly, but that didn't hide the soft way her smile curved her lips.

"I'm Silver."

"Margr... Mags.. Maggie." She fumbled for the right words which only drew a melodic laugh from Silver, his eyes glimmering with mirth.

"Come, come sit by the fire. I'll feed you all." He gestured towards the flames and Julie eased Maggie's grasp from her arm so her sister could follow the young man. Amor leant against a nearby tree, arms folded. There was something like pity or perhaps sympathy on his features as he watched Silver.

"So, you're the two who will be traveling with us to Seruvia?" Silver handed Maggie a bowl of something that certainly smelled enticing before making the rounds to give bowls to Julie and Amor.

"Yes, forgive me, I wasn't aware we'd all be traveling together." Julie slipped down to the grass, tucking her legs underneath her. Amor hadn't said anything about an extra traveling partner. Though, she suspected Maggie had no qualms on the matter, judging by her stolen glances at Silver.

The blue-eyed man chuckled. "Somebody has to keep this one in check." He warmly clapped Amor on the shoulder. "Besides, there's not a finer fletcher to have on hand if I do say so myself."

Julie chewed her bite of stew before she asked, "You make Amor's arrows?"

Silver nodded. "Guilty as charged." He scanned Amor's quiver. "By the looks of things, you're running a little low aren't you, Am?"

A smile threatened to break across Julie's lips. *Silver had nicknamed Amor, which sounded like a feat in itself.*

"I gathered the ones I could, but some broke in the wolf fight." Amor twisted his spoon that had yet to gather any stew.

"It's no matter, but before we leave tomorrow I need you to find some materials. Nightrose root, if you can."

Amor raised his brow. "That's not going to be at the nearest outpost."

Silver shrugged. "You may have to find the second nearest. I can't make them perfectly without it."

"Nightrose root? What's that?" Julie questioned.

"Poison." Amor said simply, like he was discussing something mundane like the weather instead of something deadly.

"A slow-acting toxin, to be exact." Silver shook his head. Pale, glimmering strands of hair fell into his eyes. "I grind the root into a concentrate. It's subtle enough at first. Oftentimes the victim doesn't realize they've been poisoned because the symptoms initially sharpen the senses. It might feel like you have a clear head, a better sense of smell and heightened hearing. Of course, that's just temporary before the... other effects take place."

"Are all your arrows poisoned?" Julie found herself asking. She turned her attention to Amor who, startlingly, had already been looking at her.

"In a sense." He ran a thumb over his jaw, his gaze pulling away from Julie's to stare into the fire.

The shiver that ran over Julie's shoulders had nothing to do with the breeze lacing through the wooded enclosure. This man was not safe. He could never be safe. He was a living, breathing weapon with agendas Julie did not understand nor was she entirely sure she wished to. Whatever gentleness she'd experienced when he caught her from toppling onto the ground must have been the imaginings of her tired mind.

It wasn't just her head that ached, but the rest of her too. Silver broke the silence again by telling Amor, "We'll need food for the road. This stew was the last of it." His pale finger tapped against Amor's half-eaten bowl.

Food... A birthday dessert... *Maggie's birthday.*

"It's Maggie's birthday?" Silver turned to Julie who stared at him in surprise.

"Did I say that out loud?"

"Yes, you did Jules." Maggie laughed from her seat by the fire, leaning over the log to watch their conversation.

Silver grinned, stepping away from the tree and back to Maggie. "I don't suppose you would do me the delight of dancing with the birthday girl? It was a tradition in my family."

Maggie flushed, "Dance with you?"

"I guarantee your toes will stay intact." Silver extended his hand to her. Maggie's hand slipped into his and Silver led her away from the fire.

"Don't you need music to dance?" Julie mused, setting aside her bowl.

"We have it. Listen." Silver gestured lightly to the woods around them. Maggie tilted her head, listening for the notes in question. Julie watched as a smile graced her sister's lips. *She heard what he did.* If Julie tried hard enough, perhaps she could too. The crackle of the fire acted as the beat. The hum of the crickets could be interpreted as the song of a violin. In the distance, a river of burbling water made the melody.

Silver danced with her slowly, spinning Maggie at certain points. She gave a squeal of delight. *Oh, Maggie looked happy.* Julie drank in the sight, memorizing the way Maggie's cheeks dimpled with her smiles.

Behind her, Amor quietly shifted. He stepped back from the fire and when she caught his line of sight, he angled his head. A silent message to follow so the tender moment remained uninterrupted. Julie gathered herself to her full height and matched his pace. Where they were going, she didn't know. Why she was willingly following him in the dark was also an excellent question for which she had no answer.

The tree line broke, showcasing the star-reflecting river Julie heard earlier. Amor unclasped his cloak and moved to the bank. "Come here."

"I'm much too tired to go for a swim." Julie hung back, hesitant. *What was he doing?*

Amor shook his head, "Fine, I'll come to you then." He dipped the soft, inner fabric of his cloak into the water, dampening it before he stalked back over to her. Julie's breath caught as his boots stalled right in front of her. The broadness of his shoulders and his height dwarfed her as they cast her into shadow.

Julie raised her chin, looking him squarely in the eye but she could not read him.

She should turn on her heel and walk away.

She must.

She couldn't.

His eyes pinned her in place. Her legs may not have wished to cooperate, but her mouth still worked fine. "Are you planning to get rid of me?"

"What?" Amor furrowed his brow. "Where is this coming from?"

"That's not an answer."

Amor sighed and pinched the bridge of his nose with the hand that wasn't holding his dripping cloak.

"No, Julie. I still need your gift. Getting rid of you is counterproductive." Amor's hand went to her chin and Julie's body stilled.

"And after?" Julie's voice came out quieter than the volume she demanded of it.

"It concerns me little what you do after we're done." Amor tilted her chin to the side, allowing the generous moonlight to wash over her skin. He raised the edge of his cloak and with gentleness that sparked chills along her spine, dabbed away the dried blood.

"My gift will still work with these scrapes, you know." Julie pried her eyes away. His gaze was too intense to bear for long.

"Best not risk it." Amor swiped lightly over the remaining cut. Once that was done he backed away from her, not lingering a moment more than necessary.

"Get some rest. The journey will be tiring." Amor said in lieu of 'goodnight.' He folded his cloak over his arm and left the riverbank. Julie kept him in her range of sight until she spotted the campfire. Her sister was contently asleep by the fire, wrapped in a fur blanket. Silver sat across from her, sharpening an arrowhead against a flat stone.

"Mind if I sit?"

Silver glanced up, "I always appreciate company."

Julie eased down beside him and was silent for several beats before she offered, "Thank you, for making tonight special for her."

Silver nodded, an almost bashful smile on his lips as he lowered his head back to the stone. "She made it special all on her own. I merely provided the choreography."

Julie propped her chin up in her hand. The words inside her bubbled to the surface, try as she might to ignore them. "You don't have a string."

"I know." He replied quietly.

Julie studied him, brows drawn together. "You know? How?"

Silver set the stone and the arrowhead aside for a moment. "Because it was my choice to leave."

Julie plucked a piece of grass from the earth and tossed it into the flames. "Why would you leave your soulmate, if you don't mind me asking?"

Silver sighed, long and slow. He tilted his head up to the sky before answering. "So she could have a better life. A fuller one. That was reason enough for me, hard as it was."

"I understand wanting a better life for the person you love." Julie drew her knees up to her chest, stretching her sore muscles. "After this, I should have enough for Maggie to experience everything she's ever wanted."

Silver hummed a response, his gaze flickering over to Maggie's sleeping form. Her head was cradled underneath her bent arm, all snuggled underneath the fur. "And you? What is it that you want?"

Julie turned to him, "For her to be happy. I can spend the rest of my days content with this life as long as I know I gave her my best."

Silver looked as if he wished to add something else that elicited the swirling emotions Julie caught in his eyes, but he didn't. "Try and sleep, we only have a few hours until dawn."

Julie was tempted to press. To ask him what it was he wanted to say but the ache in her bones and the exhaustion in her mind didn't allow her to refute him. "Goodnight, Silver."

"Goodnight, Julie."

As she laid on her side, Julie couldn't help the path her mind wandered down. The way Silver uttered, *'it was my choice to leave,'* had been pained. Like it ripped him in two to make that decision. Julie curled in on herself. She didn't know a person could sever their soulmate cord. All these years, she thought it was unyielding and unbreakable.

Was that why her and Maggie's strings were incomplete? Because no one wanted them? Or perhaps they had at one point, but changed their mind?

Julie rolled over onto her back. Sure, she had her faults. Promises she'd made and yet to keep, lying to the only family she had left so a heart wouldn't break. Those were just a couple of reasons why she could understand her string being damaged, black and blurry.

But Maggie? Sweet, glowing, beautiful Maggie?

Who would ever look at her and decide they didn't want her in their life? If anything, she would make their existence exponentially better just by being in it.

Those thoughts were more uncomfortable than the twigs and rocks underneath her back. After a while, even those couldn't keep the lure of sleep out of Julie's reach.

When she woke, it wasn't yet morning.

She awakened to the sound of her sister's cries.

CHAPTER SIXTEEN

Julie

Maggie writhed in pain. Wordless whimpers left her lips as tears beaded underneath wrenched lashes. "Shh, Maggie, I'm here." Julie tried to keep the panic from her voice as she eased her sister into her arms. Maggie's skin was damp, scalding to the touch. *Not good.*

"Can you wake up for me?" Julie coaxed. With every passing second that Maggie did not wake, her heart constricted. Another cry escaped Maggie, her body twisting in discomfort. Julie tried to rock her gently back and forth but that did nothing to quell her sister's suffering. *She needed medicine.*

Frantically, Julie whipped her head around. By some miracle, could there be an herb in the forest to lower the fever? Disappointment settled in Julie's gut as her darting search came up empty. "Silver!" Julie hissed, clutching Maggie to her chest.

Silver stirred, his eyes slowly focusing on them before he bolted upright. "What happened?"

"Maggie's ill." Julie said quickly, "I need to get her medicine. Can you watch over her until I get back? Please?" Julie would give anything for him to say yes. Before she could figure out what she had of value to barter with, Silver was at her side. He dropped to a knee and cradled Maggie in his arms. She turned her head and buried it in his chest.

"Where's the nearest town?" Julie hauled herself to her feet, ignoring the protest of her stiff limbs.

"There's one east of here but-"

Julie didn't linger to hear the rest of Silver's sentence. She unhooked Fiona from their wagon and pulled herself up onto the mare's back, who chuffed in surprise. Julie clicked her tongue, clutching the leather reins. "Go." She urged the horse, and with a kick to the mare's sides, Fiona took off.

Branches and leaves blurred past on all sides. Fiona, sensing her rider's urgency, didn't hesitate to jump across the hurdles in their path. Julie gritted her teeth, having to grip both Fiona's mane and the reins just to stay upright.

Julie ducked just in time to avoid colliding face first into a large branch. Her sleeve, however, was not as fortunate. The fabric snagged on a sharp piece of bark and tore away, revealing the upper part of her shoulder. She would have to mend that later. For now, she just needed to get a remedy for Maggie. Julie racked her brain as rapidly as Fiona's hooves connected with the ground.

'The little ones seem to be coming down with something, but so far it's only the youngest that are affected.' Julie heard Maggie's voice in her head, recalling how the children in the gypsy camp had fallen ill.

And Maggie had been there to take care of them.

The sun barely kissed the top of the cresting hills, illuminating the town which bustled with life. Julie bit back a groan of discomfort as she dismounted Fiona. She quickly reached out and caught the reins to keep her legs from buckling. The mare, panting, turned her head to nudge Julie's side. "I'm fine. Just tired." Julie stroked Fiona's sleek muzzle, before tying the reins to a fencepost attached to a brick-laid building.

This town must have an apothecary, but where? Every building looked similar and there were hordes of people moving too fast for Julie to pin one down and question them.

Julie's hand drifted to her pocket and her being was filled with sudden dread. She turned the pockets inside out to reveal nothing. In panicked haste, she'd forgotten to bring any aurums at all. Julie twisted to look back at Fiona who pawed at the dusty road with her hoof. Julie didn't have the spare time to ride Fiona back to camp, and she certainly couldn't return empty handed.

Julie curled her hands into fists. The sensation of her nails digging into her palms helped distract from the mounting pressure in her head. Julie slipped to the sidewalk, tracking everything from the movements of passersby to the signs above each shop. Julie's throat went dry as she saw an opportunity. *A young woman who set her coin purse down on the side of a fountain as she busied herself with retying her little boy's shoe.*

It was right there. She could take it to buy Maggie's medicine. Julie hesitated. Taking a wagon from a cruel ringmaster who'd done nothing but mistreat them was different than stealing an innocent mother's coins. *That wasn't how father raised them.*

Julie breathed out trepidation and inhaled conviction. *Father wouldn't want his daughter to suffer without relief.*

She took a step off the sidewalk and was immediately caught by a young man who was more blur than body.

"You have ten seconds to convince me why you need that moneybag you're eyeing." He stated, whirling Julie around.

"What?" Julie blinked at the stranger. His blue eyes shimmered with a sort of mischief that betrayed his cool exterior.

"Five seconds." He tapped his wrist, although there was no watch there to refer to.

Julie wasn't sure why on earth she complied, but her words poured out in a rush. "My sister is sick. I need to get her medicine, but I don't have the money."

The young man tilted his head, light brown hair sliding across his forehead in feathered swoops. He studied her features as if truth and lie could be read on her face before he blew out a breath. "I love a good sob story. Watch and learn, hazel-eyes." He flashed a grin and sauntered onto the street as if he owned it. He dropped to a knee in front of the little boy and his mother. "I am sorry to interrupt your afternoon, but I just had to say, you look exactly like my nephew, Liam."

The child laughed when he winked. "Quite a lovely mother you've got as well. I don't suppose I'd be lucky enough to gather a name?" He lifted his eyes to the young woman who flushed a blooming pink.

"Marianne."

"The pleasure is entirely mine, Miss Marianne. I do hope it's 'Miss?'" A coy smile played on the stranger's lips and Julie's jaw hung open slightly as the woman played right into his hands.

"You would be correct." She gently giggled as she took her son's chubby hand and picked up her coin purse.

"I won't keep you from your day, but I do hope to run into you and this little man sometime." He told her. *All charm and no bite.* Which was ironic, seeing as his incisors looked unnaturally sharp.

"Perhaps." She flashed a shy but flirtatious smile in his direction and walked past him.

What was he doing? The purse had been right there! Julie wanted to dart into the street and capture the little drawstring bag herself. Every one of her thumping heartbeats reminded her of the passing time.

The blue-eyed stranger strolled back, not even sparing a glance in the direction of the woman's retreating form. Julie pressed a hand to her pounding head. "This was a waste of time."

"Okay. First, ouch." The man leant casually against the wall of the alley. "Second, catch." He flicked his wrist and flung an object into Julie's face. She gasped as she caught it. *The coin purse.*

"But how? I saw her walk away with it."

The man laughed. "You've never pickpocketed anyone a day in your life, have you, hazel-eyes?"

Julie held back her glare and did not answer. "Thank you for your help, now I have to find the apothecary." Julie tucked the drawstring bag into her pocket and picked a direction to walk in.

"Uh-uh, you're going the wrong way." The man called, a smug smile on his face. Julie turned her head to the sky, wincing against the sharp pain of the sun in her eyes. She changed course but had no sooner placed her boot down that the man whistled. "Oh, yikes that's absolutely not the right way."

"What is the right way, pray tell." Julie locked eyes with the snarky stranger.

"The other way." He chuckled. "I can take you, if you'd like. I mean hey, it's your choice if you want to go toward the Potter's district alone. But, not to be rude, you look like you might tip over."

At the mention of her physical state, Julie's body ached. "Okay. But quickly."

The young man took hold of her forearm and steered her in the correct direction. To the Potter's district, apparently.

From the corner of Julie's vision she saw patches of red... bright, blinding and abrupt. When she did a double take, the color she witnessed dancing across her field of vision was mundane and lifeless. Julie loosed a breath, digging her nails into her closed fist. She didn't have time to be sick. She would force herself to be fine. Maggie needed her more.

"Here we are." The young man drew Julie to a halt infront of a particular shop boasting beaded curtains instead of a door. A peculiar scent tickled Julie's nose, wafting from the swaying glass strings.

"Are you sure this is it?" Underneath an array of abandoned bird's nests, lay a faded purple sign covered in looping script.

Madam Clara's Oddities & Remedies

"The one and only." He grinned, waving a showy hand in the direction of the building. A much grander gesture than the place itself appeared to deserve. "Come on, time's a ticking." The blue-eyed man lightly poked Julie in the back to push her forward. A black bird burst free of the clinking curtain and squawked its way out into the street, startling Julie enough that she stumbled backward. She recovered herself and climbed the creaking wooden steps, parting the beads with her hand before stepping through.

Her guide sputtered behind her, the beaded curtain flinging back into his face.

"Sorry." Julie offered a slightly apologetic raise of her shoulders as he pulled one of the strings free from his black shirt.

"Ah! He deserves it, the scoundrel." A woman materialized from the back, running over to them in a fury of dark cloth and thick necklaces. The lines around her aged but matronly face deepened as she struck his side with her clasped fan. "Darcy sensed you coming a mile away! You scared him off with all your troublemaking." Bracelets of gold and raw tumbled stones clacked against each other as she set her hands on her hips.

Julie's guide shrugged and stuffed his hands in his pockets. He would have looked innocent if it weren't for the smirk that made a single dimple deepen on his face.

"I didn't spook your old bird, I came to bring you some business." He stepped aside, deftly picking up what looked like a sphere made entirely of quartz.

An intrigued sound burbled in her throat, and she spun around on her heel. The situation with the blue-eyed rascal and her bird now forgotten. "What do you need, dearie?" She looked Julie up and down. "Lotion? Jewelry? Ach, you're too skinny, you need a belt." The woman reached weathered fingers to pinch Julie's waist.

"No, nothing for me, thank you." Julie gave the woman a tired smile and backed away a step to free herself from the woman's clutches. "My sister contracted an illness and has a very high fever."

"Ah!" The older woman wagged her finger in Julie's face and shuffled to the counter laden with various objects. She rifled through a shelf that held vials in various colors and shapes. "You came to the right place, dearie. You'll find no finer an elixir than this one." She proudly displayed a small, corked bottle. "House recipe."

The man made a face, "I can attest that it works but I hope you don't value your tastebuds too much."

"Ach." The woman took a pebble sized gemstone and threw it at him. "Who cares about taste when it's effective."

Julie pressed the money bag onto the counter. "Is this enough?"

The woman lovingly set down the bottle and proceeded to paw through the coins before she squinted at Julie. "This is your money?"

Julie's throat went dry, her palms slickening. "Is it not enough for the elixir?"

The woman made a thoughtful hum. "That delinquent helped you, didn't he?" She jabbed her finger in the air toward Julie's guide who watched the scene unfold with amused delight.

"Please, madam. I'm running out of time." Julie pleaded.

"I'll take that." The woman's fingers traced the worn crimson ribbon that kept Julie's braid from coming loose. From seemingly nowhere, she produced a brown paper bag and slipped the bottle inside, rolling the top and pushing it into Julie's grip. "And you can take this."

Perhaps it was the fog that encroached the corners of Julie's mind, but something wasn't adding up. "Don't you require money? What could you want with my old ribbon?"

The woman smiled, a mischievous quirk of her lips. "I like things with stories." She said vaguely. "And you look like you'll have a good story to tell."

Julie shook her head as she pulled the ribbon free and dropped it in the woman's open palm.

"Good. Now Casimir, get your thieving self over here." Her eyes shot to the man who sauntered over and leaned casually against the counter, tossing and catching the stone sphere.

"Take this back to whoever you stole it from." Her eyes narrowed as she refilled the bag with its coins and planted it into his chest. "You don't have to do this anymore." She wagged her finger, as if she was scolding a child who got his hand caught in a cookie jar.

Casimir grinned, displaying his sharp white smile. "I got bored."

"Ach." She grumbled. "Shoo, and if you find Darcy bring him back. *And* bring me some customers with real, hard-earned money next time."

Casimir swept himself into a bow. "Yes, grandmother."

Grandmother? Julie looked between the two. *That explained their familiarity with each other.* "Thank you both for your help." She clutched the bag to her chest and nodded a goodbye before slipping out into the street.

Hold on, Maggie.

Julie pushed her way through the crowd that seemed to have multiplied since she'd been inside. Finally, she broke past the throng and retraced her steps from the streets Casimir had guided her through. She brushed her forehead with her sleeve, dampness forming on her skin despite keeping to the shadows. She just needed to get to Fiona. Julie could already see the dark mare's silhouette.

Julie gasped, her legs buckling as stripes of red flashed across her field of sight. Jagged bits of gravel pinched her palms as she tried to gain her bearings. "Get up." She told herself, gritting her teeth. Whistles vibrated through the dusty air, forcing Julie to lift her head. Her heart stammered in her chest as her vision cleared.

Three masked figures sprung from the shadows. They stalked towards Fiona, slipping her lead free of the post and securing their own rope around her neck. Fiona's whinnies and snorts of panic spliced the air. "No!" Julie yelled, gathering every bit of strength to stumble forward. *They couldn't take Fiona.*

The bandits swiveled their attention, laughing at her struggle. Julie threw her weight into the closest one, but her sluggish efforts did little against the sheer solidity of the thief. In the chaos, Fiona bucked, stamping her hooves against the building's wall in an attempt to gain freedom. Like her rider, she was unsuccessful.

"You're a little sparkshow aren't you?" The bandit Julie had flung herself into swept her arms behind her, pulling her flush against his chest.

The earth began to pitch, ground and sky were easily blurred. "Let us go!" Anger and nausea made for a wretched combination in her gut.

Her captor's companion wrangled Fiona's thrashing with a sharp tug of her lead and spoke, "Might as well take advantage of this two-for-one deal. What do you say, boys?"

Julie's breath came in sharp bursts, sweat glossing her skin from her effort to wriggle out of his grip. *No. Maggie needs... Please...*

"She's a little spirited, but nothing the right encourage-ment can't fix." He greedily smiled as he lowered his face to Julie's ear.

"Please…" Julie's head drooped, her shoulders sinking.

"Oh, she's pretty when she begs." His grip tightened on her arms. Out of the corner of Julie's eye, she watched as Fiona was led away by his other two companions.

Now. It was now or never.

Julie summoned her last scraps of strength and slammed her head upwards, bashing the man's nose inside his mask. Blood seeped through the black cloth like spilled ink against paper. He cried out in pain and thrust her to the gravel in favor of bracing his broken nose.

Julie curled in on herself reflexively just before she con-tacted the earth. Her skin tore when she landed, judging from the lashing stings that roped her forearms. A tiny sliver of satisfaction broke through her pain when she didn't hear the sound of shattering glass in her pocket. Maggie's medicine was still intact.

The furious growl behind her was incentive enough to crawl toward the edge of a building, shakily hoisting her-self up by a white-knuckled grip on the bricks. *It was too late to get Fiona back.* Julie's stomach formed a knot at the thought of never again seeing the mare who served them so well. But she had no time to allow regret to creep in, not with the crunch of gravel underneath heavy boots still in earshot.

"Get back here!" The footsteps grew louder, along with several hurled insults. Julie staggered into the crowd.

Where she found the strength to heave her limbs forward, she didn't know. She refused to succumb to the weakness that crept over her like a nightmarish shadow. Julie pressed on through several winding alleyways, only allowing herself a reprieve when she could walk no further. Her hands curled into fists in front of her knees, breaking the blades of grass from the hill outside the city square.

Get up.

Stand.

Pull yourself together.

A hiss slipped through her clenched teeth as she raised her head, using the ground as an anchor to rise. Her limbs nearly gave way again, but this time it was not from pain.

Her gaze swept over the city from a vantage point higher than she realized she'd climbed. The back of Julie's shaking hand pressed hard against her mouth to stifle the strangled cry that built in her throat. Cords of scarlet waved through the entire city. Ribbons invisible to all but her floated every which way, making the world look stained by a sea of red.

It was too much.

Everywhere she turned, the strings followed. They were in the sky, scattered through the blades of grass, and rushing through the air towards her like vipers ready to strike.

It hurt. It hurt so badly.

The world tilted, taking its infinite crimson threads and strangling her with them.

Before darkness encroached upon her vision completely, Julie made out the dark form of a masked man storming towards her. His silhouette blurred into undefined edges. Julie could *feel* his anger, see it in the way his steps picked up speed when she crumpled.

When she stopped seeing the strings, she saw the stars.

CHAPTER SEVENTEEN

Amor

It had taken him four hours of traveling to the third-closest outpost before obtaining the Nightrose root. Even then, Amor pursued less than savory means of pocketing the little blue velveteen bag now attached to his belt. It shouldn't take Token too long to prepare the arrows, then they could be on their way. The crackling of a dying fire met Amor's ears as he re-entered camp.

"I brought food and the root. Don't get the bags confused." He said, expecting Silver to already be awake and prepared like he usually was on travel days.

As he scanned the small enclosure, he found something he *hadn't* been expecting. Silver knelt beside an unmoving

Maggie, dabbing damp cloths over her skin. His brow pinched in worry while he brushed the curls from her face.

"Silver." Amor dropped the bag and came to his friend's side. "What's wrong with her?"

Silver peered up at him with eyes laced in dark rings. "She's ill. I just recently got her to stop crying." His words were tinged with a type of sorrow Amor couldn't understand. The type that comes from longing for something that will only slip away. Silver tipped the younger woman's head up enough to ease a bowl of water to her cracking lips.

Amor's gaze immediately snapped to where Julie had fallen asleep the night before. "The other one, where is she?" *She wouldn't leave her sister, not in such a state.*

Silver sat back on his heels after pulling a blanket over Maggie. "Julie went to the nearest city to find medicine for her." Silver's hand hovered over Maggie's shoulder.

An odd and unwanted sensation twisted through Amor's stomach. "On foot?" His vision flicked back to the place beside the fire as if she might magically materialize there if he willed it.

"Horseback. She left an hour ago."

A muscle feathered in Amor's jaw. "You just let her go? Did you consider she doesn't know where she's going?"

Silver scrubbed a hand over his jaw. "She would have gone regardless of what I said, Am. She'll do anything for her sister." Silver's eyes locked with Amor's. A thousand words were spoken in that glance.

A thousand, aching words.

"If she winds up dead, I'm going to kill her." Amor frustratedly pulled his mask up over the bridge of his nose.

"That's counterproductive." Silver commented off-handedly.

Amor pocketed several knives in replacement of the scarcity of arrows in his quiver and started east. The ground crackled underneath his boots as his pace quickened with each newly racing thought. *Why couldn't she just stay in one place? He could have gotten the medicine for her sister with haste, and wouldn't be wasting time trying to bring her back.*

He needed her. His revenge was a flame, and she was the match.

Amor planted his hand against a thick tree trunk on the outskirts of the town to brace himself. His breath came in sharp pants, his muscles straining under his cloak from the fact he'd run the entire way. Julie was somewhere within the city limits, charming her way through the crowd no doubt, and he was intent on finding her.

He pushed away from the tree and stalked forward, the town's cacophony filling his ears. His line of vision darted to the posts and corrals where travelers hitched their horses, but Julie's coal-dark mare was not among them.

Amor's frustration with the entirety of the situation only deepened the further he pressed into the crowd. Distracted individuals toting bags and crates shoved into him, hindering his progress as he weaved through the chaos.

This was why he preferred rooftops. He could garner a better vantage point from a distance. Amor ducked into one of the adjacent alleyways, locating a ladder leading to the flat upper level of an older building. He climbed it swiftly and crouched at the ledge, scanning the sea of bodies below. There were a few women with Julie's golden-brown skin and long onyx hair bustling about, but none of them were her. *Not even close.*

Amor dragged a hand through his hair, a few pieces hanging low over his eyes. He found himself growing desperate to see a flash of her red dress or the glint of her glass jewelry. She usually stood out among all crowds like an ember in the dark without even trying. *She would certainly be easier to track down in such a colorful arrayment.* Everyone else down there suffered from a lack of originality which Julie seemed to carry in spades. Amor bolted toward the next rooftop, boots scuffing against the surface as his landing stirred up chalky dust.

Perhaps, if Amor had Julie's soulmate in his possession, he could simply shoot the man and follow his string. But Amor did not know who was stuck on the other end of her string nor where to find him. Julie, of all people, should be privy to such information and Amor found it odd that she hadn't sought him out. He shook his head to clear the unhelpful thoughts, and his gaze happened to flit to a stumbling form at the edge of the square. *Drunkard*. He readjusted the strap of his bow across his chest, prepared to switch rooftops but froze when he lingered on the inebriated silhouette. Someone shouted after them and they turned their head just enough for Amor to see their face.

Amor's stomach dropped and a sensation akin to claws of ice crawled over his skin. *Julie*. She looked like death yet frightened enough as if death was the one after her.

She staggered away, as she made a break for the hills that surrounded the western side of the city. Amor leapt off the rooftop, barely giving himself time to compensate for the fall before he was running toward her. "Julie!" He called out. *You are not allowed to die.* Her name tore from his lips again as he got closer. She barely glanced in his direction before she crumpled, like a flower unforgivingly stomped on.

"Julie. Get up." He commanded, taking hold of her shoulder in an attempt to rouse her awake. Her neck lulled to the side, dark lashes weakly fluttering against her cheeks. Amor tightened his jaw to the point it ached. *What use could she be in such a state?* He drew in a breath and exhaled slowly. *She shouldn't be in this state at all.*

Amor slid one arm under her back and the other beneath her knees, settling her limp body against him. He noted the sheen on her paling skin and the blood dripping down her arm. His thumb and forefinger shifted over the material of her torn sleeve which flapped loosely in the wind. An unexpected spark of fury ignited in his gut. "Who dared to lay a finger on you?"

Julie didn't respond, unless her slight moan of pain could be considered a response.

"Come on, argue with me. Surely, I've done something to aggravate you that you'd like to air out." Amor stood to his feet, limp girl in tow. Julie's arm only drooped over the side of Amor's forearm as he carried her.

"Alright, I'll give you something to fight me over." Amor shifted his grip on her, ensuring her head would rest against his inner shoulder instead of succumbing to gravity. "It's absolutely stupid to trek into an unfamiliar town alone. Your horse is nowhere to be seen, and you could have been killed." Amor glared down at her closed eyes.

For a moment, a glimmer of hope flared when she sluggishly moved her hand to her pocket and mumbled something that vaguely sounded like Maggie's name. Then her consciousness fled, rendering her still and silent once again.

Amor looked down at the faint outline of an object in her pocket. *That must be the medicine she risked herself for.* He wished she would demand to be set down with fire in her eyes and a temper of similar heat.

"If you don't look at me, I'm going to take ten aurums out of your next payment." He grumbled as they crossed closer to the tree line. The mouth of the forest beckoned him closer with promises of shade and refuge. Julie's breathing was becoming irregularly shallow as her body trembled.

"You're going to fight this with sheer spite, you hear me?" Amor stopped at the beginning of the river and lowered Julie to the ground long enough to unclasp his cloak. Whatever illness her sister had contracted, clearly sunk its fangs into Julie. Amor wrapped her in the emerald fabric, still warm from his own body heat.

Once Julie was nestled in his grasp, Amor headed in the direction of camp. "I'm going to hold you closer until you push me away." He threatened lightly, emphasized by the slight press of his arms into her side. *Surely, that'll get her.*

The wind nearly fled his lungs when she instead curled closer.

"Oh Fates, she's not..." Silver's eyes were wide and worried when Amor came into view.

Amor shook his head. "She's not dead, but it looks like she has the same ailment Maggie does."

Silver swiped a hand over his jaw, looking older and more tired than when Amor last saw him. "She must have tried so hard to get the medicine."

Amor eased down onto one of the log benches, plucking the bottle from Julie's pocket, which wasn't difficult with her still in his arms. "She did get it."

Silver's shoulders slumped with relief. "Incredible." He said under his breath, gratefully taking the bottle from Amor's hand. He poured some of the concoction onto a wooden spoon and eased Maggie's head up to slip the medicine past her lips. Maggie pursed her mouth, as if the taste offended her senses. A smile broke out on Silver's features at the scrunch in her nose. "I know." He brushed a thumb over the pinch in her brow. "You'll feel better soon, promise."

Amor glanced down at Julie, "Can you give her a dose too?"

Silver nodded and leapt to his feet. He grabbed another spoon and measured the dark liquid. "Did you chew her out for leaving yet?" Silver mused, tilting Julie's face enough for the medicine to trickle down her throat.

Amor gave his friend a sharp look, "I'm going to when she wakes."

"No, you won't." Silver disagreed, resting his arm over his bent knee. "You're grateful she's alive, aren't you?"

Amor shifted uncomfortably on the wooded bench. "Yes." He said simply. "With my powers fading, I can't finish what I started without her."

"You've started to care for her."

Amor's eyebrows drew together in refusal. "Silver, I can't fault you for what you feel for her sister. I know Maggie's..." Amor wrestled with his wording before settling on a sigh. "I know you've missed her. But you have to realize after we're done, we'll never see them again."

Silver cast a glance over his shoulder to where Maggie rolled onto her side. "It seems rather cruel, doesn't it? To provide a sense of safety and then take it away from them."

"We're not here to be their friends, Token." Amor lowered his voice. "I don't want you to get hurt."

Silver loosed a breath and stood to his feet, digging the toe of his boot into the dirt and lightly tossing the broken earth onto the unlit firewood. "You know, Am, I'm alright to walk away from this with a broken heart. If it could only be hers for a little while, it would be worth it."

Amor opened and closed his mouth, unsure of how to respond. He couldn't pretend to sympathize with the type of loss Silver had experienced. It was far different than his own. But, seeing the smile Maggie put on Silver's face did make Amor's heart lighter. Amor's fingers absentmindedly brushed through the ends of Julie's hair as it spilled over his leg.

"Did you recognize Maggie the minute you saw her?" Amor offered his friend a slight, knowing smile.

Silver's icy blue eyes twinkled like starlight. "To be honest, I thought I'd been dreaming again. You know a few of my memories from before are starting to fade, but not the ones of her. She's even more beautiful up close."

"You made the right choice." Amor nudged his friend in the shoulder.

Silver's smile faltered, a more somber expression pulling at his features. "Sometimes the right choices are the hardest ones."

"Do you regret it?" Amor questioned, his gaze drifting past Silver's shoulder to the shadowy trees beyond.

Silver tilted his head skyward and swallowed. "No. The fact that she was granted a full life will always be more important to me than the fact I can't have a life with her."

Amor couldn't help the twinge of pain that lashed through his battered heart. Although it was hard, and surely a difficult thing to live with, at least Silver's wish had been granted. No one ever said fate was a fair judge.

Silver motioned to the space beside Maggie. "Why don't you lay her down? They can rest, and we can finish preparing for the journey ahead."

At the mention of relinquishing his hold on Julie, Amor's arms tightened around her subconsciously. Silver's eyebrow flicked upwards, a questioning smile on his lips. "I thought you said you didn't care."

"I don't." He rose from the bench and settled Julie beside her sister. Amor didn't expect the absence of her warmth against him to feel like a punishment rather than relief.

"Right." Silver said thoughtfully. "That cloak is more hers than yours at this point." He vaguely waved to the dark fabric that Julie was swaddled in.

"She was shaking, I'm not *that* heartless." Amor replied, his tone short.

Silver chuckled and clapped Amor on the back warmly, saying nothing further on the subject. "Should I expect you to stay down here tonight instead of up in your tree?"

Amor rolled his shoulders. "I wished to leave this afternoon, but I don't see that happening now."

Silver grabbed his fletching tools and the blue bag of Nightrose root before sitting closer to Maggie. "In their condition, we may be delayed several days."

Amor massaged the sides of his temples. "That's what I was worried about."

"Worried about getting to Seruvia on time, or worried about her?"

Amor dragged a hand through his hair, his hand flexing at his side before a slow exhale left him. The forest was silent for several beats before Amor spoke again.

"Both."

CHAPTER EIGHTEEN

Julie

"Tell me another one, Papa!" Julie bubbled over with laughter.

"Another one, hmm?" He smiled as he stroked his close-shaven salt and pepper beard, pretending her request would take a great deal of thought.

Julie grinned. "Don't tease, Papa!" She stood on little legs and did a twirl. "Tell me the one about the sleeping princess."

"Don't you have that one memorized, Mija?" A rich, melodic woman's voice met Julie's ears from the kitchen where her mother stirred a pot of stew. Julie flashed her mother a mischievous smile. She watched in delight as the pretty red string that only she seemed to see floated from her mother's ring finger to meet her father's hand. Julie had tried to catch their string, but she was yet to be successful. Her small fist only captured air with each attempt.

"We have our own sleeping princess over there." Julie's father laughed as he cast his gaze to the toddler with dark ringlets spilling over her face. Julie's baby sister was asleep in her hand-carved wooden high chair, using an empty plate as a pillow.

"Maggie doesn't count!" Julie argued with a pout. "I mean the story, Papa."

"Alright, alright. Let's see, little one." Her father gave into her sweet demands and lifted Julie up onto his lap. "Once upon a time, in a faraway kingdom, lived a beautiful young princess. She always wished to venture outside the walls of her castle, but she was warned not to because of the-"

"The monsters!" Julie blurted, a giggle bursting from her.

Her father reached forward and used the end of her braid to tickle her nose. "Yes, the monsters. The entire kingdom feared their nightmarish legend. But this princess was brave, braver than the king's finest guards and knights."

"I'm that brave. I didn't even cry when I fell out of the tree!" Julie puffed out her chest proudly.

Her father chuckled warmly, "Yes, you are, little one. Now, the princess realized she was running out of time to escape before she was to wed a prince she'd never met. Seizing the opportunity when it struck, she snuck out of the palace with only the moonlight to guide her."

"And Julie, what was wrong with this princesses' plan?" Her mother chimed in, pointing at her daughter with a steaming wooden spoon.

Julie smoothed down the stray hairs that poked their way free of her braid and answered. "She didn't take any food?"

"Very good, Mija." Her mother beamed and brought the spoon over to give Julie a taste of the stew.

Julie nodded her approval at the flavor and her father continued. "At first, the princess was delighted by all the new things she was able to experience. She was optimistic that the stories of the monsters were just that, stories. But on one particularly dark and stormy night she stumbled across an abandoned castle, seeking asylum from the rain."

"There's a monster in there." Julie said, very matter-of-factly.

Julie's mother pressed a hand to her heart, feigning shock. "Don't go spoiling the story for everyone else."

Julie giggled at her mother's silliness and her father grinned. "The princess was curious, so she explored the palace. In one of the rooms rested a magical mirror. She remembered hearing about the mirror in her childhood storybooks. The object was told to grant the deepest most innermost wish of a person's heart. They only needed to look into it. She realized she could wish to no longer be a princess. Then, she would no longer be forced to marry for duty."

"I would wish for a mountain of cinnamon buns." Julie's mouth watered at the thought of the decadent pastry.

"Well, it wasn't that simple. The princess would soon learn the mirror could not be removed or taken from its stand. It was guarded by one of the most frightening creatures of all... a cursed prince."

"But he didn't scare her." Julie shook her head.

"You're right. She befriended the cursed prince and as time passed, she started to care for him."

Julie stuck out her tongue, "But how could she care for him if he was cursed?"

Her father shrugged. "No one can truly explain the ways of love. It's a mystery how it can catch someone by utter surprise and refuse to let go."

"I don't want to be caught. I'd rather have my cinnamon buns." Julie's mouth twisted into a determined line.

Her father laughed. "Levana, do you hear your daughter?"

Levana smirked. "Let your father finish the story, Mija."

"The cursed prince didn't want the princess to look inside the mirror. He spoke of the dangers that could arise if she peered into it. But the princess was stubborn, and she argued the only way they could be together was for her to wish for freedom from the crown."

"She looked into it when he wasn't watching, right?" Julie drummed her little fingers on the arm of her father's chair.

"Yes, and what a pity it was. For when she saw her reflection in the mirror she fell into a deep sleep. It was the mirror that made the monsters and then trapped them."

Julie cocked her head, "But he kissed her to break both their curses didn't he?" Julie didn't recall this version of the story, but that was Papa. He always made slight tweaks to his tales, so she never tired of them.

A slow smile pulled on her father's lips. "I thought you preferred cinnamon buns over love?"

Julie shrugged. "I guess it doesn't hurt to have both if it's like yours and Mama's."

"He-" Her father's words were abruptly shortened by a ferocious crash outside. Julie jumped, startled as the sounds of shouting and whinnying horses burst through their cracked windows.

"Tomás?" Levana's voice filled with fear, the serene and happy expression on her face now erased.

Her father set Julie down and rushed for the window, his hands trembling as he whispered. "Raiders."

Levana gasped, pressing her hand to her mouth. "Julie get under the bed. Now."

Julie gulped, tears pricking at her eyes. "What's happening, Mama?"

"Go, quickly. And make no noise, no matter what." Levana waved her arm towards the bed frantically as she and Julie's father worked to blow out the lanterns.

Julie crawled underneath the bed and her mother yanked the comforter down, concealing Julie from sight. Her heart slammed against her ribcage as she watched in horror while their front door was brutally forced open, sending splintering pieces of wood across their humble home. Men with weapons strapped across their chests held drawn swords as they stormed into Julie's house. She forced herself not to cry out when they dragged Tomás and Levana outside with blades to their backs. Maggie whimpered from her high chair, the darkness and chaos around them frightening her. Julie's heart plummeted to her stomach. *Maggie.*

Julie clawed her way out from underneath the bed and ran towards the high chair, adrenaline giving her the strength to grab Maggie and pull her down. Her sister cried, burying her head in Julie's neck. They wouldn't both fit underneath the bed. Julie hurtled them towards the shadowy corner of their parents' room in a split-second decision. Maggie refused to cease her crying and as the sound of screams from voices all too familiar met her ears, a sob wracked Julie's chest too. *No. Don't take them from us. Please.* Julie clutched Maggie to her chest as the raiders stormed back into the house, their boots splattered with fresh blood. They looted the cupboards, stole Papa's woodworking tools and knives, and pocketed Mama's favorite necklace. A silver chain with a single sapphire dangling from it.

Maggie squirmed, fussing in Julie's arms. She could only pray the baby wouldn't be heard over the sound of the raider's pilfering. Through tear-filled eyes, Julie peered up into the window above the corner they were hiding in. There in the night sky, amongst a multitude of stars, one flashed with all the brightness of the sun before it fell. As if enchanted by such a sight, Maggie fell quiet, and Julie realized upon closer inspection that her sister was asleep.

The raiders swung their lanterns back and forth over the space, casting shadows that transformed innocent corners into homes for monsters. They left without a word, taking everything of value from the house. The echo of horse hooves rang in Julie's mind long after the raiders departed. On shaking legs, Julie stood with Maggie still in her arms as she made her way outside. Even the crickets in the grass silenced themselves as if they too mourned for the innocent blood that stained the earth. Levana's eyes were open and unseeing. Her face twisted in a silent scream as a dark stain bloomed across her stomach. Julie choked on a sob, stumbling to the ground beside the bodies of her parents.

"Julie..." Her father's voice weakly strained past his blood-stained lips.

"Papa! Papa please don't go." Julie cried, tears streaming down her chin. Her other arm that wasn't clutching Maggie to her chest gripped her father's shoulder.

"Be brave..." His breathing caught painfully, "Like the princess." The corners of his mouth lifted in the slightest smile, and Julie knew it was the final gift he could offer her.

"No, Papa please. I'm not brave." Julie curled closer to his side, her heart breaking with every aching beat.

"Take..." He swallowed. "Take care of her." His hand weakly raised to Maggie's cheek.

Julie's small shoulders shook, and she wrapped her arms around Maggie's sleeping body. "I will. I swear I will."

Her father gave her one last labored smile. "Good."

"Papa? Oh, Papa…" Julie could barely make out his life-less form through the blurriness in her vision.

Suddenly the world shifted. Julie was no longer the small, broken girl bent over the form of her father. She was watching her through the eyes of the young woman she'd grown into. Julie tried to take steps toward her younger self, but she was rooted to the ground by a weight on her legs. When she looked down, she screamed.

Maggie, her sweet Maggie, was pale and limp in her grasp. Crimson seeped through the heart of her cotton dress, pierced through with an invisible knife. Her soft gray eyes were turned to the stars, a tear slipping past her lashes.

"Maggie!" Julie screamed, shaking her sister by the shoulders, her hands cupping the younger girl's cold face. "Help!" She cried out, begging for someone, anyone to hear her. "Help me!"

It seemed with each scream tearing from her throat, the world only grew quieter until no sound came from her cries.

She was going to break, right here and now.

She couldn't breathe.

She couldn't see.

She couldn't feel the arms around her, holding her tightly enough to keep her heart from fleeing its cage.

Chapter Nineteen

Amor

Her screams would haunt his memory for the rest of his miserable life. The sound was utterly broken and defeated. An echo of a boy on his knees, making promises and wishes to the very stars that took everything from him.

She cried for help, gasping for breath and twisting atop the blanket. As if she could wrench herself free of the horrors that plagued her. Amor found himself running to her, regretting his decision to wander to the lake a mere hour ago. Silver was already beside Julie, trying to soothe her, but none of his efforts were working. "I can't wake her." He said to Amor, his face drawn in worry.

"She's trapped." Amor drew her thrashing body into his arms, even as she tried to claw at him to free herself. It shouldn't have been his first instinct to hold her. He was the last person she needed, but in that moment he wanted to be the only one she clung to.

The back of his hand brushed her cheek, tears transferring onto his skin. "I've got you." He said quietly.

Julie's inhales were as shaky as her exhales, her cheeks flushed with fever. Only wordless whimpers passed her lips.

"Do we have anything to lower the fever?" Amor looked to Silver who rifled through his basket of poisons and herbs.

"I gave the last of the yarrow to Maggie when Julie left this morning."

Amor bit down on the inside of his cheek, "I have an idea. I'm taking her to the lake." If the fever worsened, it could have lasting effects on her abilities. He couldn't risk it. *She was his last option, and he needed her alive.*

The heat seeping from Julie's body bled into his own, her face glistening in the wash of the moonlight. "I would think with how stubborn you are, you'd be trying harder to fight this." He placed her down on top of the soft grassy bank. He was almost frustrated that she allowed anything to have control over her. Amor stared at the way her black hair splayed against the grass, some locks clinging to her neck and forehead. "But then again, you've been fighting for a while haven't you." He said with no one to hear him but the wind and stars.

Amor pulled his shirt over his head and ripped it into pieces of cloth. The sound of tearing fabric matched the hitches in her breathing. Amor knelt and placed the strips in the lake, dampening them with cool water. "Look what you've done, made me ruin my best shirt." Even though his words held a sigh in them, the corners of his lips lifted. He raised her head to place the fabric at the back of her neck, settling strips over her wrists and her forehead. The breeze that rolled over the lake would be good for her too, he supposed. Amor eased down next to her, drawing one knee to his chest and slinging his arm around it. His gaze scanned the tree line across the lake. He watched the gentle lapping ripples in the water before ultimately returning to her face.

She was quite lovely when she wasn't glaring at him. Amor didn't scold himself for noting it, after all it was an observation like anything else. He was focused, not blind. Try as he might to refute the thought, he hadn't been able to purge her scent of sweet almonds from his senses since the night of the wolf attack.

It took a lot to stun him, but it had deeply unsettled him when she flung herself in his direction to prevent his head from being bitten off. His first instinct was to break her fall when they hit the earth. Even after Julie scrambled away he couldn't bring himself to move for fear the sensation of her might dissipate. She'd saved his life that night. Amor didn't particularly enjoy being indebted to anyone and as his fingertips grazed her cheek he said, "Now we're even."

Those words seemed to be the ones to rouse her from her feverish slumber. Slowly, glassy hazel eyes blinked open to see him watching her. Julie drew in a breath, looking around as much as she could without moving her head.

"Where am I?" Her voice was raw and raspy.

"The lake." He replied, readjusting the cloth on her forehead to expose the cool side to her skin.

"Maggie?" Julie swallowed in an attempt to make her voice less hoarse.

"Sleeping." She'd been crying out for Maggie, but her sister's body was too exhausted with the toll of recovery to be roused.

Julie's moonlit silhouette visibly relaxed as she heard confirmation that her nightmares lied to her. "Why are you here?"

Amor turned over the cloth at her wrist. "To make sure you don't die before we get to Seruvia."

Julie's eyes closed. "We'll go... in the morning."

Amor's hand hovered over her other wrist. "No."

She cracked one eye open. "What?"

"I can't have you falling over on the road. Besides, you're without a horse and I'm not about to carry you the entire way." He said simply, leaving out the fact that it hadn't been a burden to carry her back today. She'd fit a little too well in his arms, like a puzzle piece finding its perfect spot.

Julie groaned, which turned into a cough. After she'd regained her voice she added, "There were bandits, they took Fiona and tried to take me with them."

Amor was silent for a few moments, taking the cloth from her left wrist and re-dipping it in the water. "How did you escape?"

"I think I bashed his nose in?"

Amor's brow flicked up. Now he knew who to pin his anger on. A man with a shattered nose and shame in his eyes. "Good." He said, draping the fabric along her wrist once more.

Julie turned her gaze to the night sky, tracing the constellations behind the swiftly moving clouds. "At least everything's not red anymore." She said to herself. Or, she thought she only said it to herself.

Amor looked at her questioningly. "Was it red before?"

She pursed her lips, unwilling to answer. "It's nothing."

Amor slipped his hand to the back of her neck, easing her head up so they were nearly at eye level. "You're wretched at lying."

"It..." She swallowed again, drawing Amor's attention to the fact his thumb was tracing the side of her neck as he held it in his hand. "It was just a side effect of whatever this is." She gestured loosely to herself.

"Julie, tell me." His gaze searched her own. He could count the individual green and golden lines in her irises. *It was a strange phenomenon, to see the sunrise at night.*

"I saw all the strings." She whispered. "There was no end to their power. I thought I would drown in them."

Amor bit back a curse. "Can you still see them?"

She looked around to confirm. "There's none here."

Amor's brows furrowed. "You can still see yours can't you?"

Julie was quiet for several seconds before she said, "I can." Her gaze flicked from her hand to just past Amor's shoulder. He couldn't help but wonder what the person on the other end of her string was doing right now.

Did that man know his soulmate could have been in danger, that she was sick?

Did he have the slightest clue of Julie's love for her sister or how her eyes sparked with gold when she tried to reign in her temper?

Had he ever cradled her to his chest while she cried from a nightmare?

Surely not, because then he would never have let her go.

"Am I interrupting something?" Silver's amused voice met their ears from behind them. Amor's body tensed as he realized his hand was still at her neck and she hadn't pulled away from it, until now.

"No." Amor said, a muscle feathering in his jaw for reasons he didn't want to explore.

"Good." Silver looked like he was biting back a smile, and Amor suppressed his urge to glare. "It's time for your next dose, how are you feeling, Julie?"

"Tired." She shifted uncomfortably on the grass. "I want to see Maggie."

"Lucky for you she just woke." Silver stepped over the twigs and thin tree branches on the ground to reach them. "Need help up?" His blue eyes briefly slid to Amor, a silent question in them.

Amor pushed himself to his feet and offered his hand but Julie grasped Silver's instead. Silver steadied her when her legs buckled. "You can lean on one of us if you'd like."

Julie pushed her shoulders back a bit. "I can walk on my own, thank you."

"Let him. You're weak from fever." Amor nodded towards Silver without breaking her gaze.

The defiance in her spirit flared and Amor watched as she raised her chin in his direction. "I'm not as weak as you believe." She started forward, slowly but wholly unsupported by anyone.

Amor swiped a hand over his jaw. "She's the most irritating thing."

Silver hung back, keeping Julie well within sight. He shrugged. "You do typically go for the throats of those that irritate you."

Amor shot a dagger-sharp look in Silver's direction, to which the man only grinned. "I jest. For once I would like to see something on your face besides a scowl."

Julie nearly tripped over an overgrown root which drew both men's attention, but she righted herself and kept walking. Amor lowered his voice and said, "Watch them both. I'd rather not hunt her down again. I have something to take care of."

"Will you be needing your arrows? Not all of them are ready yet."

"I'll take the ones you have." Amor replied.

Silver ducked underneath a low-hanging branch and glanced at Amor, amusement pricking at his lips. "Where's your shirt, man?"

Amor extended his hand and plucked a piece of torn cloth from a sharp mossy twig. "Here," he crumpled the cloth between his fingers, "and on that log, and back at the lake." He jerked his thumb backward.

Silver chuckled. "She may irritate you, but she is the only woman who's ever gotten you to remove your shirt."

"I'm going to leave you behind when we go to Seruvia." Amor said darkly.

Silver tipped his head back and laughed deeply. "Let me know how that works out for you, Am." He patted Amor's shoulder like a brother would.

Amor rolled his eyes, the flickering campfire now within view. Silver knelt beside a satchel and dug through it. He produced a dark, balled-up object before tossing it directly at Amor. "The arrows are in your usual spot." He said over his shoulder.

Amor unraveled the cloth projectile and slipped the shirt over his head. The black cotton garment was snug, but it would serve its purpose. "Don't listen to her, whatever she tells you. Tie her to a tree if you have to." Amor made a pointed look towards Julie across from them. She was crushing her little sister in a hug with whatever scrap of strength she had in her body.

Silver held his hands up in surrender. "I don't want to get on her bad side."

Amor slung his quiver across his back, clamping down his agitation for the situation he had landed in. "Just keep her alive, okay?"

"That I can do." Silver dipped his chin once. Amor tightened his grip along the smooth wood of his bow as he stalked away from camp and vanished into the darkness.

In the distance a storm was brewing.

And it was following him.

CHAPTER TWENTY

Julie

There was no greater relief for the lingering aches in her body than to see her sister alive and smiling. Julie threw all her energy into her legs to propel herself forward, wrapping Maggie up in her arms.

"Oh! Where's this coming from?" Maggie lightly squeezed Julie back.

Julie buried her face in her sister's shoulder. She needed to replace the image of a blood-soaked Maggie with one of her sister unharmed. "You scared me to death."

"I'm sorry, Jules. I didn't do it on purpose, promise." Maggie moved to see Julie's face better. "But you look worse for wear than I feel." She pressed her hand to Julie's forehead.

"Which is why she needs to take this." Silver crouched beside them, a spoon in hand as he tilted the medicine bottle onto it.

"Give it to Maggie." Julie pursed her lips. She had gotten the remedy for her sister in the first place, and she knew the worst of her own illness had passed.

Silver gave her an apologetic smile. "I was strictly told not to listen to you."

Annoyance sparked underneath the remnants of chills in her muscles. "You can't be serious."

Maggie massaged Julie's arm. "My fever broke, and I've slept enough to last me a month. Take it, for me."

Julie's shoulders sagged. "Don't use the, 'for me' loop-hole."

Maggie smiled, "It's purely out of love that I will utilize every loophole in the book." She said matter-of-factly.

"Fine." Julie conceded and accepted the spoon from Silver's hand. The liquid scorched her throat and made her tastebuds revolt. "He was right, that tastes awful."

"Amor?" Maggie questioned.

"No, Casimir… it's a long story." Julie dragged her hands over her hair, smoothing it.

"Before you regale her with the story, eat." Silver handed both girls plates of bread and broth. It smelled good but Julie wasn't sure if her appetite was up to par. It was the flitting memory of Amor believing her to be weak that urged her fingers to curl around the spoon. If she forced herself to eat, perhaps she would regain her strength faster.

As Julie chewed on the bread, she attempted to sort through the memories that slipped past her in a blur of nightmarish haze. She remembered running and being caught in arms far too dangerous. Julie certainly needed to keep her wits about her, because it was terribly wrong to associate a feeling of safety with those arms. A shiver ran over her shoulders and Maggie set her empty bowl down to pull a blanket over Julie.

"Thank you." Julie leant against Maggie's side.

"Thank *you*." Maggie said, pulling the blanket tighter against the night's chill.

"After the day you two had, something sweet is in order." Silver came over to them with a smaller bowl in hand. In it, rested a cinnamon pastry topped with powdered sugar that glittered in the firelight. Maggie gasped. "Where did you get this?"

Silver passed the plate into her hands. "I didn't. Amor brought it back this morning from the outpost."

"Amor brought it?" Julie couldn't keep the surprise from her voice. She thought he would have been the last person to spring for a dessert. Poison, yes. Sweetness, no.

"Even he will make exceptions when birthdays are involved. So, I know we're a little late but..." Silver took a smooth, match-like piece of wood and allowed it to catch flame before placing it on the cinnamon bun.

Birthday. "Oh, Maggie I am so sorry I slept through your birthday!"

Maggie laughed. "What do you call this? Our favorite childhood dessert and my own candle. It's perfect." Maggie leaned over and kissed Julie's cheek.

"Wait!" Julie drew in a breath, realization hitting her like a spark taking flight. "Give me one second before you blow that out."

Julie scrambled out from under the blanket towards the leafy curtain enclosing their camp. She pulled open the door of their wagon and climbed in. Thankfully, the small package was undamaged when Julie withdrew it from its hiding place. She hopped down from the wagon, pressing the gift to her chest.

As Julie parted the vine laden entrance, the sight she was met with made her pause. Silver tucked a wild curl away from Maggie's eyes, his knuckles grazing her cheek.

And Maggie... Oh, how she smiled.

Julie's little sister who wasn't so little anymore, beamed up at the young man with blue eyes brighter than the stars.

Silver murmured something in Maggie's ear when he saw Julie hanging by the entry.

He waved her forward with a smile. "Come now, don't keep us in suspense."

Julie went to her spot beside Maggie, sitting on her heels as she presented the gift. "Now, you can blow out your candle."

Maggie's face lit up. "Julie you didn't have to-"

"Yes, I did." Julie cupped Maggie's cheek. "Blow that out before it burns straight through."

"Make a wish." Silver said softly. He watched Maggie in a way that made Julie wonder if he was trying to memorize every freckle on her face.

Maggie's lashes fluttered shut as she thought about her wish. Suddenly, she blew out the flame. The smoke curled into the air, taking her secret wish with it.

"Happy birthday, Mags." Julie hugged her sister by the shoulders.

"Happy birthday." Silver echoed.

"Thank you." Maggie's grin was all the radiance of lost magic. "Can I?" She peered down at the carefully wrapped package.

"Absolutely."

Maggie gingerly slipped the bow free of the box. A soft gasp left her when she looked upon the contents. Her fingertips grazed the vial of rose water and she held it up to her nose. "Have you ever smelled anything so delightful?" Excitement and awe seeped into her voice as she made both Julie and Silver take turns sniffing the perfume. Maggie was not fully satisfied until she'd dabbed a bit of it on both their wrists as well. Maggie's gaze landed on the last item in the package.

"Julie this is… incredible." Maggie breathed, draping the necklace over her hand. The delicate three stars with blue stones fastened into their centers danced with firelight. *Something glimmering and sparkling, just like her.*

"It looks like mother's." Julie took the silver chain from her sister's grasp, pulling Maggie's curls to the side to fasten the necklace.

Maggie placed her hand over the stars as they settled just underneath her collarbone. She then turned and threw her arms around Julie. "Thank you, Jules."

Julie held her tightly. Perhaps one day, even after Maggie was surrounded by all the pretty things she could ever desire, she might still wear this necklace.

Maggie would have that and so much more.

It would all be worth it. The circus, wolves, uncertainty, illness and lies.

Julie would keep her promise to Papa, whether it took till the end of their journey with Amor or the rest of her life.

Hours passed as they exchanged stories by the campfire. Maggie curled up next to Julie, utterly enraptured by the tales Silver spun. Between the low hum of Silver's voice, the warmth of the blanket, and the certainty of her sister's form beside her, Julie found her eyelids growing heavy.

Julie jerked just before she gave into the allure of sleep as an awful stomping filtered past the leafy veil that concealed them. Footsteps, too many to count, made Julie press her arm against Maggie's body to shield her.

Silver's hand reached for the dagger at his hip. If Julie looked hard enough, past the slight cracks in the vines, she swore she could see a man in a mask.

The bandits had found them.

Chapter Twenty-One

Amor

Amor itched for a fight. Gravel crunched underneath his boots as he trekked down the worn path. He was miles from camp, yet her voice clung to his thoughts. Amor pressed the heel of his hand to his temple as if he could physically restrain the memory. *It should not be this difficult.*

'*They took Fiona, and they tried to take me with them.*' Julie had told him. The pride he felt when she mentioned how she bashed in one of their noses was tangled with confusing sensations of guilt.

Besides, he offered her his hand and she accepted Silver's. That's all there was to it.

Amor's gait slowed. A fire dwindled by the side of the road where three men lay snoring on the grass. Tied to a tree was a certain night-dark horse with her head lowered. Amor's focus settled on one man with dark bruising along his eyes. The cartilage of his nose was bent at a misshapen angle, making him wheeze.

Good girl.

Amor planted his boot directly into the man's chest, whose dark eyes flashed open with a mixture of shock and fear.

"A pretty little bird told me you tried to take something that didn't belong to you." Amor said lowly, applying harsher pressure. *He could crack a few ribs, but that didn't seem punishment enough.*

The man tried to heave himself out from underneath Amor's foot, but he was pinned. He pushed both hands against Amor's shin and shoved his leg away. The commotion stirred his two other companions, and a chorus of confused grunts tainted the quiet. The bandit with the broken nose scrambled to his feet, unsheathing a dagger and brandishing it.

"What's all this?" The other bandit asked, annoyed at being roused from his slumber.

"Which one of you stole that mare?" Amor jerked his chin in Fiona's direction.

"Stole?" One bandit rubbed his unshaven jaw, his voice still gravelly from the late hour. "We've had these horses for months."

"You'd best be getting on your way." The man with black rings under his eyes scanned Amor's form, lingering on the quiver at his back.

"No, I don't think I will." Amor's lips pulled back from his teeth as he turned towards the man and connected his fist with the thief's jaw. A crack echoed in the air as the first bandit stumbled backward, cursing colorfully while blood dribbled down his chin. He tried to throw a punch in Amor's direction, but he was disoriented, and Amor was quicker. The side of the man's head was an excellent place for Amor's strike to land and he fell ungracefully to the dirt.

With a growl, his traveling partner whirled around, attempting to swipe Amor's legs out from underneath him. Amor grabbed onto the second assailant's shoulders and drove his knee directly into his stomach. He doubled over as a grunt of pain escaped him along with the air in his lungs.

It was the glint of silver in Amor's periphery that had him ducking, narrowly avoiding a dagger to the neck. The instant after Amor dropped into a crouch, he leapt forward, lunging for the bandit's center of gravity. The man twisted the knife in his hand, thrusting it forward towards Amor's heart. Amor grabbed the man's wrist, wrenching it away and squeezing until the sound of snapping bones reverberated through the night's breeze. The man howled in pain as his wrist bent to the side and Amor swiped the silver knife from where it had fallen. Amor glared down at the men, one still struggling to refill his lungs and the other cradling his limp wrist with deadly malice in his eyes.

Then he turned his attention again to the one who had tried to take her. The scene kept circling his mind. Julie, on the brink of collapse, fighting with every fiber of her being to escape this man's clutches.

He and Julie were nothing to each other. They were only two ends of a bargain struck from desperation. Yet Amor advanced, flashes of her hazel eyes stabbing him to his haunted core.

Not again. Never again. When this was all over, her life full and their paths separated, he would keep watch from the shadows. That's what he was good at, the darkness was where he belonged. She belonged in the realm of light and fire and treasure. Those two worlds were never meant to collide. He stalked forward, his deliberate steps the replica of the heartbeat he could practically hear shuddering in the man's chest.

Amor gripped the bandit's collar, blood stained and torn as he hauled him upright. Weak mumbles of protest slipped over his lips as he faded in and out of consciousness. Amor plopped him in front of a tree, dropping his body like a sack of potatoes. That was about how much this cretin's life was worth anyway.

Amor's voice was unsettlingly even, as his fingers curled around the man's wrist. The man groaned, weakly trying to pull his arm free but it was a useless and sorry attempt. "I want you to remember your mistake every time you see your hands. I want you to regret putting them on her." Amor took the point of the silver knife and made two deliberate slices into the man's palm. One curve, and one line. The sudden pain made him jerk, grasping onto his consciousness with wide eyes. "Stop!" He hissed.

"Something tells me you didn't listen when someone else begged the same." Amor released the bandit's first wrist, capturing the next. Despite the man's efforts, Amor didn't relent until mirrored gashes were drawn into his skin. Blood poured freely from the marks that would certainly form nasty scars with time. The man moaned in pain, cradling his hands to his chest, further covering his shirt in crimson. Just before he hid his palms completely, the moonlight caught onto the edge of Amor's work.

Two J's. Etched forever into the hands of a thief who tried to take what wasn't his. Her initial, branded into flesh as a constant reminder and warning.

Amor left them there. None of the bandits willing to go another round as they were all battered, bruised, and actively bleeding. He went up to Fiona and loosed her lead from the trunk. The mare chuffed and bowed her head against Amor's chest. It was almost like the gentle beast was saying, *thank you.*

Amor wrapped her reigns around his fist and took them both to an adjacent tree that bound another horse. This one was moonlight gray, with a long mane and speckles along her flank. Amor untangled the rope and walked in front of both horses, moonlight and shadow trotting behind him. The girls would be thrilled to see Fiona. He could almost envision the relief that might lessen the weight from Julie's shoulders. He wasn't sure what to call the new gray one but perhaps Maggie would be up to the challenge of naming her. It was the girl's birthday after all.

Eventually, they reached the canopy, the leaves on the outside slightly illuminated by the light of a waning fire. Fiona, perhaps excited to be back in a familiar environment, stamped her hooves. Her behavior rubbed off on the gray horse who mirrored Fiona's actions. Amor was about to re-attach Fiona to the wagon when the leafy canopy parted. Silver was there, brandishing a blade pointed outwards before recognition clicked and he lowered it. "Am?"

Amor tugged down the black cloth covering the lower half of his face. "Do people usually stop by and bring you horses, Token?"

Before Silver could respond, Amor looked behind him where Julie appeared with her hand cocked back, a rock clenched in her fist.

Was she planning on throwing it at him?

"It's me." Amor told her, stepping aside and out of range were she to throw it anyway.

"I thought you were the bandits." Julie sighed, unfurling her fingers from the rock and letting it fall to the ground.

The bandits will never come for you again, Julie. You're safe. Amor wanted to say those words, but he didn't.

Because it didn't matter.

Julie suddenly gasped in surprise, before she ran towards the mare who previously blended in with the night. Her hands stroked Fiona's muzzle, resting her forehead against the horse's long face. "You found her."

"And you found one we didn't lose." Amusement curled around Silver's tone, as he let the gray horse sniff his palm.

"I figured we could use them both," Amor told Silver. His gaze never strayed from the way Julie's lips pulled into a relieved smile as she continued to pet her horse.

"Was this what you needed to take care of?" Silver dropped his voice to a murmur, standing at Amor's side as the two watched Julie interact with Fiona.

"They would slow us down without a horse, and I knew they wouldn't want to leave their wagon." Amor withdrew the silver knife from his belt, cleaning the edges of the blade with the hem of his shirt.

"Yes, I'm sure they wouldn't." Silver replied. Amor didn't have to look at him to know there was mirth dancing behind his eyes. "It certainly has nothing to do with the fact that losing that horse would have eaten at her everyday."

"She would have recovered." Amor slid the newly shining knife back into the sheath at his belt. "Don't read too much into it." He warned, which only pulled a smile onto Token's face.

"My friend, it's hard not to when the book is out in the open for all to see."

Amor gave him a flat look, making his way toward the vine-laden curtain. "I'm going to bed."

"Goodnight." He mused, lightly chuckling.

CHAPTER TWENTY-TWO

Julie

"What do you think about the name, 'Pepper?'" Maggie asked. The sunlight poured through the canopy, casting a halo behind her damp, dark curls. She had been trying to conjure up a name for the new horse since breakfast. Then, she spouted off a list while the girls washed in the river.

"Pepper is cute." Julie pulled the brush through Fiona's mane as the mare tossed her head lightly. Julie's fingers curled through a lock of Fiona's mane. She thought for certain they would never see her again. When Amor brought Fiona back, Julie had felt the near overwhelming urge to wrap her arms around his neck and thank him.

Obviously, that only stemmed from a rush of adrenaline and a surge of relief. She knew that.

Yet, it hadn't stopped her eyes from following him when he slipped inside camp, words on her tongue that were never uttered but instead swallowed.

"What about her middle name?" Maggie's voice drew Julie out of her head.

"Even Fiona doesn't have a middle name." Julie chuckled.

Maggie began to braid Pepper's long, gray mane. "Sure she does. It's Daisy." Maggie looked at Julie as if she'd suddenly sprouted two heads.

"Daisy? Since when?" Julie turned her body towards her sister, amusement written all over her face.

"We drove through a field of daises the night we escaped *The Circle of Lights.*" Maggie grinned, and Julie could tell with her sister's vibrancy that her strength was returning. However, Silver informed them that they wouldn't depart until tomorrow, so the girls could fully recover.

Julie shook her head, smiling. "It'll come to you, Mags. Who knows, you might get inspired on the road."

Maggie was about to respond when the sound of rustling leaves filtered through the air and her lips split into another smile. "Hi, Amor."

Julie whirled around, slightly unsettled by the fact his eyes knew exactly where to fall into hers before she fully turned.

"Are you busy?" He asked Julie.

Julie looked between the brush in her hand, Fiona, and then back to him. "I'm brushing Fiona at the moment."

Maggie hopped down from the dead tree stump she'd been using as a stool and swiftly plucked the brush handle from Julie's clutches. "I've got it."

Julie opened her mouth to protest but Maggie proved her point by beginning to detangle the ends of Fiona's mane.

"Alright, I guess I'm not busy." Julie shrugged, sparing her sister a light look.

Amor held open the vines, creating a partition large enough for her to duck under. When they were inside, he spoke again. "I noticed you last night."

Julie lifted a brow. "I noticed you too, I thought you were a bandit. We've been over this."

Amor's emerald eyes looked at her sidelong. "No, I mean I noticed you planned to launch a rock at what you thought was an intruder's head."

Julie dropped her arms across her chest. "What are you getting at?"

"What if it hadn't been me last night? What if there really had been someone that could've hurt you?"

Julie watched him. "And you couldn't hurt me?" That thought was nearly laughable. He was over a foot taller and much broader in build. He had the ability to snap her in two.

Amor paused in front of her. "I can, and I would like to know what you could do against it."

"I'd run, probably." Julie said simply.

"Won't work, you can't outrun an archer. Especially not a sharpshooter."

"Okay... I would hide Maggie first and then-"

"No." Amor interrupted her. "If your life is in imminent danger your first thought cannot be to protect someone else. If you die, she dies."

Julie blinked at him, dumbstruck by the absurdity of that statement. "If I'm in imminent danger and I have the opportunity to get her to safety, I will take it. Either way, I die in this scenario." Julie tapped her foot impatiently against the dirt.

"Or you take the third option which is to fight so neither of you dies." Amor pulled an object from his belt, a dagger still trapped in its leather sheath. "Do you know how to use this?"

Julie pinched the bridge of her nose. "Do I know how to use a sharp object against a threat? Well, you're still standing here so clearly I do." She challenged, drawing both their minds back to the night of the wolf attack.

"An arrowhead that's already poisoned is different." Amor pressed the sheathed weapon into Julie's hands. "In close proximity with an attacker, you can't fire a bow." He picked up a blade that Julie recognized as Silver's and stood behind her. "Unsheathe it and show me how you'd use it against me."

Julie's eyebrows drew together, and she turned her neck back to look at him. "You want me to stab you?"

"Preferably not but I do want to see what technique you would use."

Julie sighed and slipped the dagger free of its confinement. *This shouldn't be so hard. All it takes is-*

His arm wrapped around her waist.

Julie's breath hitched as she was pulled slightly back into the solid pillar that was Amor. "What are you doing?" She scolded her voice for sounding so faint.

"An attacker won't just stand idle waiting for you to fight back." Amor said, his other arm pressed against her upper shoulders, holding the flat side of his knife near her collarbone. "You need to learn how to escape if someone bigger literally has you backed into a corner."

The thumping of his heartbeat against her back was wildly distracting from the blade at her neck. If she moved forward, the blade would prick her. She couldn't move back any more as there was no space between them. Amor's hand and arms were making sure of that.

The dagger in her hand felt quite like a useless piece of metal. At this point, it would better serve a purpose as a fancy paperweight. She needed a plan.

Amor's grip on the knife faltered when Julie's head leant back against his chest.

"I'm waiting," He said quietly, his voice low against the shell of her ear. A shiver that had little to do with the breeze around them trailed down her spine.

"Working on it." She huffed a laugh, or an attempt at one. She was in a dangerous situation. One wrong move and she could spill her own blood. One right move and she might spill his.

And that felt very, very wrong.

If she couldn't go forward, and she couldn't move back, her only other option was to drop.

She heard Amor draw in a breath when she went limp, slipping free from his hold before she stood and held the dagger out in front of her as a barricade. "I did it." Julie said, feeling slightly out of breath which didn't make sense. All she had done was fall.

"Good." Amor cleared his throat. "Next time, you need to take my legs out. Depriving someone of their balance can often give you a precious few seconds to regroup."

"I thought about it."

Amor looked at her, confusion knitting his black brows together, "So why didn't you?"

Julie stuffed the dagger back into the leather sheath. "Look where you were standing. If you'd fallen back, you would have hit your head on that log."

He glanced over his shoulder, something passing across his features when their eyes locked that Julie couldn't decipher.

She extended the dagger back to him and swiped her palms on her pants. "What about this?" Julie walked straight for his bow at the base of the tree he always slept in. It was nestled atop soft grass with little blooming wildflowers.

Amor slipped both knives into the belt at his hip. "You want to shoot my bow?" He asked, a hint of surprise in his voice.

"Well, seeing as it's the main weapon you travel with and we're travelling with you, I probably should know how to use it." Her fingertips grazed the smooth curve of the black bow. Even when it wasn't in Amor's grip, it looked lethal. "Who made this?" She questioned. The detailing along the bend of it and the utter beauty of the weapon made it look unearthly.

"It was a gift." Amor said, leaning against the side of the tree next to her. Julie hadn't realized he'd moved so close.

"Silver made it for you?" Julie picked it up, tracing the swirling pattern engraved within the bow.

"No." Amor's voice sounded withdrawn. When Julie looked up she noticed his gaze was stuck on the bow. "It's a long story." He pushed off the tree, slung his quiver over his shoulder and beckoned for her to follow. "Come on, you need a wider space to practice."

He left his bow in her hands and Julie wondered if perhaps that was significant. The weapon he was never without, now in her grasp. Amor led her to the clearing by the river. "See that tree? I want you to shoot the knot in the middle." He pointed towards a decently thick trunk with gangly branches and a lack of leaves. Amor produced a few arrows and brought them to her.

"What are those laced with?" Julie peered down at them, but it was difficult to determine exactly what they could be coated in.

"They're not. I'm never going to give you poison." Amor told her.

"I suppose that would be unhelpful since you still need me." Julie nocked an arrow into the bow before continuing, "For what reason I haven't fully grasped yet, but the fact remains that I have leverage."

Amor twisted the arrow's slender shaft between his fingers, "You have leverage? I have a bow and arrows with poison tipped arrowheads. You see magic strings and have pretty hazel eyes. Which one of us do you think has more leverage?"

A little jolt went through her, as if she had touched metal while being covered in static. She shoved the sensation down and answered, "Me, now that I know you think my eyes are pretty."

Amor's silence gave Julie the opportunity to tack on, "Besides you don't have your bow and arrows right now." She flashed a triumphant smile. "I do."

"You are so devoted to frustrating me." He grumbled, stepping to the side.

"I'm devoted to a lot of things. Frustrating you is just a bonus." Julie tried to level the bow, focusing on the knot in the tree's bark.

"You're leaning too far forward." Amor's fingers splayed against her abdomen, straightening her.

"It's the only way I can make this level." Julie countered, her focus ripping into shreds at the feeling of his hand on her waist.

"If you were to fire right now, the arrow would go directly into the dirt." Amor's hand slipped away from her stomach. Instead, with a pressure gentler than she thought possible, he lowered her raised arm. "The fletching should brush your cheek." He murmured. "Right about there." The side of Amor's knuckle grazed Julie's face and she held her breath. *How was it that the feathers on the end of the arrow were less soft than the way he just touched her?*

"Take a breath before you let the arrow go." Amor said quietly, the heat from his palm seeping through the fabric of her sleeve.

That would have been excellent advice if she wasn't struggling to remember how to breathe. She looked away from the tree and to him. His eyes were so rich, so intense. It was nearly overwhelming that the entirety of his focus was pinned on her. Before this moment, Julie would have sworn that it was a death sentence to be on the receiving end of Amor's attention. But now it was like gravity didn't exist. The only thing keeping her rooted to the ground was his touch and the intensity with which he looked at her.

"Should I let go?" She whispered.

"Yes." Amor answered, equally quiet. Julie released the arrow, her aim forgotten.

"I don't think that hit the mark." Julie's words were embellished with a small smile. Not the kind reserved for those who showed up to their wagon or when she wanted to convince Maggie it would all be okay. Just... *a real one.*

"It didn't, but I'm starting to think you were right when you said you had leverage over me."

"What made you change your mind?" Julie lowered the bow to her side, turning more toward Amor.

He was silent for a few heartbeats before he answered, "I saw you smile."

CHAPTER TWENTY-THREE

Amor

The hours had slipped by since their departure at dawn. The sun now hung at its highest point above their heads. Maggie walked with Silver as Pepper trotted alongside them. Amor could hear pieces of their conversation, at least the parts that weren't drowned out by the sound of Fiona's hooves.

His mind wandered to yesterday. Amor stared ahead towards the brimming horizon. Yesterday had been a mistake. It shouldn't have mattered whether or not Julie knew how to use weapons. Once he no longer needed her gifts, she could find her soulmate and he could show her how to protect herself. Or perhaps, the man would protect her so she never needed to reach for a knife.

The wind began to pick up, ruffling his hair into disarray much like his thoughts. In a rare, unguarded moment, he had spoken a foolish thing. To admit her smile held any power over him had been thoughtless, irrational and nonsensical. He couldn't afford any distractions.

There was a line in the sand between them. He hadn't realized it until she'd been so close he could have breathed her in. Amor let the corner of his bow dig into the soft, fine ground beneath them as he walked. *It would be easier to fall into a chasm of his own design rather than reach out blindly and hope a hand on the other side might catch him.* Julie sat tall on the bench seat, reigns in hand as she kept her gaze trained on the path ahead. So determined, so steady, even when the world around her was wreathed in the unknown.

Suddenly, she turned her head and saw him. Fates, she made that little smile. It was almost enough to warrant the defenestration of the entire plan he had concocted.

Almost.

"Am! There's a stream up ahead. We can let the horses take a break and drink." Silver called, turning and walking backward. It was a perfectly timed interruption. Now, he didn't have to worry about being locked in her gaze.

"Alright, we'll stop."

Julie pulled Fiona to a halt when they neared the pond's bank, the wheels of their wagon groaning in protest. Around them, the wind licked at their faces. Amor glared up at the sky, noting the rolling clouds. A storm would only slow them down. Just when his resolve would strengthen, she would walk by, and it would falter again. Julie unhitched Fiona from the wagon and led the mare toward the water. Amor watched Silver kneel down and flick a little sprinkle of water in Maggie's direction. The gray-eyed girl tossed several dandelions at him with a bright grin on her lips. The breeze swept through their small group and Julie pushed black strands of hair out of her face. Amor suddenly found himself right behind her and gathered her tresses into his hand.

"I'm not going to fall in." Julie lifted a brow, looking back to see him standing precariously close with a fistful of her hair. *Julie's hair was heavy, how did her neck not buckle under the weight of it all?*

"I wasn't worried." Amor answered, separating the majority of her hair into three sections.

"What are you doing?" Julie tried to sneak a glance over her shoulder.

"It's windy."

She gave him a look, "I can see that. But I'm just curious why you're holding my hair hostage."

That's an excellent question. Amor draped the sections over each other, being careful not to pull on the strands.

"I'm braiding it. It'll get tangled otherwise." It was the logical thing to do.

"Do you have something to tie it with?" Julie asked, reaching back to run her fingers down the texture of the braid.

Amor pinched the end with one hand and plunged his other into his pocket, producing a small piece of leather. "This ought to hold it." He said as he secured the improvised tie. It wasn't the fanciest braid in the world, but it would serve its purpose. She pivoted toward him as he brought the plait over her shoulder.

He thought now that her hair was secure, she would walk away. But Julie instead perched upwards on her toes and brushed errant waves from his brow. Amor drew in a breath as the pads of her fingertips grazed his forehead. "What are *you* doing?"

She didn't seem satisfied until the unruly locks were mostly brushed back. "Like you said, it's windy. You'd barely be able to make anything out with your hair in your eyes."

"I can see just fine." Amor spoke. He could see too well now. Clearly enough to distinguish the individual black lashes that fanned over her eyes and the slight cracking of her bottom lip where the wind had roughly kissed her.

Rather than question why he'd lingered on the mouth that loved to frustrate him so, he turned and grabbed the water canteens from Silver's pack. Silver stepped around Amor's knelt form. "Did my eyes deceive me or were you playing with her hair?"

Amor dipped the canteen into the swiftly burbling water, "I wasn't *playing* with it." His eyes narrowed briefly as he tightened the cap on the newly filled container. "Wearing it down was impractical for travel and the weather."

Silver picked up a small stone and cocked his wrist back, sending it skipping across the surface of the stream. "It is a real issue. I've heard stories of women having to cut off all their hair because the knots were too difficult to deal with." A cheeky smile tugged at Silver's lips. "So, I'm glad you remedied that for her." He tacked on.

Amor threw one of the water containers at Silver who caught it in midair, the water inside sloshing. "How about you focus on getting us to Seruvia."

Silver had the audacity to smirk. "Did you forget I used to be excellent at watching over multiple things at once?"

"The key words are, *'used to be.'*" Amor stepped aside to avoid being nudged in the shoulder by Pepper.

"Some things are too blatantly obvious to ignore." Silver chuckled, his eyes straying to the far side of the bank. Amor followed where his gaze stopped. Maggie was weaving flowers through Julie's braid, making his simple plaiting look like something out of a painting. Splashes of blue and purple, with tiny sprigs of white and green curled themselves amongst a cascading river of black. "Impractical." Amor sighed.

"Then why are you staring?" Silver asked quietly, lingering for a moment before walking toward the women. Amor didn't have an answer for him. The words to refute weighed heavy on the tip of his tongue and stayed there.

The wind kicked up, sending Amor's hair tumbling back into his eyes. He raised a hand to push it back like she had. It allowed him another instant to watch the way she made the landscape around them pale in comparison simply by standing in it. Not even a field filled with flowers of every color could aspire to be as lovely as how they looked in her hair.

"Time to go." Amor's voice didn't sound like it belonged to him. It pulled itself from his throat against his internal protest. He didn't deserve to imagine putting one of those flowers behind her ear. That privilege would belong to a better man. A man who certainly would be his opposite in every way. For her sake, he hoped that was true.

As they continued their trek the wind began to lash at them. Clouds the color of ash stretched out over their heads, snuffing out the sun like air to a candle's flame.

Amor had to raise his hand in front of his face to block the wind's wrath. The horses tossed their heads nervously, expelling swirling particles of dirt from their nostrils as they clomped forward. Julie struggled to keep her grip tight on Fiona's reigns as the mare tried to bolt. A rumbling encased them, and Amor turned just fast enough to see the billowing plumes of dust devour everything at their backs. Trees and boulders disappeared underneath the floating mass which approached with every passing second, swallowing the road.

They only had one minute before they were blinded.

Chapter Twenty-Four

Julie

Everything happened between the span of one blink and the next. Amor shouted over the roaring wind for Silver to grab Maggie as the hot air became heavy with dust. Then he had his bow slung over his shoulder and his hands wrapped around Julie's waist, ripping her down from the bench seat. Julie collided into him, braced only by Amor's arm that kept her firmly pinned until he was certain she had her footing. His movements were that of lightning, unhooking Fiona from the wagon and gathering her lead.

"We have to move!" Amor called over the thundering that filled Julie's ears. Silver had taken Pepper's lead, but kept Maggie tucked into his side, shielding her from the dust that poured over them.

"The wagon." Julie gritted her teeth against the harsh gust of wind that threatened to keep them from advancing further. "I can't-"

"You have to," Amor readjusted his grip on her arm. "We'll come back for it."

The dust enveloped them, and Julie could no longer see two feet in front of her. The only thing that grounded her was Amor's hand acting as an anchor even as the earth was being devoured underneath their boots. Julie's vision was pummeled with dust and sand. It felt like they'd been pushing through the storm for hours.

"Amor! I think there's something out there!" Silver yelled back, his words split by a muffled cough.

"Hold on!" Amor pulled Julie alongside him, fighting the wind that kept them caged in its clutches.

"Julie, are you okay?" Maggie's voice rose to be heard over the droning and before Julie could answer she had to spit out the sand that clung to her lips.

"I'm okay!" Julie ducked her head against the whipping gusts.

"Up ahead!" Silver shouted, and Julie's other hand become encompassed by one that was unmistakably Maggie's.

"I see it." Amor's arm went around Julie's shoulders to steer her in the right direction. The ground shifted beneath her feet before she saw what they did. Instead of dirt and rocks, her boots scuffed against wood. Regardless of what the structure was, it was a refuge. Silver fumbled with the door handle and ushered Maggie and Julie inside. The men followed after they tied the horses to the railing attached to the porch. Julie prayed the mares would be alright out there with no barn to shelter them. Maggie coughed into the crook of her sleeve, her slim shoulders shaking. Silver brushed the sand and dust off his hands and clothes. Amor didn't release Julie's arm until he scanned their new surroundings. Julie's chest heaved as she caught her breath, swiping tears that slipped past her irritated eyes.

As Julie's sight adjusted to the dimness, she saw many others in a similar predicament. Some had chosen stairs to plop down on, while others leant against banisters and walls.

Outside, the storm howled, shutters clattering against the façade of the inn. The only thing that clacked more fiercely was the sound of a woman's hurried steps tearing down the stairs. "Eric? Eric!" She scanned the bodies gathered at the foot of the stairs but from the distraught and panicked look on her face, she did not locate whomever she was calling for. "Please, have any of you seen Eric?"

A chorus of grumbled and tired 'no's' weaved through the space, accentuated by several yawns. The woman looked like she was on the verge of tears, frantically swiping her palms over the front of her apron.

"Who are you looking for, ma'am?" Julie questioned, weaving past the throng of weary travelers to reach her.

"My son! Oh, please miss, have you seen him? He's this high." She gestured with her hand at her mid-thigh. "He ran outside to play just before the storm rolled in."

"Where does he usually play?" Amor's voice sounded behind Julie.

"The well behind the inn," she choked out. "But it's been too long, he could be lost out there."

The storm was worsening by the minute. Who knew how terrified that little boy might be? "Don't worry, ma'am. I'll find him." Julie squeezed the woman's shoulder reassuringly. A small sliver of hope was better than none at all.

"Julie you can't go back out there, it's dangerous." Maggie's hand gripped Julie's sleeve, with an imploring look in her gray eyes.

"I'll stick close to the inn, I promise." Julie pulled her sister in for a quick hug before relinquishing her to Silver. Both worry and understanding crossed her sister's features. As Julie started for the door she heard the sound of cloth being ripped and suddenly something soft and dark green was tied around her wrist. *Amor had torn the bottom of his cloak to make a rope that would tether them together.*

"Why did you-" She started before he cut her off.

"If you think I'm letting you face a storm alone, you're severely mistaken." Amor gave one harsh tug to the knot, testing its durability before pushing the door open.

Julie knew it had been a smart idea on his end. He still needed her, and their journey was not yet finished. It would all be for naught if she was lost to the dust storm. So, it made sense that he bound them together. *She just wished it didn't make so much sense.*

"Eric!"

"Eric! Where are you?" Julie's call a near echo to Amor's as their ears strained to pick up even a hint of a cry or small voice.

Julie's foot caught on an overturned rock. She tripped, the ground reaching up for her.

"You're usually much more graceful." Amor caught her before she made contact with the earth. "Losing your touch are we?"

"Hilarious." Julie's foot smarted from where it had banged against the stone. Amor's hand ran alongside the exterior of the inn, using it as their guide. "Eric! Make a sound so we can hear you!" His voice carried across the wind, fiercer than Julie thought necessary.

"He's going to think you're mad at him." Julie poked Amor's arm. "Could you sound a little less grumpy? Or you'll scare him into not responding." Julie reasoned, calling the child's name again.

"What do you want me to do, get him a puppy?" Amor gave her a look that she could see clearly even through the dust and dirt raining down on their heads. "If he cries, we'll at least be able to hear him." The cloth-cord grew taut between them as Amor continued further.

"You're really going to be father of the year someday." Julie grumbled.

A scoff rolled over Amor's lips. "The last thing this world needs is more of my blood. What's in my body is a waste already."

Julie stopped in her tracks, words about to slip past her tongue to refute him. Before she could consider why she wanted to say them, the faintest sob broke through the wind's howling. Julie and Amor's eyes flashed to each other, and they ran in that direction. "Eric!" They called in unison.

Curled up against the well's stony curve, sat a little boy with sand coating his black hair. His knees were drawn to his chest, small arms wrapped around them. Eric's shoulders shook as he cried, and continued to shudder even after Julie pulled him close. "Shh. You're fine now."

"Julie." Amor knelt in front of them, his back acting as a shield against the storm for both she and Eric. "There's blood on him." Amor moved the boy's hair back from his temple, revealing a trickle of crimson.

"We need to get him back to his mother." No sooner had the words left Julie's sand-laden lips that the wind growled its refusal. Amor braced his hands on either side of their heads as Julie saw the vague outline of debris shooting past. "We can't take him through this until it calms down."

Eric whimpered and burrowed his face into the crook of Julie's neck. "What do we do?"

"Wait it out." Amor's voice was tight. "Protect his head."

Julie's bound hand cradled the little boy's head. From her periphery, she saw Amor's hand inch higher to ensure she was guarded from any flying fragments.

But if she had Eric, and Amor had her...

Who was protecting Amor?

Julie's free hand snaked behind Amor's head, her fingers spread through his hair.

"What are you doing?" Amor's eyes settled on hers, his voice quiet as his head dropped lower underneath her hand. That simple movement cost them inches of space they previously had between each other and yet she found it impossible to pull away. When he turned his head just the slightest amount, his lashes grazed her cheek.

There was something here. An unspoken spark that glimmered in the dusk. Being blinded on all sides wasn't as frightening when he was so close. She guided Amor's head to rest against her own and he didn't resist.

She had to know...

She needed to know.

"Is this all in my head?"

Around them, the wind itself seemed to take a breath as if the worst of the storm might pass were Amor to answer. It took seven heartbeats of silence for him to respond. "It has to be." Her heart stammered when his lips ghosted over her temple. "Dream of something better, Julie."

"Then why haven't you moved?"

His breath was soft and warm at her cheek. "Because I'm not a good man, and you're the best dream I can think of."

Her heart fluttered in her chest, and her tongue was rendered too heavy to form words. With every passing second that Julie didn't respond, he began to recoil into a mask of indifference. In a desperate attempt to reach out and grab onto that vulnerability before it was concealed she started, "Amor-"

"I'm sorry." He interrupted her, his head pulling away from her ear. Dusty wind filtered in through the newly made gap where his whispers had been a mere moment ago. "That was wrong of me."

Julie's hand slipped out from his hair, the only warmth now was that of dry air settling around them like fog. "It's alright." She watched the tension return to his shoulders. She hadn't realized they'd relaxed even in the face of a swirling storm. Or maybe they never had, and she imagined it just like she'd imagined everything else.

Imagination was for children. She couldn't forget why she was here. *This was all for Maggie.* This was a means to an end of a necessary journey to fulfill her promise. "It's best you don't dream of something you're paying for, right?"

Amor's eyes fell on her, sharp and hard. Julie wasn't sure which was worse, the storm they were trapped in or the one warring behind shards of emeralds.

"Right."

It might have been minutes, it might have been hours. Eventually Amor's hands fell away from either side of her head, and he instead offered one of them to help her rise.

Julie didn't take it.

It took a considerable amount of effort to stand up with Eric in her grasp, but she did it and all without Amor's help.

If she were honest with herself, perhaps part of her refusal was simply because if she took his hand, she might have been inclined to keep it. The fact of the matter is, you simply cannot keep something that was never yours to begin with.

CHAPTER TWENTY-FIVE

Maggie

They hadn't gotten lost, which was a blessing. After the initial wave of relief at seeing Julie unhurt ebbed away, Maggie truly took in her sister's state. Her braid was fraying, strands had been harshly dragged free, and there wasn't a single wildflower remaining.

"What do you think happened out there?" Maggie whispered, leaning slightly to the side where Silver stood. They hung back enough to allow the child's mother room as she hugged the boy and sobbed out words of gratitude.

Silver tilted his head, an action Maggie found rather endearing especially with how it made his hair swoop over his brow. Even dusty and tired, Silver was the most handsome man she'd ever seen. "I'm not sure, I'll have to ask Amor later."

"Does he usually give you a straight answer?" Maggie quipped, doubtful someone so ornery would be forthcoming with his feelings.

Silver's lips twitched at the corners. "On occasion. Although judging by the hand he keeps flexing, he's in no mood to answer me right now."

"You've picked up on all his tells haven't you?"

Silver chuckled, low and melodic in a way that made her skin flush. "He's not that difficult to read if you just look closely. Oftentimes, people forget that closed doors can be opened."

Maggie snickered. "Julie would tell you his door is locked."

Silver took a seat on one of the lower stairs, leaving ample space beside him for her. "Locks have keys." He mused, watching Amor and Julie step to the adjacent side of the room to untangle themselves from each other.

Maggie dropped her chin into the palm of her hand, studying her sister. "Would they be terrible together?"

Silver hummed thoughtfully before saying, "Undoubtedly."

"How come?"

"Well, the same defiance in her chin matches the stubbornness that makes him stand so rigidly. They're too alike. They would be like a shipwreck, I suppose."

"A shipwreck?"

"Beautiful treasures lie within, but they're hidden underneath so much destruction."

That part was true, at least on Julie's end. There was so much Maggie knew her sister kept inside. Maggie tried desperately to make her see she didn't need the grandeur Julie talked about. She just wanted her sister with her and the rest would sort itself out.

It had been years since she'd seen Julie's face light up. But the morning they had been brushing their horses when Amor came around, Maggie caught it. It had been quick, flashing like a candle sparking to life but it was there.

"Well, I've always had a thing for love stories that defy the odds." Maggie brushed some of the dust out of her curls.

"Here." Silver chuckled, making that sparkling butterfly float around in her stomach again. He used one hand to comb through her hair, and simply let one of her curls wrap around his finger. "How many odds do you think one has to defy to become one of the stories you love so much?"

Maggie smiled as Amor and Julie finally pulled apart.

"All of them."

Chapter Twenty-Six

Amor

The silence of night settled over the inn. The mother whose son they'd rescued turned out to be the owner of the establishment. She wasted no time in allowing the tear-tracks to dry on her cheeks before she was escorting travelers into rooms upstairs and sweeping dusty footprints off her hardwood floors.

April was her name. Amor only gathered this information after hearing one of the visitors shout over the railing for towels. Thankfully, she hadn't ushered he and Silver into their rooms yet. Amor wasn't certain about attempting to sleep in a small, enclosed space. He hadn't done that since he was a boy. Perhaps he could reach the roof from the window.

Left to his own devices, which was rarely a good idea, Amor wandered into a room flickering with lantern light. A brief scan of the space told him it was the dining hall, boasting tables and chairs that gleamed with polish. It was nice to have peace and quiet again. But, for the first time Amor realized how lonely the silence truly was. After all, what is silence but the company of words unspoken?

Fates. He was starting to sound like her.

He pictured her hazel eyes in his mind, searching straight through him for something he could never give. Amor perched on the edge of a stool near the spotless wooden counter, taking the hem of his cloak in hand. It was unraveling thread by thread, a mockery of everything inside him.

He hadn't thought twice when he ripped the fabric. All it had taken was the mental imagery of Julie lost within the throes of the storm. The calluses on Amor's fingertips caught on the deep green material as he ran a hand down the side of it. A fleeting echo of laughter tickled his memory.

'You're gonna get caught!' Annaliese giggled, popping her head around the doorframe of their parent's bedroom.

'Will not!' Amor said matter-of-factly. He dropped to his knees in front of the mattress and stuck his tongue out to the side as his arm fumbled around underneath the bed for

the object of his sneaking. 'I got it!' He said in victory as he tugged on the handle of the box, sliding it across the floor.

Annaliese scanned the hall with nervous excitement before she ultimately plopped on the floor next to him. 'How do you know it's for you?'

Amor deftly unwrapped the ribbon and grinned over at her. 'Because it has my name on it, see?' Amor opened the lid of the box and sure enough, there was a card on top with the letter A.

Annaliese's little nose scrunched in confusion. 'Wait! It might be mine. A for Anna.'

Amor rolled his eyes, abandoning the box to attack her side with the tickle monster. 'It's not your birthday tomorrow, little gremlin. Its mine remember?'

Between fits of giggles and wheezes, Annaliese conceded. 'What did ya get?'

The suspense seemed to be killing her as much as it was him. So, Amor remedied the issue by plunging his hands into the box and withdrawing a mess of cloth.

'You got a blanket?' Annaliese looked at it curiously, little fingers grabbing a fistful of the emerald material.

'No, I don't think it's a blanket.' Amor said thoughtfully, standing to his feet to fully unfold it. A proud smile spread across his lips. 'It's a cloak! Just like dad's.'

'That is daddy's.' Annaliese stood up, grabbing onto the corner of its hem. 'Look, that's where I got berry juice on it.' She thrust her finger at the inside near the bottom. Amor's eyes traveled where she pointed and there in fact was the evidence of his sister's clumsiness. Momma had spent hours trying to scrub out the stain but ultimately it remained, branded within the fibers.

'He's giving me his cloak?' Amor said in awe, running his hand over the soft cloth. It was much too big for him now, but that wouldn't stop him from wearing it. If he tripped over it, he would do so proudly.

'I think you should share.' Annaliese said sweetly, before she cackled and wrapped herself up in the bottom half of it.

'No way. I'm never letting it out of my sight.' Amor smirked.

'But I've got it now.' She sang, twirling around in the cloak that positively dwarfed her.

Amor lunged and swept her up in his arms, cloak and all. 'I'll let you use it when you turn twelve, that way its fair.'

A shaky breath left Amor as he blinked slowly, pulling himself out of the trance. He should have let her enjoy it that day. She never reached her twelfth birthday. Amor peered down at the inside of the fraying hem. What fabric was left now was spotless. "I finally got the stain out, sis." He said quietly.

A steady hand clasped around Amor's shoulder. "You okay?" Silver questioned, a gentleness in his tone that allowed Amor room to evade answering if he wished. *Silver had a way of doing that, of knowing.* Amor opened his mouth, but every word hung itself before having the chance to be voiced. So, he instead moved from the stool and faced Silver.

Amor hugged him, tightly.

He embraced the man who was like the brother he never had. Silver always claimed it was him that needed a friend, but Amor knew better. Silver would have been alright on his own, but Amor might have fallen apart without him.

"Thank you."

"You're welcome. It took ten years, but I knew you'd come around on hugging." A lighthearted smirk pulled at Silver's lips as he clapped Amor on the back.

"It's not been-" Amor began to argue but then he stopped himself. "Fates, it's really been ten years?"

"To the month." Silver took a seat on the opposing barstool. "As your fletcher, I'm awaiting a promotion to celebrate my tenure." He chuckled.

"After we get to Seruvia tomorrow I'll see what I can do." Amor shook his head, folding his cloak over his arm.

"I'm afraid no one'll be travelling there tomorrow." April's words were mingled with a sigh as she swept herself into the room, catching the tail end of their conversation. "The roads are blocked both in and out of here from the storm. It'll take at least a day or two to clear the debris."

Amor drummed his fingers on the counter, "We don't have much time to spare."

April shrugged one shoulder while she swept a cloth over the tables. "I'm sorry, hon, but I just report what I hear. This inn sits at the halfway point to Seruvia. Travelers have been coming in seeking refuge from the storm because they couldn't turn around and head back into the city." April tapped her chin with her index finger thoughtfully. "You'd be amazed the things I've heard from operating this place."

"Like what?" Maggie bounded into the dining room, an easy smile on her face.

"Gossip, mostly. Plans from businessmen and merchants and the like. Many stop by here for the night to break up their journey."

"You said this place is at the halfway mark to Seruvia?" Silver slid in.

"That is correct. Prime real estate if I do say so myself." April pulled out several chairs to polish them even though they seemed clean enough to see one's reflection.

"Have you heard about something called the Seruvian gears?" Silver asked, moving from his stool to the table that Maggie leant against.

April's face twisted in thought. "Oh yes, that topic's been floating around for a while now. Why do you ask?"

"We've heard about them too." Amor started, a sense of uneasiness flickering in his gut. "What do you know about them?"

April swiped her hands on her apron, leaving streaks of furniture polish on the white linen. "They're made in Seruvia, wagon loads of them. About a year ago I over-heard some men placing an order to be sent to the Gate."

Amor's brow furrowed as Julie spoke up for the first time since they'd joined them in the dining room. "The Gate... why does that sound familiar?"

April nodded and sat down on one of her newly pol-ished chairs. "It's quite infamous and an awful place. At least it used to be. It was a kingdom of thieves and crim-inals ruled by villains to boot." April clicked her tongue distastefully.

"I've been there." Amor rested his arm against the counter. When Maggie's mouth dropped he corrected himself. "Not *in* the Gate, but Thulta." It had to have been at least seven years ago that he'd been in that vicinity. "It looks like night and day split. They have this gigantic black metal Gate that runs down the length of their kingdom. An eyesore really."

"I heard parts of it have been painted white." April hummed, wrapping her cleaning cloth around her hand and unraveling it as she recalled what she'd heard. "The King has been working to counteract the darkness within his borders. Supposedly, he's even trying to reform some of the Gate's citizens. They say he's made impressive progress in the past year."

Julie tilted her head, her hair slipping over her shoulder. "But the Gate's King is a horrible man, isn't he? I've heard the stories. They don't make it sound like he's the type to help anyone."

Amor looked back to April, the same question burning in his own head. The last he'd heard, the Gate had been under the crushing thumb of a horrific Prince.

April's lips twitched at the corners, displaying a deep dimple in one cheek. "I'm afraid your sources aren't up to date. I'm talking about the new King. He's turned everything on its head. Caused quite a stir when he announced his marriage to a commoner too. It was so sudden, as if she woke up one day and was suddenly crowned Queen." April leant forward in her seat, a mischievous smirk on her face at the opportunity to share her bits of gossip. "Some people say his Queen wasn't even from the Gate, she was a Thultan."

Julie's brow flicked up. "Wow. How did they make that work?"

April shrugged again, folding her arms across her chest. "Who knows. Love works in strange ways. I like to think of it as a patchwork quilt. Stitched together by the threads of time and the cloth of shared experiences."

Amor shook his head, rubbing at his temples. "And about the gears, have you heard anything else regarding them?"

April thumbed over the stitching in her apron. "Nothing of any great importance. All their talk runs together after a while." The sound of small footsteps pattered into the space. Eric, with the side of his head freshly bandaged, came over and climbed into his mother's lap. "Although, if you're truly curious about them, the place of their origin would be the best place to start. But it sounds like you already know that."

"You aren't privy to the location where the gears are produced are you?" Silver questioned, absentmindedly playing with the ends of Maggie's curls.

"I'm afraid no guest has shared that, but I'd be happy to keep an ear out for you."

"We'd appreciate it." Amor added, his gaze flicking to the window overhead. *It was too dark to even see the stars.*

"You all stumbled across us at quite a fortunate time. Seeing as the roads are closed, and tomorrow evening is our inn's anniversary festival, you should come!" April clasped her hands at the thought.

"Thank you for the invitation." Amor brought his gaze back to her. "We'll have to see." A festival sounded like a dreadful waste of time. Honestly, he was too tired to either encourage or discourage the idea. "I'm going to turn in."

"I showed Silver where your room is, but I'm happy to take you as well." April offered.

"I've got him." Silver smiled warmly and stepped away from Maggie after whispering something in her ear that made her eyes dance.

"What did you tell her?" Amor questioned as they ascended the flight of wooden stairs, the steps creaking underneath their boots.

Silver gave a playful shrug of his shoulders. "To wait up for me." He led Amor down the hallway to one of the rooms.

"You really like her, don't you?" Amor pivoted on his heel halfway after crossing the threshold.

Silver leant against the doorframe, arms folded. "My friend, the only difference between you and me is I'm not in denial."

Amor's brows furrowed. "What is that supposed to mean?"

"Exactly." Silver accentuated his sentence with a wink. "Goodnight, Am."

Amor mumbled a semblance of something similar but once the door was closed he ran a hand through his hair. "Denial." He grumbled to himself. "I'm not in... what do I have to be in denial about?" Amor crossed the small room to the window and shoved it upwards, a breeze making the curtains rustle. The sound of Julie's soft chuckle echoed from outside as April walked with her down the hallway, distracting him. Amor shook his head and slipped out into the night.

One Year Ago

The Prince's brother brought a beauty into their lair. Her presence was distracting. She would be his undoing if their kingdom's darkness didn't seep through the cracks in her smile. It's delicious, how fate weaves us all together.

CHAPTER TWENTY-SEVEN

Julie

Julie sputtered as cold water splashed aggressively on top of her head. "That's like ice!" She ducked under the surface of the bubbles.

"It's what you get when you stay in the bath so long." Maggie tutted, hands on her hips, looking more like their mother than her little sister. "Now come up, so I can put this in your hair."

Julie sighed in the water, small bubbles escaping through her nose as she resurfaced. "I could be content to stay in here for the next few weeks."

Maggie gave a half laugh as she weaved a sweetly scented lather through Julie's tresses. "You would be more prune than Julie if you did that."

"Then I'd be a happy prune." Julie hummed, flashing her sister a smirk.

Maggie reached into the water and flicked droplets into Julie's face. She then took Julie's head and dunked it back underwater to purge the suds from her hair. Julie held her breath as water filled her nostrils before she could come up for air again. "Towel off and change and then I want to brush your hair."

"Can I ask why I'm getting this princess treatment to-day?" Julie swiped water from her lashes, reaching for the towel resting on the edge of the tub.

"You can ask but I won't tell you, yet." Maggie beamed with mischievous radiance as she grabbed the brush from the counter and went into the adjoining room. Julie pulled herself from the aromatic water and wrapped her body in the towel.

After changing, Julie ran the soft material over the damp ends of her hair and hopped up on the bed's edge. "I think I would like to sleep early tonight." She said, flopping backwards onto the mattress, causing Maggie's frame to jump with the movement.

"Not tonight, Jules." Maggie grinned and pulled Julie up by the wrists. "You have a festival to attend."

"I don't know, Mags I-"

"Come on, Julie. You desperately need a night free from worry." Maggie ran the brush through Julie's tresses. "If you're concerned about me..." Maggie interjected right as Julie opened her mouth. "Don't be. Silver said he wanted to talk to me about something. He said it was important." Maggie's lips pulled into the softest love-struck smile.

"I'm not going to know anyone there." Julie tried to show Maggie the flaws in her plan.

"Amor's going to be there. Silver managed to convince him."

"Oh, Amor." Julie's eyes fell to her lap. Maggie paused tugging the handle of the brush and touched her sister's shoulder questioningly. "Amor... he said something yesterday."

"What was it?"

Julie hesitated, then she reached for the tattered piece of his cloak on her nightstand and wrapped it around her fingers. Amor was unable to untangle them fully and Julie was left with a remnant of the rope knotted around her wrist. It was a strange sight to see her black and blurry soulmate-string dangling off one hand and a fraying emerald-green scrap on the other. She'd managed to free herself from the improvised bracelet the night before. Julie woke up with the ripped cloth tucked against her chest. She didn't know at what point in the evening she reached for it. *Or why.*

"He said I was the best dream he could think of." Julie admitted quietly.

"Why do you not sound happy about that?" Maggie resumed running the brush through Julie's waves, easing out any tangles.

"Because almost immediately afterward, he said it was wrong, and you could *see* the regret all over his face."

Maggie made a thoughtful noise. "Well, what did you say when he told you that?"

Julie unraveled the bit of cloak, staring at it. Her thumb flicked over a stain engrained deep within the threads. "I... didn't."

Maggie sighed a laugh. "Alright, you definitely need a fun night. I don't want you to think about anything else except for enjoying yourself. Can you do that for me?"

"I don't have anything to wear." Julie gestured to the loose cotton shirt she'd changed into.

"Well... about that." Maggie's smile made the sparkle of diamonds dull in comparison. She leapt off the bed and pulled the closet door open. Inside, on a shelf, was something crème and neatly folded. "April brought this, as thanks for finding Eric. She thought you were a similar size to her when she was younger and hoped you'd wear it tonight."

Julie ran her fingers over the waist of the dress. Lace adorned the sweetheart neckline, making way for a delicate ribbon at the top that graced the fitted bodice. The sleeves were sheer and tapered at the wrist. "It's lovely."

"Now you have no excuses." Maggie grinned, her giddiness practically palpable.

Julie couldn't help feeling this was not the best idea but still let her sister fuss over the dress and her hair. Maggie bubbled over with happiness like an overfilled glass of champagne as she steered Julie toward the standing mirror in the corner of the room. "Look at you."

Julie listened to Maggie's gentle demand. When she did so, her breathing faltered. Perhaps this mirror held some sort of enchantment within its glass like in father's story. *To peer inside might show a person what they wanted more than anything.*

The woman looking back at her had bold, fearless hazel eyes. She had long, midnight hair styled to be pulled back halfway on either side, leaving curling wisps around her cheeks. She had steady hands, a determined chin. A sort of wildness in her gaze that dared any flame to rival her.

The woman trapped in the mirror was her mother.

Julie had never before realized how much she looked like her. "You're an artist." She leant her head against Maggie's shoulder.

"The art was already there, I just polished it." Maggie whispered playfully, squeezing Julie's shoulders. "You should get down there, I can already hear the music."

It was quite impressive how fast the inn pulled everything together for the festival. The dust had settled. A space cleared of debris and broken branches glowed warmly from tiny hanging candles shining within paper lanterns. Three minstrels sent an energetic melody rippling through the small crowd that gathered. Among them, however, she didn't find any familiar faces. Though halfway through her search, she had the uncanny sensation of eyes on her back. Julie swiveled around, checking each direction. There was no one whose attention wasn't already taken by lively chatter or easy dancing. Julie took a slow breath and let it out rather sharply, turning her attention away from the dancing couples and laughing friends. To her left, stood a wooden refreshment table boasting punch and wine. There were also pieces of fruit, arranged to look like different types of flowers. She picked up one such arrangement held together by a thin wooden skewer.

"Why are you upset?" A low voice sounded behind her. The owner of that voice was suddenly close enough that both their shadows intertwined. *Where did he come from?*

"What?" Julie rolled the toothpick between the pads of her thumb and forefinger as she glanced up. She nearly wished she hadn't, because now it was going to be difficult to pry her gaze away. Amor's hair was still slightly damp at the ends. It was as if he'd tried to tame the dark waves back, but they fell into his eyes anyway. He'd found a crème shirt that laced up at the front in crisscrosses, revealing a swath of smooth golden brown skin underneath. It looked like they coordinated outfits, except Amor wore fitted black pants tucked into his usual boots. He carried no bow and quiver, only a dagger concealed by a leather sheath at his hip.

"Who upset you?" He asked again, green eyes shifting from hers to land on each head around them as if perhaps they could answer his query.

"No one." Julie cleared her throat, slipping a grape free of the fruit kebab and popping it in her mouth. It was much easier to focus on the little fruit flower than him. Julie pressed the sharp end of the pick into her fingertip. If this was where her mind wandered when she wasn't constantly worrying, she needed to re-evaluate some things. Amor sighed and tipped Julie's chin back toward him

"Was it me?"

"No. Although you do irk me quite often." Julie pointed the fruit stick in his direction, pretending like he didn't still have her chin between his thumb and knuckles.

Amor's brows drew together briefly. "But Silver said..." He trailed off, blinking and slowly taking the rest of Julie in. His lips parted, looking stunned. Even his hand fell back down to his side.

Julie couldn't help herself. She put a grape in his mouth. "Looks like Silver pulled a fast one on you."

Amor snapped out of whatever spell he'd drifted into. His mouth shut, giving her a look as he was forced to bite down on the fruit. "Did you seriously just feed me?"

"Can I do it again?" Julie tilted her head with playful challenge.

"No." Amor said with finality. Julie was about to turn back to the table when Amor leant over, his arm trapping her on one side. "It's my turn."

His scent of pine and crackling fire caressed her senses as he leaned forward. It was dizzying. Like gravity was being pulled out from underneath her. Amor's thumb brushed down her bottom lip, and a piece of tangerine was suddenly dancing on her tastebuds, sweet and tart all at once.

Amor looked rather pleased with himself. Julie had the sudden feeling she might need one of those glasses of wine after all.

"I've been given strict instructions to think about nothing for one night." Julie said as her fingers curled around two wine glass stems. "And you might as well, if we're going to be here together." She handed him one of the glasses.

"Think... about nothing?" Amor repeated, as if the very concept was foreign to him. Judging by the tension coiling taut in his muscles, Julie didn't think the guess was far off.

"Exactly. Maybe it's easier if we pretend." Julie sipped on the wine. It tasted floral and fruity, with a hint of plum. "Let's pretend we don't have to leave tomorrow. Say we just met here tonight at this festival." She stepped over a rock toward a grassy hill, turning to ensure he was following behind.

"So, this is our first impression of each other?" Amor questioned, taking a tentative sip of his wine.

Julie nodded, extending her hand in greeting. "Julie Seir, nice to meet you."

Amor shook his head, but he accepted her hand and shook it. "Amor Vela."

"What are you doing around these parts, my good sir?" Julie bit back a smile as she took another sip.

"We-" He started and then tilted his head skyward before returning his attention to her. "I've come to sell my leatherworks."

Julie studied him. Of course he would want to work with leather. She should have known from the bracelets on both his wrists, and the tanned strips he always seemed to have in his pocket. "Did you make Silver's pack?"

Amor came around to her side. "I'm afraid you don't know Silver. We've only met this evening have we not?"

Julie chuckled. "Right. But, say I did. Was that your handiwork?"

Amor scratched the side of his chin before conceding. "Yes. I always wanted to make leather goods. To be the best saddle craftsman in the land."

"Why didn't you?" Julie asked more quietly. The music still strummed below them, but Julie found herself tuning it out to only hear the baritone of Amor's voice.

He cleared his throat, sidestepping the question. "It's your turn again. What are you doing around here?"

A flicker of regret went through her for setting such rules in place. Maybe she should have allotted space for reality to mingle into the fictional. Then she might have learned why he had chosen this path instead of the one he'd dreamt of. "I'm traveling for my sister's wedding. She's having it in a grand palace and she's going to wear a beautiful dove gray ballgown, with diamonds in her hair." Julie wove the tale, and perceived it coming to life in her mind's eye.

"And you? Do you have a date to escort you to this grand wedding?" Amor leant back against the only tree on the hill, running his finger over the lip of the glass.

Julie flashed a smile. "Yes. He's an archer I met at the circus and I'm going to wear my best red dress because I know how he *loves* the color." The wine was making her head light and her laugh airy. Nothing she said mattered, it was all pretend.

Amor's eyes softened, which was excellent of him to play along with her fantasy. "I'm sure he does, because you look magnificent in red."

Julie's heart kicked up a beat and Amor continued. "And in crème and white and whatever color you decide to put on because you give everything a vibrance that was never there before."

Nothing he said mattered. It was all pretend.

"I thought you didn't notice such things."

"How can I not, Julie?" Amor took two steps closer. "How can I not when you make the sunset jealous?"

The songs beneath them shifted into something sweet and gentle. A melody made out of glittering stars and the evening breeze. A tune for wishes and whispered confessions. Julie took his wine glass, setting it down on a flat patch of grass next to her own and slipped her hand into his. "I've always wanted to dance under the stars."

"Then can we pretend I'm the man you're dreaming of dancing with?" Amor's other hand slipped to her waist, strong and steady.

Nothing they said mattered, it was all pretend.

"You are." Julie murmured as they stepped in time to the lull of the music. It was exhilarating in the way she imagined floating might be. A new thrill fluttered through her with each sway and turn. The past and the future were mere concepts tonight. Julie didn't want to lose sight of the present anymore. She wanted to dance into oblivion with him.

She wanted time to stop, so she could memorialize this feeling in the very glass their moment was made of. Amor dipped her as the song ended, and never once did she feel she would be dropped. Not with his arm hooked around her waist or his hand behind her neck.

He slowly eased her back to her feet, but he didn't let go. If anything, he held her closer. "Was the dance all you hoped it would be?" His fingertips tucked wisps of hair back behind her ear. The very hands that were dipped in lethality, now tangled in her tresses.

"Not yet." Julie's hands slid up from his chest until she'd captured his face in her grasp. "Can we pretend I really am the best thing you can dream of?"

Amor's hands tightened on her waist, his eyes brimming with longing as his voice caressed her skin. "You're unraveling me."

If this was what dreaming meant, she never wanted to wake. "If you're going to unravel, do so in my arms."

So Amor did. His lips crashed against hers, the colliding of night and day to form the sparks of dawn. Warmth surged through her as colors burst behind her eyelids. It wasn't a tame kiss, one for fireside stories and fairytale books. It was wild and free. It was the flight of a blazing arrow finding its mark and piercing her through.

It was everything.

It was over too quickly.

Amor broke away first, catching his breath while Julie's mind reeled, taking all semblance of reason and balance with her. He staggered back, his hand pressed over his lips as he looked at her with stunned, haunted eyes. "I'm sorry. I didn't..."

Julie's smile faded. "That was too far." She echoed the words etched on his face. *His face.* The one drawn into a look of guilt and remorse. The ghost of his kiss still warmed her skin, though it was beginning to slip away.

"That was a mistake." Amor shook his head, stepping backwards. His heel knocked the wine glasses over as they clinked and tumbled down the hill.

Julie hadn't realized how much she'd let her walls come down tonight. Maybe that was partially aided by the drink, but it had been even more credited to him. With every step that he retreated, one more brick was laid in the fortress surrounding her heart.

Amor muttered something she couldn't quite make out before he was lost to the shadows. His absence stole away a moment she once thought perfect. It shouldn't have stung like the bite of ice into skin. She should have known better. Julie wrapped her arms around herself as she quietly walked back to the inn.

After all, nothing they said mattered. It was all pretend.

When she saw Maggie standing at the door, her shoulders slumped. *She could really use a hug from her sister right now.* "Maggie, tonight was-"

"You lied to me." She said solemnly, her soft features pinched with hurt.

That sobered Julie up completely. Her arms slipped from her chest as she paused at the stair. "What?"

Maggie's eyes were distant, her spine rigid. "You lied to me. All these years."

Julie's heart stumbled. Down, down, down. "Maggie you don't understand, I-"

"I don't understand?" Maggie's words held a note of disbelief. "I don't understand?" She walked forward, standing on the stair above Julie. "You're right, Julie. I don't understand. I had to find out from *Silver* that I don't have a string."

Julie's throat tightened. "Mags, please if you just let me explain." Julie reached for her sister's hand, but Maggie wrenched it back.

"I trusted you. I've believed in your gift, I've told you over and over that I never wanted anything but you beside me." Maggie sighed a bitter laugh. "You looked me in the eyes and told me you could see my string. 'Oh he's not here, Mags, he's not close.'" Maggie mimicked Julie's words from what now seemed like a lifetime ago.

"I didn't want to hurt you."

"Yes, well, it's a little late for that." Maggie's gray eyes turned steely, hidden behind a layer of glass.

"I promised to protect you, Maggie. I didn't want you to think there was something wrong with you. Don't you see? I did it for you."

"You do not get to decide what I can and cannot handle." Maggie looked at Julie as if she was a stranger. "There is no room for lies in love." Maggie brushed by Julie as she descended the final stair. She paused at the end of the banister to say, "Our lives have never been constant. There's always been a new town, new faces, new routines. Every day is an unknown and I've not minded it. But the one thing that's always been steadfast was you. Now, I even question that."

Maggie was gone before Julie could pick up the pieces.

Chapter Twenty-Eight

Julie

Their room was a hollow echo as she shut the door behind her. Every corner of it seemed to house one more shadowy monster lying in wait to feed off her loneliness, her guilt. Julie staggered forward, her breathing coming in ragged shakes.

Julie stumbled to her knees, a heavy weight on her shoulders. It crushed her, seeping into her bones until they ached. "I'm sorry." She whispered as tears splashed onto the floor. Julie didn't know who the apology was meant for. Maybe it was to her father, for breaking her promise to always protect Maggie. Maybe it was to Maggie, for the deceit Julie believed necessary in the grand scheme of her sister's happiness.

She had tried. *Oh, how she had tried.* Julie drew in a gasping breath as she glanced up through her blurry vision. She'd stumbled in front of the mirror, except this time she knew exactly who she was looking at. She was looking at a scared, broken little girl with tear-streaked cheeks. The girl who had clutched a baby sister to her chest while she gripped the hand of her dying father. Julie's palm lifted to the glass, pressing into it like she could shatter the image if only the mirror would crack.

But what she saw only warped, like a reflection in a twisted mirror from *The Circle of Lights*. The little girl shifted into a woman, strangled by red and black soul-strings with shredded ones at her feet. "Take it back!" Julie pounded on the mirror, rattling the stand it rested on. "I don't want to be this!"

Everything would be different if she couldn't see the tauntings of fate. They could have lived their lives in ignorance like everyone else. "Take it back!" Julie's voice cracked as her palm banged against the mirror a final time before she slumped against it. She didn't know who she cried out to or who would even care to listen. She doubted anyone would.

Julie laid there for hours, curled against the mirror in a tangle of quiet sobs. Then the feelings of hurt slowly ebbed away like the tide rolling out. In its stead was something harder, sharper.

None of this would have happened, Julie realized, if Silver had just been quiet.

She pulled herself to her feet, swiped the dampness from her face and took hold of what settled in her gut like an ember burning. Her pain was a shadow of her anger, and the source was somewhere on these grounds.

Chapter Twenty-Nine

Silver

Tonight had not gone the way he'd hoped. Silver sat on the grass with his back to a tree as he sharpened an arrowhead. The stars above offered him enough light to work. Amor would need the arrows ready for tomorrow. The last time he'd seen him, he looked as if he had misplaced his own heart.

Silver sighed through his nose and rested his head against the bark, staring up at the tiny glowing glimmers. "She's going to be angry, isn't she?" He asked them, expecting at least one to wink in response. As per usual, they were silent. "When did you all stop being such busybodies?" Silver reached his hand up as if he could snatch a few stars and sweep them into the palm of his hand. Only silence sang back. He couldn't say he was surprised, not after breaking nearly every rule he'd been given. If Silver hadn't cast himself down from their array, they might have done him the favor.

Maggie had at least taken the news well... Silver rolled the arrowhead over his knuckles, making it disappear and reappear between his fingers. Well, she had for a moment. Then he watched as realization settled within those gray eyes of hers. It was easier for her to believe his words, which to any other person would have sounded insane, than it was to swallow a different fact.

A fact approaching him at that very moment. Every step Julie took was filled with intent, determination and the type of fury that could only be borne of pain.

"How could you?" Julie stopped in front of him as Silver rose to his feet. Wisps of her hair clung to her wet cheeks and still damp lashes. "I was going to tell her."

"When, Julie?" Silver's voice softened. "It was time to tell her, she needed to know."

"No..." Julie shook her head slowly, anger making her hands vibrate. "*You* decided it was time. She is *my* sister. You didn't have the right."

"Julie, listen to me. What I told her had nothing to do with you." Silver locked eyes with her. He needed her to see the sense in this. She was hurting, and he knew it was always easier to blame someone else rather than yourself. It's an easy escape.

"Do you love my sister?" Julie asked suddenly, looking past him to something in the distance.

Silver put a hand on her shoulder. "Yes, I do." *More than Julie could fathom.*

Julie shrugged his hand off. "You could never love her like I do. You won't ever be able to care for her like I can." Her hazel eyes were as sharp as jagged gemstones. "We're going to reach the end of this road and you're going to leave her alone. We will *all* go our separate ways. Do you understand?"

The way she placed an emphasis on the 'all' made Silver think this wasn't the only thing breaking her heart. "I can't promise that."

"She is all I have! Don't you get it?!" Her anger flared and her voice rose, echoing into the night. "You've made her hate me!"

Silver cupped her shoulders firmly even as she tried to jerk away. "It's not me you're angry with, Julie."

"It is! I wish you and Amor had never found us." Her hands curled into fists, planting them against his chest. "I *wish* you would stay away from her, forever."

Silver felt invisible shackles prick at his skin, clamping around his wrists while their chain weighed his heart down. *No, not like this.* "Julie, you don't know what you're asking." Her pain was great enough for the wish to take root and he was now bound to it, eternally.

Julie's anger fizzled out too late. The damage was done. Her hands went slack. "I... I don't know how to fix this." She whispered, tears pooling in her eyes yet she blinked them back refusing to let them fall.

Neither did he. Silver glanced down at the heavy, luminescent cuffs no one could see but him. He drew in a breath and ran a soothing hand up and down her arm. "First, you need to understand you can't fix someone else if you're breaking inside. My family had a saying. 'We cry because our emotions are too great to be put into words. So my darling, in your tears, you become the greatest poet of them all.'"

"I don't want her to see me cry." Julie's head hung low, and Silver saw a tear roll off her chin to water the grass at their feet.

"It's alright." He shifted his arms to draw her in so she could tuck her face in his shoulder. "It'll be our secret."

One of many he now carried.

Chapter Thirty

Julie

Maggie sat in front of the fireplace with her knees tucked against her chest. The room was dark, save for the silhouette of a gentle face, steady hands and curly hair being absentmindedly braided.

She always did braid her hair when she was upset. The spherical object in Julie's hands had more weight to it than it should have. Or maybe it was all in her head. The scent of citrus should have calmed her but what if Maggie didn't remember?

What if Maggie never wanted to speak to her again?

No.

Julie had loved Maggie with an intensity that rivaled daybreak for far too long, to be afraid now. If Maggie never forgave her, then Julie would keep on fighting to the edge of forever. Julie's memories flickered over their lives like a spinning carousel dressed up in black and white. Wherever there was color, there was Maggie. Julie thought of every smile Maggie gave too soon, every frown replaced too quick. Each time Maggie put her trust in Julie's hands. Not because she thought Julie would find a way, but because that's what sisters do. Love is the placement of blind trust into hands that have the power to wring every drop of blood from your heart.

Julie crept closer, her shoes scuffling against the hardwood. "Do you remember when we were little and worked at that awful Mr. Peterson's manor before Pierre found us?"

Maggie's back was turned away, but she stilled her plaiting. "It was the only place that would take kids our age as servants." Her usually bright and airy voice sounded flat and even.

Julie inched closer to her sister. "We got in trouble several times."

"*I* got in trouble. You always took my blame." Maggie interlocked her fingers. "Like... that one day with Mrs. Peterson's skirt." She said quietly.

Julie lowered herself to the ground, a handbreadth apart from her knee touching Maggie's. "She was furious. There were bubbles everywhere." Julie tried a half smile, remembering how scared she had been to know their mistress's dress would now be eternally damaged. She was even more terrified to think that Maggie would receive both the blame and the punishment of no food for two days. At the time, the girls were just trying their best to stay off the streets. Julie had seen the chance to accumulate their measly savings slip away with each drip, drip, drip of a wet, ruined skirt.

"I couldn't stand how snobbish she was. How she treated you and the other girls. I saw that bucket and kicked it purely out of spite." Maggie's lashes grazed her cheek as she peered down at the knots in the flooring. "I didn't think about the consequences. Not until you told her you tripped over it. That it was your fault."

"I didn't go hungry that night, though." Julie shifted the object in her palms. "Nor any night after that."

Maggie's gray eyes lifted to Julie's hands, the firelight licking up the fruit's shadows. "An apology orange." Maggie's shoulders lowered, the corner of her lip ticking up just barely. "You remember."

"I know it's not the same and we're very far from Mr. Peterson's manor and it can never truly fix my mistakes..." Julie cupped the back of Maggie's hand and placed the orange in it. "But I need you to know I'm so, so sorry." Julie whispered, her throat tightening again. "I thought happiness was attached to a fairytale ending. But it's not. It's made of grit and determination and every little moment that makes you smile, regardless of where the moments come from. Maggie, *you* are all my little moments."

Maggie stared at it for a minute. "You sound like the stories you've told me about papa." She shifted to the side, angling her body away from Julie. Her heart sank, like it wished to settle deep in the earth and grow roots and tangling vines to keep it there.

But then Maggie turned back around and the invisible vines around Julie's ribcage sprouted flowers.

In her left hand was the orange Julie gave her.

In her right, sat another one. Plump and bright and fragrant, the perfect twin to Julie's, 'I'm sorry.'

Julie's fingertips reached for the orange, but Maggie drew it back, holding it high out of reach. "No more lies. No more promises, and no more masks."

Julie could have wept from relief, but she threw her arms around Maggie's neck instead. "I love you whole."

"I love you whole too." Maggie squeezed Julie's back. "Now eat, before April wonders where her oranges went."

Julie swiped the dampness from her cheekbones with her sleeve and curled into Maggie's side, beginning to peel the citrusy fruit as Maggie did the same.

"Have you had the inclination that our traveling partners might be on the magical side of things?" Maggie questioned suddenly, flicking away the white strings of the orange. She looked like a bubble about to burst into a thousand fizzing sparks.

"I suppose, I mean we watched Amor shoot an arrow through a man and it disappeared like nothing happened-"

"Silver's a Star." Maggie blurted, interrupting Julie and making the partially unwrapped orange topple in her palm.

"He's a *what*?" Julie blinked. Surely her sister had misunderstood. Stars were glittering lights in nights made of ink for travelers to see by and children to wish upon. They weren't people with grumpy best friends that lived in forests and concocted various poisons. Maybe they should be, it would at least make the answering of wishes much more interesting.

Maggie bit her lip and took a breath, "He's a Star, a real one. They aren't like what we think. It's a whole different world up there and they've helped watch over us since everything existed. Oh, Julie... you wouldn't believe the things he said."

Julie chuckled, "I'm not so sure I'm believing this." *Couldn't it make sense, though?* He certainly looked how Julie would imagine a star to appear if given human form.

"The Stars see every different path and direction a person's life might take. They act as guiding hands of fate to steer a person onto the path they were meant for."

Julie chewed the inside of her cheek. "Okay, say he is a Star, why is he here and not..."

"And not in the sky with the rest of his family?" Maggie finished, her voice taking on a regretful note. "Because he made a wish, and Stars aren't supposed to make wishes for themselves. They took that part of him away in exchange for-" Maggie fidgeted with her thumbnails, the half-eaten orange forgotten on her lap. Julie placed a reassuring hand on Maggie's shoulder, gently urging her to continue. The next words out of Maggie's mouth left Julie reeling.

"He made a wish to save my life."

CHAPTER THIRTY-ONE

Julie

"The night the raiders came to our house was sup-posed to be my last night too." Maggie said grimly. "My crying would have given us away."

Julie's hands went cold. *Huddling in a corner, clutching Maggie to her chest, silently begging her to cease her cries... footsteps growing closer and-*

"They would have let you live. You were old enough to be useful and when they discovered your gift they would have used you for profit. A hysterical toddler, however, would have been nothing but a hindrance." Maggie continued, shaking her head. "Silver had one chance to make his wish and he took it."

Julie could see it now. *Huddling in a corner, clutching Maggie to her chest, silently begging her to cease her cries... Looking out the window, seeing one star burn more brightly than the rest.*

It falls.

Silence.

"I remember the falling star." Julie swallowed, blinking away the memories from that night. "But why us? Why use such a great wish at such a high cost for a stranger?"

Maggie's eyes softened and Julie's gaze drifted to her sister's hand. "Unless..." She reached for the invisible cord tied around Maggie's ring finger. "Unless you weren't a stranger." Julie whispered.

She watched Maggie's string rest in tatters, as if it had been severed. Ripped away by a force greater than the might of any human.

Fate had destroyed Maggie's soulmate string.

"Fate requires something in exchange for a life altering wish. Silver's something was to be cut off from me and cast out." Maggie stared wistfully into the dancing hearth. "He said he knew it was me the night we first showed up to their camp. He'd never forgotten my face."

Julie hooked her arm through Maggie's, leaning closer. "My sister, the fate-defier." Julie rested her cheek against Maggie's shoulder. "Did he say anything else?"

"He said he loves me, and always has." A smile crept its way onto Maggie's lips. "Oh, Julie. I love him too."

Another prickle of regret for how she lashed out at Silver in her anger ate at her. Maybe she was learning that fear was a miserable enemy to love and all its dealings.

Maybe it was time to stop being afraid.

"I kissed Amor." Julie confessed. This time, it was Maggie's jaw that dropped before she grinned.

"Yay!" She exclaimed, clasping her hands together. "I was wondering what was taking so long. The way you two look at each other could practically light a fire."

"No, not *yay*." Julie gave her sister a look. "It was an accident. Wine, attraction, and a lapse in judgement."

Maggie stretched out her legs in front of the fire. "Are you sure that's all it was?" She raised a brow. Julie brushed the pads of her fingertips over her lips. If she closed her eyes she could remember the soft imprint of his mouth on hers. The thought sent a tingle down her spine. But before Julie could form a response, something crashed that sounded like the roof caving in upstairs. The racket ricocheted down the steps and spilled out into the hallways like angry thunder exacting its wrath. Even the warmth from the fire seemed to retreat into the corners of the room, leaving Julie suddenly filled with ice.

CHAPTER THIRTY-TWO

Amor

Amor pushed himself up by his forearms from a puddle of blood. The air turned sour, a sordid scent of rusted metal and decaying hope. His fists bunched up pieces of black grass, tearing them from the earth. *Why was he here?* He did what they asked.

He-

The grass underneath his feet began to ripple like a lake disturbed by a rock carelessly tossed in. Five ripples ebbed closer in waves created by five masked figures. *That wasn't right. Grass wasn't supposed to act like water.* Amor reached for his bow, but it was gone along with his quiver.

All he had was a pitiful dagger hanging off his belt.

Even that was broken.

"What do you want?" Amor called out, but the figures only continued to advance. "Answer me!" He growled.

The wraith-like figures answered in one, droning voice. Yet, Amor could single out their individual voices if he strained his ears. "Do you realize what you cost us?" Their tones grated against every nerve in Amor's body. "We should never have trusted a child with something so delicate."

The figures were closer now. With every inch the distance between them shortened, the clouds above flickered with blood-red lightning. The thunder sounded strange as well, but Amor couldn't figure out why. *Was it saying his name?*

"I don't know what you want from me." Amor searched for an escape. *Why was he on the ground? He would never choose the ground in a situation like this. He knew better.*

"You will know soon." They hissed in unison and raised their hands to strike him. Right as they lunged, so did Amor. Their bodies were like that of shadow, visible but impossible to catch. They merely dissipated like fog through his fingers before reforming again.

The black grass shifted into thorns, digging its way into Amor's ankles with the promise of drawing blood. A fierce blow sent Amor hurtling towards the dirt, the thorns as inviting as a bed of nails. Vaguely, Amor understood he was bleeding. His heart stopped beating when one of the figures removed their mask and knelt down in front of him. *Elias.*

"Such a pity. You showed such promise."

The thunder rolled in, growing more shrill. It sounded like the sky was wailing.

No.

It wasn't the sky.

The other four shadows parted to reveal the source of the cry. It emanated from a small body with a tear-streaked face and purpling bruises all along her hollow cheeks. Black hair hung limply over her face as she struggled to reach him. The thunder amplified her plea. "Amor! Amor!"

No! Amor didn't know if he thought it or shouted it. He fought with every fiber of his being to get back up, but his limbs were stone, his heart leaden. "Annaliese!" His scream rivaled the storm above them. "You'll be okay, don't be scared. I'll find a way-"

They snapped her neck.

The crack reached Amor's ears as Elias leant down and whispered, "Run."

Amor shot upright in bed. He reached his hand up to his face, somewhat aware of the fact that his fingers were shaking. His cheeks were damp with tears and his eyes still burned with the weight of them. He needed to get out. It wasn't high enough. It wasn't open enough. The window slammed upwards, the night air turning his skin cold where his tears had fallen.

Before he knew it, he'd pulled himself up into the branches of one of the taller oaks. The rough bark scratched against his palms, but Amor didn't care. He just wanted to breathe. His heart pounded behind his ribcage. *He hadn't had a nightmare like that in...*

Well, since he'd stopped feeling anything.

At that moment, Amor nearly preferred being numb.

The nightmare hadn't been exactly truthful about what happened, but it was as if his mind saved the worst parts to torment him with and discarded everything else. Amor swallowed and closed his eyes, leaning into the whisper of the night's breeze. It was like a soothing balm to his shattered soul, peace and quiet and-

Rustling?

Amor's eyes flashed open.

Someone was climbing up into his tree.

CHAPTER THIRTY-THREE

Julie

Amor broke one of April's windows, that's what caused the crash. One look at the torn sheets and rumpled bedspread made a seed of worry sprout in Julie's gut. She peered through the shattered window and caught a dark silhouette breaking into a run for a tree.

The very tree she was now attempting to scale.

A knot in the side of the trunk seemed like a great place to jam her foot and she reached up, hoping to latch onto a sturdy branch. She repeated the process a couple times, stepping in the crevices of smaller branches where they protruded from the rough trunk. She only paused when she glanced down and realized how far up she had managed to travel.

Heights. *Why did he have to like heights so much?* Julie didn't like them. She could have been content to never climb another tree. She'd nearly fallen to her death when Pierre made her cross the tightrope in *The House of Roses* as punishment.

"What on earth are you doing?" A low voice sounded from above her. When Julie examined the shadows, a glint of emerald shone through.

"I figured looking for squirrels was an excellent way to spend my night." She deadpanned.

"I could have gotten one for you. I wasn't aware you wanted a pet. We already have Silver." His lips curved the slightest amount.

"I was looking for you, but you sound fine so-" Julie's next words were pierced by a yelp as the branch she stood on creaked. She hugged the trunk, shutting her eyes against the way the ground appeared to be reaching up for her. *This was a bad idea. How was she even going to get down?*

"You're afraid of heights." Amor noted, tilting his head to the right, studying her.

"No, really? You're so observant." Sarcasm dripped from her voice, but it wobbled a bit too much to sound the way she intended.

"Don't fall," he said. Julie heard something shift in the branches above before there was a hand wrapped tightly around her waist. "Although, I'm sure you would try if you thought it might frustrate me."

Julie's gaze flicked over him. He was standing on a sturdy branch with one black boot planted. His other leg balanced carefully on a lower tree limb so he could reach her. All the while being cast in moonlight from the gaps in the leaves overhead. He wasn't supposed to look like a hero. But, Julie couldn't help thinking that if he was to be anyone's hero, she would want him to be hers.

"You could fall too." She reasoned, tilting her chin back to look him fully in the eyes. It was easier than looking towards the ground and calculating the least painful way to land.

At least that's what she told herself.

"I've never fallen," said Amor, "but I might plunge after you if you slip."

"Well, would you and your impeccable balance kindly get me down?" It was hard not to lean into his hand at her back, it reminded her too much of the way he'd held her when they kissed.

Julie had another thought. Heroes only kiss their girl once before choosing to sacrifice her for some greater cause. It's the villains that carry their love through ash and ember, who forsake all else for one more kiss.

It was as if Amor could read her mind like a book left open on a table. He drew her closer. A sturdy arm pressed against her shoulders.

"Why did you come looking for me after..." He trailed off but Julie heard the rest of his unspoken sentence. *After I said our kiss was a mistake.*

"I suppose concern took precedence over my fear." Julie answered honestly.

Amor was quiet for a pause then he said, "Heights don't have to be scary. Look up instead of down. Look forward instead of..." his brow drew together as if he was pondering something, "instead of backward."

Julie glanced up and then past his shoulder. "No, it's still scary."

He chuckled, deep and soft. Familiar, like curling in front of the hearth as a child, wrapped in a cozy blanket. It was the first sparks of a fire as it breathed into life, igniting something in her that longed to hear that quiet laugh again. "Watch the stars with me, Julie."

She studied his face and this time she was certain his gaze lost its sharp edges when it fell into hers. She remembered thinking once that he was a living weapon, and his arms were the last place she should have sought refuge. If she were to reconsider now, maybe a weapon was only deadly in the wrong hands. In the right ones, it could be lifesaving.

Amor took her silent nod as reason to pick her up and bring both of them back to his original tree limb with more grace and finesse than a man his height should naturally possess.

"You can't just pick people up without asking." Julie chastised lightly, glancing backward as he situated her in front of him on the branch, his arms bracing her sides so there was no room for her to fall.

"What if I like picking you up?" Amor's leg swung down off the side of the oak's wide arm as if he was merely lounging across a chaise.

"I didn't know you liked anything." Julie found herself resting her head against the solid wall of Amor's chest.

"I like this." Amor's chin rested atop her head.

"You never told me how we ended up in a tree tonight."

The arms around her tensed but instead of pulling away Amor's thumb brushed up and down her arm. "I had a nightmare."

That would explain why his bed was practically torn apart. "What was it about?" She asked, doubtful he would answer but-

"My sister." Amor answered lowly, halting her thoughts.

She didn't know he had a sister. "What happened to her?"

Amor took a deep breath. His chest rose, fell and faltered against her back, like the stronghold surrounding his heart was being breached. When he spoke again his voice sounded distant, like it belonged to someone he buried a long time ago. "Our parents took ill and passed away when I was thirteen. She was only eight. I worked several odd jobs to provide for us. One day I met this man who offered more money than I'd ever seen in one place, if I would just be his messenger boy. I was never allowed to read the messages. Little by little the requests shifted until I was doing his dirty work." Even Amor's leg stopped swinging off the branch as he paused. "I was in too deep. I didn't know how to get out, but I knew if I stayed with him and his men I could feed Annaliese. Eventually, they needed me to kill someone. A person who was apparently a hindrance to some dark plan of theirs. When it came time to do it, I couldn't. But I made it look like he'd been..." Amor debated his wording, "dealt with."

"Did you get away with it?" Julie turned to look at him. Although, something told her from the somber look in his eye and the way a muscle feathered in his jaw, that he hadn't.

"No, they found out. My mistake cost them something valuable, though they never told me what it was. They took Annaliese and hurt her as an example to me."

Julie's heart ached from the pain in his voice. She found herself reaching up to his forearm and placing a gentle hand there. "Did she..." Julie didn't want to finish that sentence because she feared she knew how the story ended. It was difficult to imagine Amor as a child, without his bow or his arrows promising to carry death on swift wings.

"I tried everything I could to save her. I knew I wasn't strong enough to fight them all. I needed a miracle, so I-" Amor loosed a controlled breath. "I made a wish."

Julie's eyes traveled to the inky expanse above them, to the handful of glittering lights tossed across it by unseen hands. Amor continued, "The stars grant wishes. The all consuming, down-on-your-knees, heart aching, fists-bleeding kind." He wrapped a lock of her hair around his hand and unfurled it. "The type of wish that can only stem from the worst type of pain."

"The Stars gave you your bow, didn't they?" Julie thought back to the ornate etchings of ethereal beauty. Never once had she thought his bow could have been crafted by the hands of a mere man. *Now she had evidence.*

Amor nodded once, wisps of black falling into his eyes. "A weapon in the hands of someone desperate is rarely used for good. I used it to get her out, but by the time I fought my way in, they had nearly beaten her to death." Amor's voice tightened. "I remember grabbing her and running into the forest. All the while she was slipping away from me. I tried to keep talking to her. I told her so many lies that she would be okay until I realized she couldn't hear me anymore." Something damp splashed onto her shoulder. As she twisted in his arms she saw the tear track on his cheek. She took the side of his face in her cupped palm, swiping away the watery inscription his pain left on his bronze skin.

Amor leant into her hand, "It was the same forest we camped in before making this journey."

Julie's thumb faltered against his cheekbone as a memory surfaced. *In Trace's story, two children ran into the woods one night. What if it had only been one boy running while his sister died in his arms? The voices in the forest had only been Amor telling Annaliese that she would live and not die.*

"Why go back to a place that hurts you so?"

"I wanted to be close to her." Amor admitted. "I buried her underneath the tree I slept in at night."

"I'm so sorry, Amor." Julie whispered.

"I can hardly remember a time before I turned into an extension of Fate's hand," Amor said bitterly. "I am just one of the mistakes that Fate has made." Amor's voice lost its bitter edge as his hand crept up to her own, his thumb dancing along the ridges of her knuckles. Julie's breath caught in her throat. *How could a person be so affected by something as slight as the brush of a hand?*

"Have you ever met him?" Amor asked, studying her hand like it was some great puzzle he'd lost the most vital pieces to.

Julie's head spun at how quickly he changed the subject. "Who?"

Emerald eyes collided with hers, ropes of gold woven through them, brimming with questions. "The man on the other end of your string."

"Amor, I-" *How was she going to explain that she didn't know? After all he shared with her... she should tell him the truth.* Right as she opened her mouth to admit that her soul-string led nowhere, he stopped her.

"I actually don't think I want to know right now." He tucked a piece of hair behind her ear. "What was it that you said about pretending? It's... easier." Amor's fingertips ghosted over her jaw, till he held her chin between his thumb and forefinger.

It wasn't easy anymore. It was real. There was nothing fictional about the way he'd kissed her like she held the key to every lock he secured around his heart.

Chapter Thirty-Four

Amor

The air was crisp on his skin as they descended the gravel road toward Seruvia. Suddenly, Julie stuffed Fiona's lead in Silver's hand. She flashed a smile that Amor could only describe as ridden with beautiful mischief before darting off the path.

"Where is she going?" Maggie laughed, curls bouncing with each slight shake of her head.

Amor watched as Julie's form retreated further down the path, her raven hair glinting like molten onyx in the sunlight.

"Maybe you should go after her." Maggie offered thoughtfully, tapping her chin with her index finger. The bitter voice in his mind attempted to whisper that they didn't have time for this. For once, he shoved it back. Amor's boots fell against the dirt faster and faster until he was running. *He couldn't remember the last time he'd run for fun.*

He had to admit, the sensation of wind at his back was much more exhilarating when a threat wasn't looming at his heels. When Amor ran, however, he always ran with a target in sight. His target just so happened to be weaving her way through the crowds of a bustling, colorful market. Julie paused only long enough to check behind her, grinning when they locked eyes. *This woman was going to be the death of him.* Amor found himself smiling back at her. Julie took off into a section of the market that boasted strips of fabric and cloth in every color, size and pattern. There were ribbons of gold, rivers of teal and bronze, and heaps of burgundy. Overhead, various scarves hung across wooden arches that either sparkled with tiny jewels or flecks of gold. Amor reached up and pulled one down before lunging forward and wrapping it around Julie's waist, stopping her in her tracks.

"Caught you." He said, breathless. Though, it had less to do with how hard he'd run, and more the way she beamed at him.

"I see that." Julie laughed through her strive for oxygen as she glanced down at the rope that bound them together.

Red, like tumbled rubies. *The color suited her.* It always had. Julie ran her fingertips over the scarf in awe, soaking in each detail on the cloth.

"Now," Amor tightened his grip on both ends of the scarf that hung at the back of her hips, "care to tell me why you decided to gallivant off the beaten path?"

"I couldn't remember the last time I did something for no reason. Besides, I *might* have wanted to see if you would run after me."

"Oh, you *might* have, hmm?" Amor raised a brow.

"I was right." Julie smirked in victory.

Before Amor could respond, an apparent *'ahem'* sliced cleanly through the air. His eyes begrudgingly left Julie's face and flicked to the woman who'd cleared her throat.

"Sir, if you're not going to buy that for your wife then kindly return my merchandise." A blonde woman with hair tightly wrapped in a teal scarf clasped her hands atop her stall's counter.

Wife? Amor couldn't say he'd ever thought of the word as anything other than something reserved for other people. However, the misunderstanding sounded... rather nice.

"I will take it, actually." Amor unraveled Julie from the scarf.

"We don't need that, Amor." Julie attempted to stop him, confusion knitting her brows together.

"I think we might." Amor withdrew a handful of aurums from his pocket. "How much for the scarf?"

The blonde woman eyed them, "Five of those gold coins you got there."

"That's too high for a scarf." Julie came up to stand beside him, surveying the piece of glittering fabric with light scrutinization.

The stall-keeper shook her head, the stones on her woven necklace clicking together. "The red dye is made purely from cochineal extract and the glitter is fine gold flakes. You won't find prettier gemstones anywhere else. Plus, it was imported from Cyrath. Your wife will be the belle of the ball anytime she wears it." The blonde turned her attention to Amor, her smile revealing a gleaming gold incisor.

"I'm really not going to be attending any balls-"

"Sold." Amor tossed the coins onto the shopkeeper's table, which she greedily lapped up like a dog seeking water on a hot summer day. The ghost of a smirk flit across Amor's lips as Julie balked. "Come on, *wife*." He teased, delicately picking up the scarf again.

As soon as they were out of earshot Julie stepped in front of him. "Amor you didn't have to do that. You know she was just trying to swindle you out of your money right?"

"Don't worry, there's still enough for your next payment." Amor rocked back on his heels watching Julie's mouth open and close, ultimately struggling to provide him with a good reason why he shouldn't have done it. So, Amor placed the scarf in her hands. "Do you not like it?"

"I love it, I just…" Julie cradled the fabric as if it might shatter into a million tiny threads were she to clutch it too tightly. *An accurate representation of his heart as well.*

"You just…?" He waited patiently. "I've seen you get presents for Maggie, but not once have I seen you buy something for yourself." Something treacherously close to longing lingered in his voice. "Now you'll have something to remember us by when we part ways."

A myriad of emotions twined across her features, there and gone quicker than the snap of a bowstring. *Since when had she become unreadable? At what point had he started trying to decipher every mystery that was her?*

"Our journey isn't over yet, right?" Amor swore he heard something akin to hope in her tone, like she wasn't ready for their story to be over.

If Amor was honest with himself, neither was he.

"We should get back to Silver and your sister."

Julie wrapped the scarf around her waist like a belt, her fingertips dancing along the border of gemstones. *Maybe she would wear it when she gave readings back at her cart. Perhaps it would grace her shoulders on the day she met her soulmate.*

Amor's hand flexed at his side as they ventured forward. He didn't like that thought. There were dangers in playing pretend. At some point, fantasy will always unravel for reality to peek through. As he cast a sideways glance towards the woman beside him, he was painfully reminded of something.

His reality was unfit for a beauty like her.

CHAPTER THIRTY-FIVE

Julie

They made it into the city just as dusk was beginning to kiss the day goodbye. She hadn't expected Seruvia to border the water, or for the tangy smell of fish, salt and metal to permeate her nostrils. One half of the city dwelled high above the rest, seemingly untouched by the low hanging fog and gloom flickering through the streets. If Julie cocked her head back and squinted, she could see the outline of a nearly pearlescent castle in the distance. The remainder of the sun's fingertips caressed the structure, trailing over the rest of the upper portion of Seruvia. The top half of the city resembled a pile of treasure, while the lower half appeared to be caked in dirt.

The ground was littered with black cobblestone, a well-weathered road boasting looming buildings on either side. Children ran past, darting through alleyways and around chipped fountains. The little ones weren't laughing and playing, however. They kept their heads ducked, looking around cautiously. They surveyed Julie and Amor's group with the type of scrutiny usually seen in the eyes of an adult. It unsettled her, and judging by the mirrored look Maggie cast in her direction, her sister felt similarly.

Amor glanced to the rooftops of the buildings they moved past. Julie knew he would much rather be scouting up there than down here. "Where should we start looking for those gears?" Julie tapped Amor's forearm, drawing his attention.

"Not we, me." Said Amor, steering them into a desolate stable with a thatched roof. "Rest the horses. Silver will stay behind with you both."

Silver looked uneasy but resigned to the fact that he wouldn't convince Amor otherwise. Julie crossed her arms. "You're not going alone."

Amor furrowed his dark brows. Once, Julie thought the gesture made him look like he was consistently scowling, but now it looked rather endearing. "I'm merely going to have a look around."

"Fantastic, then you could use an extra pair of eyes." Julie led Fiona over to the watering trough and Maggie brought Pepper.

"I need you and your eyes to stay put, Julie." Amor's voice sounded from behind her.

"I'm coming." Julie said with finality, her hands planted on her hips.

"No, you're not. Silver, where's the pouch with the Nightrose?" Amor turned his attention to the other young man and Julie glared at Amor's back.

"What if you need my gift while you're out there?" Julie reasoned, bringing Amor's emerald eyes back to hers.

"Not tonight, you'd be more of a distraction than a help." He walked over to one of their bags, the one Silver was not currently rifling through.

"Allow me to translate, he means he'll worry about you when he needs to focus." Silver offered helpfully, leaning back on his heels.

"I just don't see why you can't focus with me around." Julie grumbled under her breath as she turned away, petting Fiona's flank. There was silence, then shifting as Maggie and Silver suddenly found the other side of the stable very interesting.

"Did you ever stop to consider that you make me lose all sense of reason with any word that comes out of your mouth, Firelight?" Amor's words were a low hum against the shell of her ear. "Do you realize how detrimental that is when I need to be alert?" The rest of the stable, and everything else faded away until the only thing Julie was aware of was their proximity. Memories of their dance, their kiss, came whirling back like swarms of excited butterflies.

"Did you consider that two heads are better than one?" Julie turned slightly, cemented in place by the intensity of his gaze. Amor brought his hand to the side of her head, cradling it. "I've considered that this one is very precious and until the day the privilege is stripped from me, I'm going to protect it."

Julie's heart tripped, then beat faster as if it longed to break free of its cage and join his. Her eyes closed as the ghost of his lips danced along her temple. The sensation lingered but when she opened them again, Amor was gone.

Chapter Thirty-Six

Julie

"Where did I put the Nightrose pouch?" Silver scratched the side of his jaw, glaring at one of his satchels.

"Do you remember what bag it was in?" Maggie tossed her hair into a bun and opened one of the packs.

"I could have sworn it-"

"Found it!" Maggie beamed as she shot her fist in the air, the little leather pouch in her grasp.

A cross between relief and urgency washed over Silver's features. "He didn't leave long ago, I might be able to catch up to him." Silver gently took the Nightrose root from Maggie's fingers and turned for the stable's entrance.

Julie shot upright from her seat in the hay. "Wait! I'll take it."

"Julie, I don't think that's a good idea." Silver barely got his sentence out before she snatched the small satchel from his hand. She cast an apologetic smile over her shoulder as she ran outside.

The night air caressed her neck, dipping over her skin like cold hands. If she was Amor, where would she be? Her eyes snapped to the rooftops. *Perfect.*

Julie tucked the pouch into the scarf tied at her waist, before locating a thinly rung ladder on the side of a building. As she ascended, an incisor found the flesh of her inner cheek. *Heights were definitely worse when his arms weren't wrapped around her.*

Julie made it to the first roof and peered down over the road. Several rooftops down, she spied Amor's silhouette. If she didn't pick up the pace, she'd lose him in the city. Julie sucked in a breath, gauging the distance between rooftops. She needed to jump at exactly the right time in order to land successfully. The alternative looked like shattered bones and bruised skin. Her feet pounded underneath her as she began charging forward. *Jump.* The voice in her head sounded reminiscent of her own voice when she was a child. That girl had climbed trees without fear and leapt from banisters because it made her laugh.

She just needed to learn how to become that girl again. With each pulse of her legs and every time she leapt, it became easier. Her lungs burned with crisp air and her veins buzzed with electric adrenaline.

Julie landed on the final rooftop and climbed down onto the dark street. Amor stood with his side pressed against the façade of an adjacent building, tucked into the shadows. Just as she nearly approached him, the clattering of wagon wheels against cobblestone racked through the air. She watched Amor's jaw clench, his hand inching its way around his bow.

One covered wagon appeared, followed by another and another until seven such carts rolled by in succession, pulled by huffing, stocky mules. Every cart was surrounded by male guards with longswords strapped to their hips. They must have housed something that required a careful watch.

Amor loosed himself from the shadows, striking one guard behind the head. The man soundlessly crumpled into a heap on the ground. Amor deposited the guard's body into the alley, concealing him in a blanket of darkness. He removed the man's coal-colored cloak and sword, donning them both. He pulled the hood over his head, fluidly adopting the identity of the fallen guard. The other men appeared to be none the wiser as each wagon rattled forward and Amor fell into step behind them.

Now was her chance. Julie just needed to slip the pouch into Amor's pocket, without him realizing she went directly against the one thing he'd asked.

"We switch out here." A scratchy, gruff voice met Julie's ears as one guard stalked down the line. He was dressed differently than the rest and held his shoulders back with a sense of superiority. *Perhaps he was in charge of this strange, midnight caravan?* "You know what to do, men."

The wagons stalled. Julie flattened herself against the rough stone siding of the closest building, watching the first four carts veer toward the west. Their respective guards followed suit, leaving three wagons behind to stand stationary.

"Thornbeck. Whistler." He stopped in front of the second closest cart and withdrew a worn leather book from within his cloak. When Amor didn't approach, the man with gravel in his throat glared impatiently. "Whistler, would you like to keep the ears you're using to ignore me?"

Amor stalked forward. *No doubt imagining many colorful ways to run the man through with the spoke of a wagon wheel.* There was no way she could slip the Nightrose root to him now. Not without both of them getting caught. She *could* return to the safety of the stables with her sister and abandon this mission, but she was unwilling to let Amor follow these men to an unsure fate. Not without her.

With determination planted firmly in her mind, Julie crafted either a great or a horrible plan.

Her eyes darted to the men whose backs were turned just enough for her to slink to the opposing side of the closest cart. Her fingers clutched the edge of the dusty tarp. The sound of paper ripping coincided with the gap Julie forged between the covering and wagon bed. As she climbed underneath, her cramped limbs encountered jagged, sharp objects and the stale air smelled of metal. *The Seruvian gears. But where were they taking them? And coincidentally, her?* Julie lowered the wagon's cover, before one of the guards could resume their post. Her fingernails dug into the stitching of the bag of poison as she held her breath. The cart began to roll again. The steady gait at its side made Julie's lips lift at the corners in relief. *She knew the sound of that walk.*

Determined enough to charge forward into the fiercest storms, sure enough to be unmovable, and powerful enough to wrangle the night into submission.

She had to admit, she liked when she heard his footsteps traveling in her direction. She also liked when she couldn't hear his steps, but she turned around and he was just there. Julie hoped he wouldn't decide to relinquish tracking these carts.

Being alone in the dark with only her thoughts for company and the occasional gear poking her side, made Julie give into her imagination. If Amor did break away and head back to the stables, what would be his reaction at discovering her disappearance?

Would he be angry?

Would he run outside, searching for her frantically, unable to rest until she was found and back in his arms? Would he hold her or chastise her?

Would it stem from worry or frustration?

Julie twined the pouch's strings through her fingers.

Sometimes, the intensity within his emerald eyes as he looked at her made Julie wonder if he might set fire to the city to get her back, never allowing one ember to singe her face or one flame to lick her skin.

At the start of their journey, Julie believed he only wanted her for her gift. But now... if her powers were to suddenly flee from her, she wanted to believe he would still find her valuable. Would he guard her with the same intensity if she had nothing to offer him but her heart?

The wagon stopped abruptly, causing the gears to slide around, her body their only obstacle. The sudden halt pulled Julie from her thoughts and her heartbeat quickened as the wagon bed flooded with light.

Chapter Thirty-Seven

Amor

Startled hazel eyes stared up at him from her curled position in the bed of the wagon. Amor's stomach lurched in a way he'd never experienced before, even when jumping down from the tallest heights. Perhaps because that was falling with a sure landing. This was more like colliding with a wall of swords, their blades piercing directly through his body. In her fist sat the familiar pouch of poison, but the realization she'd snuck away into a dangerous situation made Amor feel as if he himself had ingested the Nightrose root.

"What are you doing?" He hissed, grasping her forearms and pulling her from the cart. "What did I say about staying put?"

"You didn't specify for how long." Julie offered a slight smile with the raise of her shoulder. The sight shouldn't have had the power to quench the frustration that washed over him like a wave. Maybe that was because his frustration sounded a lot like fear with a different name. "You have to-" Amor growled under his breath, his gaze darting around them. He was going to say, *'You have to go,'* but where would she go? There was no way in all the world he'd simply set her loose in an unfamiliar place. Subconsciously, he held her arms more firmly, daring anyone to try and pry her out of his hands. "Come on." He ushered her forward. They slipped around the side of a rectangular, torch-illuminated building. Amor had grown warier the further they traveled towards the edge of lower Seruvia. Their destination was set miles apart from any civilization. The structure in question was far too large to be considered inconspicuous to the wandering eye. A row of similar wagons like the one he'd walked alongside littered the front-facing exterior. Curved archways were carved into the east wall, where guards currently unloaded wooden crates from the carts and carried them inside. Amor pulled off the secondary black cloak he'd taken from Whistler, adjusting it instead over Julie's frame. He tugged the hood down to conceal most of her features. The cloak was loose-fitting, so her figure would not be easily distinguishable. "Follow my lead." He whispered, flicking his line of sight toward the crates.

If Pascale and Varian were going to be anywhere, they would be here overseeing the delivery of the Seruvian gears. To find them meant they needed to be inside. Amor and Julie both lifted a crate and followed the dark, firelit outline of the guard in front of them. The crates were being stacked in the central room. The sheer amount of wooden boxes made Amor uneasy. *What were they going to do with all these gears? And why?*

As soon as they were alone, Amor and Julie ducked into an alcove leading into a hallway glowing with flickering torchlight. Julie tried the handles of each door to their left but none of them budged. Amor shook his head silently and gestured to the next corridor.

Before he could take a step in that direction she latched onto the cuff of his sleeve and yanked. She pressed her finger to her lips as her eyes flew to the entrance of the next hall. Voices, both male and growing closer by the second, floated down the corridor. Julie hurriedly fumbled with the last door handle and Amor raised his bow, prepared to shoot their way out. He had expected Pascale and Varian to be in the main room where the crates were being deposited, but he'd been proven wrong. Perhaps they weren't there at all. Right as he nocked an arrow, something clicked behind him and Julie pushed the door open. In a heartbeat, she pulled him inside and locked the door. Synchronized bootsteps loudly thumped outside until they faded away into a mere echo. Both he and Julie exhaled in the quiet.

"Amor?"

"Yes?" He answered quietly.

"I can't see anything in here." Hesitancy colored her voice.

He looked around, arriving at the realization that they were without any form of light. Amor could see fairly well but he'd always been able to see better in the dark. It was as if a thin veil of perpetual moonlight always remained in front of his vision, helping him to see what others couldn't.

It was ironic. Typically, she could see the things he was unable to, but tonight the roles were reversed.

There were gentle hands on his waist.

"Having fun there, Firelight?" He was glad she couldn't see the amused curve of his mouth in the pitch.

She hit him in the stomach with enough force to not be accidental. "Oops. I told you I couldn't see." The honey in her tone was layered on to mask what Amor could only translate as a flustered Julie.

It was endearing, terribly so.

"In that case," Amor placed a heavy arm at her back and the other at her knees, seamlessly lifting her against his chest.

"Woah. What are you doing?"

"I'll be your eyes while you're robbed of sight," said Amor, his thumb stroking her side. A quick survey of the room revealed that they stumbled across an office. Judging by the crates stacked to the side, the messy desk and wall of various weapons, it must belong to whomever was leading this operation. Perhaps the letters so haphazardly scattered across the surface of the desk could provide some insight.

"What are those?" Julie's hand skimmed over the paper, feeling her way along the objects she could not see.

"Letters." Amor told her, scanning the ink. Envelope after envelope, all embossed with the name of one kingdom in particular.

Esterod.

"Receipts, requests for large shipments of Seruvian gears." He continued. "Marked with Esterod's royal seal."

"Who are the letters addressed to?" Julie squinted in the dimness.

Amor unfolded the third letter, finding similarities in the requests of each slip of paper but nothing too earth-shattering. "The Duke."

"Surely, this Duke has a name to go along with his title?" She mused.

"It seems he's in charge of the gear shipments." Amor started. He couldn't recollect a singular mention of the Duke from his time associated with their foul dealings. Elias always seemed to be the leader. Now he wondered if the Duke had masqueraded under the guise of another. Amor had been too blinded by revenge and pain to fully notice that something was brewing underneath the surface. It was as if he stood at the precipice of a nightmare just before one wakes, stranded in the space between suspense and truth. Pascale and Varian were closest to Elias. There was a high probability that one of them could be the Duke. *But what would either of them want with the gears, or even the set of twins from Elias's meeting? What did they stand to gain?*

"There has to be something here that'll point us in the right direction. A name, a face, the *why* behind all these orders." Julie drummed her fingers on her knee. "Are there any candles we can light so I can help you search?"

Amor found matches in the top left desk drawer and struck one against the side of the wall. When the flame flared, it cast a golden glow over Julie's face. Amor realized that even with his enhanced vision there was nothing more lovely than the ability to see her in the light. After four candles flickered to life, Amor set Julie on her feet.

Julie scooped up one of the candles by its base and looked at it, a slight smile on her lips. "In a different situation this could almost be romantic."

Amor's eyes flicked to hers. "I'm afraid you've not known romance if this is your idea of it."

"Trysts in the candlelit dark, being quiet so we don't get caught? Is that not the stuff of fairytales?"

Amor was about to ask her where she was getting these thoughts, but the way the candlelight caught the very mischievous glint in her eyes made him reconsider.

Teasing, she was only teasing. That knowledge did little to tame the unwarranted dip in his stomach. "Fairytales are supposed to have happy endings." Amor said under his breath as he turned his attention to the wall of weapons.

Julie was silent for a moment and Amor thought perhaps she'd busied herself with searching through the clutter. Then in a voice as quiet as his she asked, "Can't ours have a happy ending?"

Amor's hand faltered over the handle of a mounted blade whose hilt looked more worn than the rest. "I'm not the type of person they make stories about, Firelight. But you are. I don't have a place in your tale."

Julie swept an object from the table and held it out. It was a pen, with a crimson feather rimmed in gold. "Then rewrite it."

Amor swallowed. The pen was such a simple object, but he pictured being handed a knife instead with the request to run her through with it. After all, wasn't that exactly what he would be doing if he said yes? Wouldn't he be taking her away from the person on the other end of her string if he took her in his arms right here and now and told her all the words he'd kept inside? He couldn't bind her to a life of uncertainty when that's all she'd ever known and desperately deserved better. Amor learned long ago that his greatest wants were fated to never come true.

His grip slipped on the dagger's handle. It should have made the blade clatter to the ground but instead it only shifted. A click echoed behind the wall, sounding as if the dagger had settled into place. He and Julie turned as one of the shelves on the bookcase slid away to reveal a hidden panel.

"I've never seen anything like this." Julie murmured, sidestepping him and pressing her palm flat against the panel. It gave and rolled away enough for the candlelight's haze to illuminate a small carved out space in the wall itself. She felt around for the contents of the little alcove. "More letters." In one of her hands, she still clutched that feathered quill, and in the other she scanned a crisp, crème envelope with midnight ink scrawled across the front of it.

"There's two." Amor withdrew its twin, attempting not to let his gaze stray to the pen in her grasp. "They aren't the same as the letters on the desk."

Julie gingerly opened the flap of the first envelope while Amor sliced the second apart cleanly. "Careful!" She gave him a pointed look. "We need to leave things the way we found them."

"I don't think anyone will notice." Amor raised a dark brow, glancing sidelong towards the mess that was the office.

"They're invitations." Julie said after shaking her head at him, "For a ball two nights from now at the Moonstone palace."

"That's the Seruvian castle." Amor offered.

"Mine is addressed to a Pascale and a…" She paused to puzzle out the looping cursive.

"Varian." Amor finished for her, reading the same line she did. "That's where I'll find them."

Julie folded the letter back into its preordained creases. "You're looking for these people in particular? Are they the ones with answers about the gears?"

"They might be. But those answers aren't why we're here," said Amor, tucking both letters into his pocket.

Julie turned the feathered pen around in her hands before she suddenly asked something that made the blood in Amor's veins grow cold. "Why *are* we here, Amor?"

"Apparently, to attend a ball in two days." The abstract truth was the first thing to spring to his tongue. As he watched the smile on her lips fade into a line of wary suspicion, his gut twisted with regret.

"No, I mean why did you need my abilities in the first place? I didn't ask before because I thought it was best not to know but…" Julie trailed off before she squared her shoulders and locked eyes with him. "It's been eating at me for days. Seeing soul-strings won't help you find out who is behind all this." She waved a broad hand towards the letters and the invitations in Amor's pocket.

"I never came for the gears," Amor said slowly. "Pascale and Varian were part of the group who killed Annaliese. I thought if I found the Seruvian gears, I might find them too."

Julie watched him with something akin to sympathy. But, her eyes were filled with so many burning questions, they rivaled the flames dancing on the wick of every candle. "I'm sorry, I still don't understand." Julie crossed her arms. "If you knew where they were, why did you need me?"

"I would have done it myself, but I was losing my power to see the threads with my arrows."

"Why did you need to see their strings at all, Amor?" She took a furtive step closer, wanting to believe the best in him but coming up empty in her search.

He could tell her it didn't matter. That it would soon all be over, but would she ever trust him again if he were to utter those words? Even now he saw whatever had become forged between them begin to flake away like sparks leaping from metal.

"I needed you…" Amor began, his mind racing with thousands of reasons why he needed her, all fully selfish and impossible. "I needed your gift so I could kill their soulmates."

CHAPTER THIRTY-EIGHT

Julie

Julie felt like her entire body was submerged into the coldest ice, forcing every ounce of air in her lungs to be painfully pressed out.

I needed your gift so I could kill their soulmates.

"Julie..." Amor lifted his hand towards her, but she stumbled back, shaking her head even as the room spun around in a violently dreadful dance.

"Tell me you're lying." Her voice came out no louder than a whisper. "Tell me you haven't done this."

"I wanted them to hurt, Julie. Like I did. Fate has made a mockery of me while giving vile creatures like them power they did not earn."

Julie's mind retreated back to the memory of the first day they'd met. She pointed him willingly in the direction of the man in the tavern's soulmate, and didn't spare more than a second thought. She offered up someone's life and all for thirty measly coins.

What did that make her?

She was no better than him and that realization sent a wave of molten fire into her veins, melting the ice. "Were they innocent, Amor? The ones you killed?"

"Julie please understand-"

"No. I don't understand." Her gaze turned steely. "I will never understand how anyone could do what you've done. And it makes me sick that I helped you." Julie threw the feathered pen to the ground, resisting the urge to crush it underneath her heel. She bolted for the exit. The glittering scarf around her hips tore as it caught on the door's sharp handle. *Fitting,* she thought. *Everything else was falling to pieces, why shouldn't the last good reminder of him be in tatters as well?*

Julie pulled the hood of her cloak over her hair as she ran. The guards and their wagons must have long since departed but Julie only vaguely registered the fact. Even if this place had been teeming with them, she would have still run.

Her feet raced past trees and boulders, through the forest and barren grass. She pressed on until her lungs could have wept from exertion if they possessed the ability.

She didn't stop even when she heard the pounding of bootsteps behind her.

When she stopped, it was not of her own volition. She was caught by arms encircling her that she feared she'd never be able to outrun.

Chapter Thirty-Nine

Amor

"Let me go!" Julie thrashed in the same hold that only hours before she'd melted into. Amor would have given years of his life for her to curl into him like that again.

"No. Not unless you swear you will stop running." His heart pounded against her back.

"I could just as easily lie." She panted, trying to jerk her body free but Amor held tight.

"Yes, you could. If you want me to chase you into eternity I will, but at least catch your breath before you continue to hate me."

Julie drew in a long, raggedy breath, perhaps weighing her options. Thankfully, she stopped twisting in his grasp like a caged tigress.

Amor slowly pulled his arms away from her and watched as Julie walked several paces ahead before turning around. "I know what happened to your sister killed you. But no amount of pain should give you the right to take someone else's life."

"If it had been Maggie instead of Annaliese, what would you have done?" The words were out of Amor's mouth before he could reign them back in.

"This isn't about Maggie-" Julie's hands clenched into fists at her sides.

"Every decision I made in my life led to her death. It was *my* fault. She would still be alive today if I hadn't done the things I did. The one common thread in all of it was them. I wanted them to feel at least a shred of the torture they put me through. I knew if there was any room for love in their twisted hearts at all, I could poison it until they were ruined."

"And now? How many deaths will it take for you to be satisfied, Amor? It won't bring her back, no matter how much blood you spill in her name." Julie shrugged off the black cloak and cast it aside before beginning to walk away.

Amor wanted to tell her that deep in his heart he knew she was right. He wanted to say that he had started relinquishing his ironlike grip on his revenge the day he'd started to fall for her.

But it was too late now. She was already leaving in more ways than one.

So, all Amor said was, "After the ball, I won't need your gift anymore. You and your sister will part ways with us, and you can imagine that none of this ever happened."

Julie froze, like an arrow suspended in flight. Her hazel eyes sharp as daggers as they met his gaze. "So that's it?" Each word fell harshly on his ears. "All of this. You dragged us into the middle of nowhere, Maggie almost died! And then you and... me..." She trailed off and Amor's throat tightened. "Maybe it will be easy for you to forget all of this, but I won't."

A muscle ticked in Amor's jaw. *How could she possibly think he would ever forget what happened between them?* As if a solitary day would ever go by that he didn't think of every word she ever said to him. But pain was easier to lean into than vulnerability. He knew pain, he was familiar with its ache and its sting. Vulnerability was something that had only sparked in her wake. She'd reached through his every wall and tied herself to his heart. Now, she was going to vanish with it still resting in the palm of her hand, leaving him empty and hollow.

"Forgetting you would be the hardest thing you could ask me to do." Amor's hand flexed around his bow. *When had he even grabbed it?* "It's not as if you'll be lacking. When this is over you can run to your soulmate. I'm sure the two of you will be very happy." His words were bitter, rimmed with hurt and jealousy.

"What are you even talking about?" Julie ran a frustrated hand through her hair.

"Come now, Julie. You of all people would know where he is. My only question is why you haven't looked for him before?" *Pain is familiar, lean into it, it'll make things easier when she leaves-*

"I don't have a soulmate string." Julie said.

Just like that, Amor's world tilted on its axis. "That's impossible, you've done nothing to sever your tie."

"It's black and faded. So thank you for the reminder that I either wasn't wanted by whoever once connected to it or they died before they got the chance to decide for themselves."

It didn't make sense. She had to be lying. Amor's eyes lowered to the bow in his hand. "You know, but you're scared to tell me because you think I'll go after him."

"I can't do this." Julie shook her head, turning on her heel again.

"Maybe I can point you in the right direction." Amor said lowly. Julie didn't look back before the arrow loosed from his raised bow and found its mark. Piercing her through the heart, before vanishing without a trace.

CHAPTER FORTY

Julie

She saw the arrow before she felt it. Its flight was a kiss to her spine, phasing through her chest in a manner that very well should have killed her. But she remained standing. Her heart continued to beat. The arrow dissolved into nothing more than a thought, and yet its invisible mark would forever remain.

Daybreak crested over the tops of the tallest trees, bathing where she and Amor stood with rose gold light. As she lifted her eyes skyward she saw something new. Where dawn reached out across the expanse of the heavens, it touched stars that burned more brightly than she'd ever seen. A new day and the old one. Each battling for the chance at staying a moment longer to bear witness to the scene unfolding below them.

Julie looked to Amor, but his gaze was immovable. Entranced by something in the sky she had missed. A gasp left her as she watched the stars shift, forming a new constellation that swept overhead, glimmering with radiance and light. The stars were moving to paint a picture of her and Amor.

The magical rendition of them showed Amor pulling her close, her dress scattering smaller stars in its path. He leant down to kiss her, and the instant his eyes closed, the scene rearranged to depict Julie's silhouette running. Determination radiated from every inch of her body. The stars exploded apart, coming together to form an arrow that sailed past the clouds and vanished in a show of sparkling light.

Julie's hand pressed against her mouth in awe as the stars collected a final time, arranging themselves to look like Amor and Julie's hands, pressed together before their fingers interlocked.

Then one by one the glowing diamonds fell all around them from the sky, raining down in a display of celestial splendor. Julie wondered if she could reach out and grab a fleeting star in her hands, but the illusion faded.

A sound akin to thunder rolled through the air at the very moment the final star fell. Light flashed so blindingly bright that Julie had no choice but to shut her eyes against it. When she reopened them, the stars were in the same position they had been since the beginning of time, nary a trace of the enchanting display they performed.

"Julie." Amor said suddenly, emerald eyes locked onto her hand.

"What-" She peered down, and nearly fell to her knees.

Her soulmate string.

It was turning red.

Julie feared if she blinked, the vision in front of her might just curl into smoke and dissipate. But it didn't. The crimson thread stretched and floated forward, reaching for something or someone.

"I can see it." Amor whispered, his grip on the curve of his bow shaky and white-knuckled. "I can see your string."

Julie's thread twisted, rising on an unseen wind before it paused in midair, merely hovering in the space between them as if it were undecided on where to go.

Or perhaps it had known all along and was merely taking a moment to bask in the reality that it was finally time to entwine with its missing half.

Julie's red thread of fate surged ahead, dancing and weaving and circling as it coiled around Amor's finger and tied itself with an inseverable permanence.

Julie heard her heartbeat rush in her ears as she slowly lifted her gaze from their string to his downcast eyes.

Amor was her soulmate.

And she was his.

"It's you." She breathed, her hand falling limp at her side. "It's always been you." Julie moved towards him, but Amor stepped back, their fated thread snapping taut between them. She had been so enthralled at the sight of her soulmate string, their soulmate string, that she'd missed how haunted Amor looked. There was a fear in his eyes that had perhaps been there when they first looked at the stars.

But why?

Was she truly that awful that it terrified him to be forever bound to her?

A torrent of emotions swept through her with every second that Amor's silence grew. At first she'd experienced sparks of shock, spanning into ripples of elation and wonder. But she hadn't seen even a hint of those feelings flash across Amor's features.

If anything, he looked prepared to wrestle with fate until it gave him a different outcome.

"Please say something." If all he could give was silence, she wanted him to at least pull her into his arms and hold her until he was able to speak again.

Amor didn't hold her. He didn't even look at her.

"The stable is a mile east of here." He said, sounding far away though he stood not three feet in front of her.

"Amor." Julie reached out and clasped his hand in her own. "Why aren't you looking at me?"

She regretted asking that question as his hand slipped out of hers. She'd never before realized how lonely a hand could feel. "Because this is wrong, Julie. We are wrong. I'm- I can't be your soulmate."

"You can't tell me you don't feel it." Julie urged. "Look me in the eyes and swear to me you don't want this." She reached up and cupped his face in her hands. Amor's emerald eyes fell into hers.

"I..."

Don't say it, it's not true.

Amor wrenched his eyes shut when he drew in a breath, like it pained him. "I don't..."

"I don't want-" Amor's hand tangled in her hair, tipping her head up, poring over every plane of her face like it was the last time he would ever see it. "Oh Julie, don't make me swear this."

Julie pulled his face down to hers and captured his lips with her own. Their past kiss had been every longing and stolen glance they refused to admit, disguised under a mask of pretending. This kiss was a confession. This kiss was the antidote to poison, the chance at the eternity he said he would chase her into.

This kiss also tasted like goodbye.

Amor broke away first, then pressed one last painfully soft brush of his lips to the corner of her mouth. His hands gripped her upper shoulders. He looked as if he might fall to pieces were he to release her. However, when he did, Julie thought she might be the one to crumble.

"I'm sorry, Firelight," he whispered. "But the one death I refuse to have on my hands is yours."

CHAPTER FORTY-ONE

Julie

A hush settled over the forest as she stood there alone. She felt equal parts numb and breakable and couldn't decide which was worse.

Perhaps if she had told him how she truly felt, he might have stayed. But all she had now was a constant, crimson reminder attached to her hand that he was there but never next to her. Julie ran her fingertips across the string, feeling its tangibility.

She'd never known you could touch one. Did he feel it when she did?

She felt strangely empty, like she was missing something she'd only just learned belonged to her, and she craved its return. Why did Amor think if he were to stay with her she would lose her life? After everything they'd been through, he had proven time and again that his arms were a safe haven carved out for her alone.

How could they ever part ways if they would always remain forever connected? And not merely by the string they shared, but by heart?

Julie wrapped her arms around herself as she came upon the stables, where she was greeted by a fussing Maggie brimming over with worry. "Julie, where have you been? We tried to look for you, but we didn't know which way you went and oh, you were gone for so long I started to assume you'd gotten lost trying to find him and-" Her sister stopped breathlessly in her tracks. "You're crying."

Was she? Julie swiped at her cheek, not expecting the damp tracks she found there. "I didn't mean to worry you."

Julie had no sooner gotten the words out before Maggie crushed her into a hug. It was the type that needed no words but offered the comfort only a sister could bestow. Julie buried her face into her sister's shoulder as Maggie rubbed her back.

"Amor gave me these." Silver approached cautiously, holding up the foiled invitations.

"He's here?" Julie couldn't stop the words from tumbling over her lips even though she knew the answer before Silver said one word.

"No, he came in just a few minutes before you got here." There was something heavy in Silver's blue gaze, pity or sympathy she couldn't tell. He turned the invitations over in his hands. "He wanted me to give you both a choice."

Julie pulled back from Maggie's embrace. "What choice?" *Now he wanted to give her a choice? Yet, he wouldn't allow her a similar courtesy when she wanted him to stay?*

"Varian and Pascale are supposed to be at the ball. We may be able to stop whatever plans they're brewing if we go in their stead." Silver reached into his pocket and withdrew a pouch clinking with metallic contents. "But, if you and Maggie wish to, you can take these coins and leave. Amor will figure out another way inside." Silver held out the pouch in the palm of his hand. Maggie settled an assuring hand on Julie's shoulder. A touch so gentle and understanding it nearly made Julie's tears brim anew. *They could take it and go away from all this.*

But did she truly want to leave?

In their time together, they had experienced a sense of home. Yes, they'd been tossed into danger, but they came out of it victorious and wiser than before. Amor's motivations, twisted as they were, stemmed from a place of hurt so deep she was certain no light could have reached there. Not until she'd unknowingly begun hammering away at the walls he kept around himself to let the light in.

Julie ran her hands down her face as she silently walked further into the stable. He'd asked her what she would have done if it had been Maggie instead of Annaliese. She hadn't answered, because she feared the answer.

What led them here was her desire to fulfill the promises made to their father while he toed the line between death's door and the last whisper of life. Julie's every motivation, her drive, her dreams... they were all for Maggie.

If Maggie had been wrenched from Julie like Annaliese had been torn away from Amor... she would grieve so harshly that her heart would be beyond consolation. She and Amor were similar in that way, Julie realized.

They both were willing to fight fiercely for that which they loved to the point of their own destruction. If theirs was a bond the stars danced to then Julie could not let go of it so easily.

She turned to Silver who held her sister's hand in one of his and the invitations in the other. This wasn't going to be the end of their story. Not if she had anything to do with it.

Julie clenched her fist around her soulmate string, her own secret to carry and her reminder of what she stood to lose.

"I believe we're going to a ball." Julie said.

CHAPTER FORTY-TWO

Julie

The walls of the Moonstone palace rose up from the ground and spiraled toward the clouds until she was certain they scraped the sky. Did they pay people to polish the castle's exterior to make it gleam? It shone with radiance by the sun's light and was surely even more luminescent under the glow of the moon.

Gilded carts, fashionable men astride well-bred horses and a variety of other guests were beginning to arrive for tomorrow night's ball. Silver had decided the girls' wagon would be too conspicuous and therefore had to remain behind in the stable with Fiona and Pepper. Julie could only hope everything was still there when they returned.

Frankly, they were not guests at all, though the stolen invitations in Silver's pocket claimed otherwise. Throughout the night they worked to concoct their plan. Silver would pretend to be Varian. Upon further investigation of the invitation, they learned he was a lord. Julie would take on Pascale's role, the role of a lady. The sisters wore their best dresses, Maggie in her gray and Julie in her crimson. They would not rival the rest of the guests on the royal invitation list by finery alone, but it was better than their cotton traveling clothes.

Pascale and Varian were not native to Seruvia, Silver mentioned the night prior. This meant they wouldn't be easily recognized. They were unsure whether Pascale and Varian were more than partners in crime. So, it had been Maggie's idea to pose as Julie's friend instead of Silver's date.

The guarded entrance boasted doors stretching to a height that she had to crane her neck backward to fully take in. Armed soldiers dressed in black with small purple flowers pinned to their breasts stood resolute on the topmost stair.

"Names and invitations." One guard thundered. He had eyes of such dark blue they looked black.

"Lord Varian, Lady Pascale, and her companion." Silver responded easily, producing the letters and showing them to the guard. The other man in question raised a thick brow and looked them over.

"You don't look like lords and ladies."

Silver looked genuinely bored. "Yes, it's been a long journey, and we would like to rest before tomorrow or before we die of old age." Silver's tone turned impatient, the haughty manner Julie would have expected from a lord.

The guard watched them warily and Julie felt her palms slicken at her sides when his heated gaze stuck on her. He then dropped his eyes to the invitations, and after scanning them thoroughly he dipped his chin. "I apologize for the confusion, welcome to the Moonstone palace. Your accommodations have been provided for you."

Silver strode forward, Julie behind him and Maggie following suit. The guard plucked the small purple flower from his armor and pinched it between his fingers, offering it to Julie as she passed. "Will you accept this, my lady?"

Why would she need something that fragile? Surely, a cut flower so tiny wouldn't last the night, much less till tomorrow evening. Regardless, Julie felt a lingering sense of trepidation at the thought of refusing it. What if it was some type of test? If she declined the flower would he realize they were not who they claimed to be?

Julie took the little purple flora without a word. Only after they were tucked within the confines of the palace did she glance down at the flower she'd been clutching so tightly. Along its thin stem were dozens of even smaller thorns and in her palm, welled four pinpricks of blood. Julie swiped the heel of her hand against her skirt, smearing the small red beads onto the fabric. She relaxed her harsh grip so she didn't destroy the flower completely.

The Moonstone Palace was unlike anything they'd ever seen. The very walls mirrored their reflections as they ascended the grand staircase. Julie was caught by the moonstone's reflective surface as she snuck a glance behind her, looking for someone she knew wasn't there. The way her cord tangled and floated far in the opposite direction wasn't her only indicator of his distance. The distinct, hollow lack of his presence left her heart aching and cold.

Would she see him again? Surely, he would return for Silver and when he did, she would convince him that he was wrong.

Amor would not have her death on his hands, despite whatever had given him such a notion. One cannot simply flee from love because of fear. If anything, love is the antidote to fear. The force powerful enough to conquer it. She didn't want him to act the hero. Amor had selfish motivations in the past, now was not the time for him to lay all of them down. She wanted him to come for her with the same amount of dangerous promise with which he seemed to handle everything.

So lost in her own thoughts, Julie realized they'd been shown to their adjoining rooms only after the doors shut behind them. *How was it possible the guest rooms were equally as grand as the main entry of the castle?* Everything was covered in gold filigree. Including the crystal chandelier that twinkled down from an arched ceiling, and the crème furniture that sunk into rugs more plush than blankets of soft grass.

"Now *this* is a castle." Maggie set her hands on her hips, turning slowly and taking everything in. "It looks like a fairytale exploded."

Julie's lips lifted at the corners as she stepped deeper into the room, running a hand over the roping posts attached to the luxurious bed. Designs of flowers and vines curled around them, as if they'd been there for so long they'd merely become one with the frame. The pillows on the bed and chaise were colored with pastels in blush pink and pale green. Everything had a theme and a place.

Maggie flopped backwards onto the feather-down mattress. "You two go ahead to the ball. I'm going to live on this bed."

Silver chuckled, "I understand, but I would hate for your gown to go to waste."

Maggie perked up, leaning on her elbows as she eyed first Silver, then Julie. "What gown?"

"Oh, you know, just..." Silver walked backward into the adjoining room and returned with a long white box, wrapped in a silver sash. He placed it on the edge of the mattress. Maggie seemed delighted with the arrangement of the bow, and giddily curious about the contents. As soon as the sash fell away and the lid was lifted, Maggie's gasp of shock filled the room.

It was the dress from Seltor. The very one Maggie had admired in a store window on the day they'd met Amor.

"Silver!" Maggie practically squealed and threw her arms around Silver's neck. "How did you do this?"

"You told me how much you loved it on the road remember?" Silver's low laugh was tender.

"Well yes, but I didn't mean you had to go buy it! It's too much, Silver."

Silver held his hands behind his back. "Why don't you try it on? Make sure it fits."

Maggie bit her lip as her smile widened and she swept herself and the gown into the other room to change.

Julie lowered her voice so Maggie wouldn't pick up on their conversation. "How did you really do it?"

Silver tilted his head, hair dipping into blue eyes. "You didn't think I stayed behind at camp all day, did you?" He mused. "Poisons sell, quite well actually. I've been saving up for it since she mentioned how beautiful it was. I was planning on sneaking her into the castle after the real ball ended to dance with her in the garden. It turned out we wouldn't have to sneak... well, not in the way I thought we would. When you spend so long looking down at the world, you get very good at memorizing where everything is. I knew this palace was in Seruvia and I wanted to bring her here."

It was cruel to remain steadfast in her belief that no one could love her sister the way she did. Maggie deserved both their love, just because she shared hers with Silver now didn't mean Julie would lose her. "I'm sorry, for what I said that night about you and Maggie. It was wrong of me."

Silver's eyes softened, "I know. Getting to love your sister has been a privilege. It was a dream I never thought would come true. I'm content with what has to happen now." He spoke quietly.

Julie's brows furrowed, "What do you mean-"

"Well, what do you both think?" Maggie's soft voice called from the doorway, drawing Silver's attention first, then Julie's.

She looked like an angel. The shimmering silk fabric swished around her ankles. It led up to a fitted bodice accented in various shades of delicately cut gray, silver, and black gemstones. Her sleeves were crafted from white lace so sheer, they were nearly transparent. "Maggie. You look beautiful." Julie smiled, reaching for her sister's hands and squeezing them.

"I second that." Silver said warmly, "It was made for you."

Maggie beamed, twirling herself around. "May I have this dance?"

Julie stepped aside, expecting Silver to step in and sweep Maggie off her feet but her little sister was only looking at her expectantly. The sight warmed Julie's heart with a wave of memories. It was the same way Maggie looked at her when they were younger. They used to dance together to the faintest echo of music, finding small joys in the spaces between surviving and simply being children.

They had come a long way since then. But, Julie knew some things would remain the same no matter how many years passed or who came into their lives and found homes within their hearts.

"You may." Julie accepted, spinning her sister around. They had traded a circus for a palace, worn-out clothing for ballgowns, and doubts for the promises of someday.

One Year Ago

"Which knife do you trust more? The one in your hand or the one in the grip of your enemy?" The Prince asked his ally.

"The one in my enemies' grasp." The friend replied.

"And why is that?" Dark eyes slid from the stained mahogany table to the other man.

"Because it's still in his hand." The young gentleman's lips lifted. "Whereas mine would be imbedded in his back."

CHAPTER FORTY-THREE

Amor

A mor was very certain something within him was broken. More than anger or the guilt he'd run off of for the past decade, was the sensation that he had made a very grave mistake.

The cold wind curled around the back of his neck as he stared at the palace from the highest rooftop he could find. It would be nightfall soon and the ball would commence shortly.

His grip on the rooftop's ledge was strained and white-knuckled. *He should be there with her.* He should have taken Varian's invitation instead of giving it to Silver. It seemed like the best course of action in the moment. Amor knew Silver would protect both of them, but Maggie would be his first priority. Julie was Amor's to protect, she... *she was his.*

Amor felt the plaster of the ledge crack under his hands. He shook his head, attempting to clear the thoughts that raged relentlessly. He saw what would happen if he didn't leave. He'd watched it play out in that awful display by the stars. He couldn't forget the depiction of a poisoned arrow being shot into her heart or the picture that came directly after of her crumpling lifelessly to the ground.

Why was Fate so cruel? He couldn't wash the stains from his hands, but he was setting down the knife and with it his vengeful agenda. Was that promise not enough to be granted even a sliver of a second chance? What must he swear in order to reverse what was scrawled in the stars?

He needed her. He needed her so much his heart ached with fervent intensity. When he saw her string reach for him, he'd felt shock, disbelief, euphoria, joy, and the fear that it was a horrible trick. Amor would rather be the victim of an illusion than hold the knowledge that somehow, someday, he would be the one to kill her. Amor wanted her heart to beat faster because of him, not stop entirely.

Not stop...

Amor's heart faltered in his chest just then, a sluggish stammer that had him grasping for the front of his shirt. The hand clutching the dark fabric was the one their soulmate string floated from. Amor stared at it in horror as his heartbeat regulated, but their string, the one attached to Julie, began to flicker.

CHAPTER FORTY-FOUR

Julie

It was nearly time to head downstairs. Julie ran her hands over her embellished satin skirt. *Pascale and Varian must have been important guests for suits and dresses in various styles were brought to their rooms for their choosing.* Maggie, of course, picked the one Silver purchased for her. Silver chose a dark blue suit with inner pockets that he utilized to discreetly carry small amounts of poison and a few blades.

Julie was left with three options. Each gown, beautiful and fine, promised an evening of enchantment but only one of them drew her eye. The rich, deep emerald skirt glittered and flowed from her hips in a river of green and gold. Her hair fell in raven waves down her back. Her shoulders and décolletage were bare, save for the thin golden necklace that dripped small emeralds as if the chain bled them.

Julie turned, her gaze catching on the red scarf at the edge of the bed. Part of the cloth was torn. It would never be flawless again but that didn't mean she loved it any less. The scarlet color matched the string looping around her finger. *How many times had she aided others in learning where their cords led? How many questions burned in her mind for years regarding the absence of her own? Julie had wished so direly for a string. Now that she possessed it, she thought she should have wished for the man on the other end instead.*

As she draped the scarf around her shoulders, a shiver went through her. The sensation was odd since no draft crept into the room. Since yesterday, she'd been overcome with random bursts of chills trailing over her skin. Julie ignored the feeling as it faded away. She picked up the small purple flower the guard had given her from the dresser. She tucked it behind her ear, wary of its tiny thorns. It was obscured amongst her dark tresses, but there was a small sense of security in knowing she had the flower if she needed it.

"Are you ready?" Maggie came up beside her, a gentle hand against Julie's arm. Silver was ready at the door to escort them downstairs. Hopefully, before the night was through, they would have some answers. Julie hoped to see a certain face in the crowd when they descended the steps, but she knew he wouldn't be there. Her eyes flicked to their red thread of fate as it drifted through the balcony windows, free and forever reaching out for a hand too far away to hold.

"Ready as I'll ever be."

The ballroom overflowed with richly decorated guests, dressed like glittering jewels scattered across the marble. Harpists lined the far wall. The melodic violin weavings danced through the air as elegantly as the couples on the floor. "How do we find who they intended to meet? There are hundreds of people here."

"If they're blending in, so should we." Silver stepped in front of Julie and extended his hand palm up.

"Aren't Stars supposed to know everything? Can't you just point us in the direction of who we're looking for?" Julie questioned under her breath as she slipped her hand into Silver's. The music swelled and he spun her around before reeling her back.

"Unfortunately, I only remember some things from before, and even now some of those memories are fading. The Stars see all the different paths that a person's life can take until the pivotal moment that cements their destiny in place."

"What if a person misses that pivotal moment?" Julie's emerald skirts twirled around her ankles as the song ebbed and flowed.

"There's always a second chance," said Silver. "It's only a matter of whether or not the person decides to accept it. You have the power to become all you were made for. If you're ever lost, look up."

Julie's line of sight drifted past Silver's shoulder to the grand staircase. Only a few stray partygoers drunkenly chattered atop its steps.

"I know what you're thinking." Silver watched her intently. "Something tells me he'll never be far if you need him."

"Perhaps..." Julie drew in a slow breath, not ready to admit what she feared. Partly because she'd been letting herself hold on to the hope that he would come. "Perhaps fate got us wrong."

"Do you really think Amor wouldn't destroy the ties of fate with his own hands if it meant keeping you safe?" The violin whispered its final note, and a chorus of applause rose into the air from gloved hands.

Julie stared at the red thread on her finger. "That's what I'm worried about." A chill crept over her skin again, a thin layer of invisible ice inching up her spine. "I'm going to get something to drink." Her head was beginning to ache much like her feet in the heels she wore. From the corner of her eye she saw Silver return to Maggie's side as she made her way to the refreshment table.

"Might I have the honor of procuring a drink for you?" A deep voice met her ears and as Julie turned around she recognized him. It was the guard from yesterday, who'd given her the little purple flower. Only he was no longer dressed in armor but a fine suit of deep blue.

"Yes, thank you." Julie pulled her scarlet scarf around her arms tighter, attempting to ward off the chill in her bones. He swiftly plucked a thin flute from the pyramid of glasses and offered it to her.

"Is this your first ball at the palace, Lady Pascale?"

Julie took a sip of the champagne. It tasted fruity with a dash of something akin to lemongrass. She decided it would be best to answer his question with another question. "What is the purpose of this event? Surely, such a lavish celebration isn't without warrant."

The guard-turned-party-guest reached for a glass of his own and leaned into the table. "You didn't hear? Esterod's king croaked. I say, good riddance. This is a celebration of life, or rather the end of his."

Julie fought her grimace. It was awful to speak of an untimely passing this way. Clearly this man and all these people held a similar distaste for the king of Esterod. Before she could rifle through the fog in her mind to form a response, he tilted his head. "You still have the flower."

"And you don't have yours anymore." Julie commented, raising her flute towards the bare pocket on his jacket. *This champagne was good. It made her heart hurt less.*

The guard leant forward and removed the flower from her hair by its petals. It dropped to the floor and was squashed underneath the toe of his highly shined boot. "I don't pride myself on wearing the same poison twice. Tacky, you know?"

Julie laughed, she couldn't help it. Such a reaction went against the claws of apprehension that dug into her lungs.

"But you knew that of course, Lady Pascale." The guard took a long sip from his flute, draining and setting it aside. "After all, it was your idea."

Julie's smile slipped, torn between the urge to run or press for information. Something about this was very wrong. "Of course, and I assume it's you that Varian and I are to meet tonight."

"Ah yes, your silver-haired friend." The guard drummed his fingers on the table's edge, deep blue eyes searching the room. "Is that not him leaving the party?"

Julie whirled in the direction he pointed. Her heart lodged in her throat as she caught the tail end of his silhouette being pushed into the shadows by three other guards. "What is the meaning of this?" She steadied her voice, attempting to sound every bit the Lady she was portraying.

"Here is what's going to happen, *senorita*." A large, rough hand wrapped firmly around her arm. "You traveled here with an archer and the moment he arrives I want you to point him out to me."

Alarm bells cried in Julie's head as she looked desperately for anyone in the crowd to notice the situation, but no one paid attention. "I don't know what you're talking about." She gritted her teeth as she tried to yank her arm from his unyielding grip.

"You do. And I am aware there are two hundred guests in this room so merely pointing at him won't do. You're going to kiss him as the signal."

"I won't." With a final yank, Julie freed her arm and took several steps backward, breaking all pretense. *She needed to grab Maggie and Silver and get out of here.*

The guard approached in a blink. He backed Julie against the wall, grabbing her chin in his cupped hand and forcing her head upward as he leant in. "You might want to look over there." He pulled Julie's face to an angle.

A guard brandished a glinting blade to a throat in one hand, while his other covered the mouth of a girl with curly hair and dove-gray, terrified eyes.

"If you don't cooperate, I'll be obliging the kingdom with its first public decapitation in decades. Ask the archer for help, and she dies."

Julie was shaking now. Whether from the cold or fear, she did not know. Her legs buckled, and the guard released her chin. Her heart stammered, struggling to produce more than a few measly beats. "What did you give me?" Julie grasped at her chest, her vision growing blurrier at the corners.

"Nightrose root. It's a lovely poison. A bag of it was dropped in my office last night. Apparently, I had some uninvited guests and well, I've always been one for irony."

"Your office?" Julie took gasping breaths and glared up from her position on the floor.

"Oh, did I not properly introduce myself?" The guard questioned thoughtfully. "The name's Varian and I must say you make a beautiful little liar."

The fog in her mind began to clear and she heard Silver's voice faintly echo in her memories. *'A slow-acting toxin, to be exact... It's subtle enough at first, and oftentimes the victim doesn't realize they've been poisoned because the symptoms initially sharpen the senses. Things like a clear head, better sense of smell and heightened hearing. Of course, that's just temporary before the... other effects take place.'*

She was experiencing the first of those symptoms. Julie pushed herself to her feet on unsteady legs as Varian stepped aside. She wished hallucinations could have been a side effect instead of seeing things for how they truly were.

Because at the top of the steps clutching a night-dark bow with beautiful vengeance written across his features, stood Amor.

"No." She whispered, though she knew he couldn't hear her. Amor's emerald eyes locked onto hers and his grip turned white-knuckled. He looked like the catalyst to the end of the world, and he was running toward her.

The guard holding Maggie captive dug the edge of his blade a little deeper into her skin and her sister let out a cry of pain before he hauled her into the shadows out of Julie's view. Just before she'd lost sight of Maggie completely, she caught a blooming stain of crimson across the side of her sister's once pristine silver gown.

Then Julie was running, stumbling, climbing before she collided into Amor's arms on the last flight of stairs. "I'm sorry, I'm so sorry." Tears dripped from her lashes as she repeated those words like a whispered prayer.

"Julie, what's going on?" Amor clutched the sides of her arms, scanning her for injury. "What have they done to you?"

"Amor listen to me." Julie drew in a raggedy breath and grabbed his face in her hands. Her heartbeat was weakening by the second, she didn't have much time. "I love you."

"Julie-"

She pressed her lips to his.

She couldn't feel her own body.

She faded away.

CHAPTER FORTY-FIVE

Amor

Was one supposed to feel their body ache to the point of breaking after death? Unless he wasn't dead. Amor forced his eyes open a sliver against the banging in his skull. But the place he found himself in was too dark to make anything out.

No... it wasn't too dark. Amor could always see in the dark.

He couldn't see at all.

His throat constricted but he shoved it aside. He attempted to sort through his fragmented memories. He knew he was missing something vital, something he needed more than air. He felt it in his very bones.

He remembered finding Julie on the steps of the castle, and being terrified as he watched her crumple. He remembered how she looked when she said she loved him.

"Julie?" He called out, his voice raw and filled with gravel. She would be here. She had to be.

No response came.

"Julie, I can't see you, please answer me." Amor tried again. When only silence answered back, he resolved he would find her even if he had to search every inch of the earth. As he moved his arms, a loud clang reverberated through the air. They'd chained him to the wall. "Julie, please-" He needed her to know he was there, he needed her to know it was...

Something clicked to his left, the screeching sound of metal settling out of place. A door must have opened, judging by the squeaking hinges.

"I always forget how dark it is down here." A male voice sighed. "Ah, you're awake."

Amor twisted toward the direction of the voice. "Where is she?" He bit out.

"Well, she's currently that heap over there on the floor but you wouldn't have known that, would you?"

"Why isn't she waking up?!"

"That's why I'm here, actually. I figure she has about an hour left before death gives her a kiss and you're down a traveling partner."

Amor's chains strained as he lunged, but his efforts didn't free him. "Save her, I'll do anything."

"Oh, I'm going to save her. It's less fun to torture people when they're already dead." Amor heard the sound of footsteps crossing the room and the rustling of fabric as he apparently knelt down. "You woke up much faster than I thought you might, of course you only had the poison from her kiss in your system. She had a whole glass plus a pretty little flower." The man chuckled, sounding delighted.

He was going to bury him alive. "Stop talking and give her the antidote." Amor growled. He didn't care if he was subjecting them both to torture, he just needed her alive and then he could think of a way to get them out of here.

A glass vial clinked against stone. "I forgot to mention, the antidote takes two hours to work." It sounded as if the man dusted his hands off. "I hope you're not squeamish about being in the same room as a body." The footsteps faded and the lock clicked back into place.

Two hours... he said she only had one. "Julie, I don't know if you can hear me but if by some miracle you can, I need you to fight. I'm begging you to live, because if you don't

I'll be beside you in the grave. I'm sorry I said I couldn't be your soulmate. I was terrified of... this happening." Amor felt something damp roll down his face. "From the first day I met you you've had this fire, this spirit. You've fought wolves and bandits, illness and fate. You fight for the things you love, and you said you love me. Please, Firelight. Fight so I can have the chance to tell you the same."

Even if Amor strained his ears, he couldn't hear her breathe. There was no way to tell how much time passed. Had it been minutes? Hours?

He just wished he could see her.

Or maybe it would hurt more to see her slipping away from him, unable to grab onto her life with everything he had until she stayed.

Then there was rustling, the clinking of metal so faint he feared he imagined it. His fear only amplified when everything was still and quiet again. He wanted her to be alive so badly he was beginning to hallucinate.

Something touched his chest.

Another brush to his neck. He knew that touch. It was burned into his memory each time, in case it was the last one she'd ever give him. "Having fun there, Firelight?" Amor whispered, his body limp underneath a wave of relief.

"I figured if I didn't fight, it would frustrate you and we both know how I love doing that." Julie murmured, leaning into his chest.

"You're okay. You're okay." Amor repeated, needing to convince himself this wasn't a figment of his imagination.

"Tired but alive." He could hear the smile in her voice. "I'm afraid I can't reach your blindfold, my hands are... occupied." The sound of metal clinking together reached his ears.

Blindfolded... not actually blind. He could work with that. "It's okay, I just want to hear you breathe."

"Then I'll be your eyes while you're robbed of sight." She said softly. "Though I'm not sure my own vision is doing us many favors. There's one candle on a table and no windows that I can see."

"Mmhm." Amor followed the sound of her voice and leant forward enough for his lips to graze the shell of her ear. Julie shivered, "And there's a..."

Amor pressed a kiss to her jaw.

"I think there's a door..."

"What else?" Amor asked.

"We're getting distracted." Julie said absent-mindedly as if she wasn't the one melting into his affections.

"Death thought you were his to kiss, I'm simply setting the record straight."

The sound of metal against metal made Julie flinch from her trance. Though Amor couldn't see who had just walked in, he had a very visual picture of what he'd like to do to them.

"I'm impressed, *Lady Pascale*." Amor could practically hear the sneer in the man's voice. "I thought for certain the amount of poison you ingested would at least leave you paralyzed."

Amor felt the heat of Julie's body press closer to his own. "What do you want with us?" She asked, that fire Amor loved roaring back into her voice.

"There's someone who wants to meet you, actually." The man replied and Amor heard him smile. "Did you really think after all your hunting we weren't two steps ahead of you, archer? I mean, I expected you to kill Elias but what I did not see coming was your targeting of our men's wives and lovers. It was good, I'll admit." The man cracked his knuckles thoughtfully. "Then you started getting sloppy, which I believe might be in part to this little beauty right here."

Amor heard bootsteps getting closer and he said through gritted teeth. "Put one finger on her and you'll be missing your entire arm."

The man laughed. "I'm afraid the Duke won't like that very much, I am quite useful in his assignments. Speaking of the Duke, I suppose now is as good a time as any to make your introductions."

A new set of bootsteps stalked into what Amor could only assume was their cell but hopefully not their grave. "Excellent work, Varian." The new voice sounded pleased.

"You can call me Matthias."

CHAPTER FORTY-SIX

Julie

The light from beyond their dingy holding cell barely illuminated the two figures towering over them. Julie recognized Varian, the fiend who drugged her and nearly sent her to death's doorstep. Who she could not place was this older man. She knew him by title alone. This was the Duke who sent all those letters they'd found in the office.

"Oh, and don't worry we picked up your friends too. No man left behind and all that." Varian slipped on a sharp smile. "One of them looks awful though, there's blood everywhere."

Julie's heart seized, though this time it was not from poison. Maggie's dress had been covered in blood the last time she saw her. She needed to make a plan to get them out and she needed it fast. All she had on her side was a blindfolded Amor, who looked one heartbeat away from tearing his chains from the wall and bringing the roof down on top of them.

"You've got the wrong people." Julie quickly darted her gaze over them, checking for any weapons they could steal. Varian and the Duke both had a dagger attached to their hips.

The Duke, or Matthias, dug around in his pocket and produced a scrap of ruby colored fabric. "You almost made it too easy to single you out at the ball."

Julie's mouth went dry. When she'd run out of Varian's office her shawl had torn. She hadn't considered that a piece remained behind.

"It's quite impressive, your ability to adopt the persona of a dead woman." Matthias leant a stocky shoulder against the cell wall. "Pascale bit into the fruit of betrayal, so we no longer had a use for her."

"We were just in the wrong place at the wrong time, surely you can't fault us for that." Julie tried again. *If she could just keep them distracted long enough to think of something...*

"We should have killed the archer when we had the opportunity. Well, here's our second opportunity!" Varian chuckled, nudging Amor's leg with the toe of his boot. "He actually gave us a wonderful idea of what to do with you, in fact." Varian's attention turned to Julie and Amor blindly yet forcefully kicked out in Varian's general direction.

"Do you know something funny, archer?" Varian knelt by Julie's side and produced a brass key from an inner jacket pocket. "In revenge, there are no winners. Allow me to demonstrate." Varian unlocked Julie's shackles and hauled her up by her waist though Julie tried to make herself limp. "I'd like to have some fun with this beauty, it would be so sweet to break her bone by bone. But, then it would all be over too quickly. And what was it you taught us with your little displays? The pain needs to linger in a more permanent way."

Amor's chains strained and Julie formed a haphazard idea. *If the circus had taught her anything it was how to be an actress.* "Don't you dare touch me!" She snapped at Varian, letting pain bleed into her voice. "You're hurting me!" Julie bit out through clenched teeth. Varian's brow furrowed, staring at her in a slight state of confusion.

"Shut her up." Matthias barked.

Varian had barely lifted his hand to cover her mouth before Julie choked on a pain-ridden sob. "What is-" Julie had a feeling he was about to ask what was wrong with her, but Julie hissed between her teeth as if he'd wrenched her arm behind her back at a horribly contorted angle.

That'll do it.

There was an awful rattling and a crash as stones came tumbling down around the place Amor's chains used to hang. He'd pulled them out of the wall. He ripped the blindfold from his eyes and the look in them was murderous. Varian cast a wary glance to Matthias who brushed the leaping pebbles from his jacket with a casual hand.

"I'd remove your head from your body, but I don't want to get your rotten blood on her." Amor curved his hand around the chain that fell from his wrist. "Though if you don't release her, I'll simply have to clean her up after."

Varian made no move to release Julie and Amor lunged. A glint of something sharp caught Julie's eye right before Amor faltered, barely reaching her. Julie screamed.

Matthias had driven his knife through Amor's stomach, the spray of blood leaping onto Julie's emerald dress. Amor's leg buckled and he pressed his hand to the wound as Matthias pulled the blade out.

"I thought we were going to torture them." Varian sounded disappointed as Julie fought against his grasp.

"No, no, no!" Julie cried, thrashing and twisting her body in an attempt to get to Amor. Blood was spreading across his shirt, dark, damp and sticky. Varian tossed her to the floor as if she weighed little more than a ragdoll.

"Leave them, we've got more pressing things to discuss." Matthias swiped his blade against the fabric of his jacket, purging it of Amor's blood.

Julie barely registered the sound of their exit, her senses filled with the sordid tang of blood. "Amor, Amor you'll be fine, I promise."

"I... prefer this over... shooting you." Amor's hand was completely coated in scarlet. Julie set his head carefully in her lap, her heartbeat roaring in her ears.

"What are you talking about?" Julie squinted in the dim light for anything she might have missed that she could use to staunch the bleeding. *Her skirt.* Julie ripped the hem of it, tearing the gown further as she balled up the fabric and pressed it to the gash causing a hiss to escape his lips.

"The stars..." Amor bit back a groan. "They showed you dying by... my arrows."

Julie's eyes fell to his face. "That's why you ran away?" She brushed the hair out of his eyes. She remembered doing the same thing before everything went wrong. She should have savored the moment. Amor's grip on her arm tightened, like nothing in all the world could pry her away from him, not while air still filled his lungs.

But what about him being pried away from her?

"I didn't deserve to keep you safe, but I was going to, no matter how it ripped my heart out." Amor's emerald eyes were glassy, wholly unguarded. "Julie," he lifted the least blood-stained hand to her cheek, "I have to tell you something."

Tears slipped down Julie's face. "No. Tell me when you're better. You're going to live. You told me to fight and now it's your turn."

"Thank you for loving all my broken pieces." Amor gave her a faint smile as his eyes closed and his head lulled in her arms.

Sleeping. He was only sleeping. "I'll be back, then you can tell me." Julie whispered, easing Amor's head to the floor.

Julie pushed herself off the floor, her palms sticky with Amor's blood as she ran for the door. It was locked, she needed some way to pick it. Her gaze flew to the single candlestick balanced atop a crudely carved shelf and she grabbed it. She blew out the only source of light they had in order to smash the candlestick against its shelf. Silver shards flew in multiple directions and Julie was left with something just jagged enough to prove useful. She jammed it into the lock, praying under her breath that by some miracle this would work.

The candlestick twisted at a specific angle and Julie heard a click. She inched the door apart to keep it from creaking and cast one last look over her shoulder to where Amor lay. He won't die. He wouldn't leave her.

There were stairs carved into the stone that Julie took two at a time. She recognized this place. This was where all the crates of Seruvian gears had been stacked. Only now, there wasn't a single wooden box in sight. The lanterns had been snuffed out and only the pale wash of moonlight aided her from cut-outs in the roof. Julie had long lost her shoes and now her bare feet pounded the halls. She didn't see any sign of Matthias or Varian but that didn't mean they weren't still on the premises. Just as Julie spied the door, the sound of muffled sobs struck her in the heart.

'Oh, and don't worry we picked up your friends too. No man left behind and all that... One of them looks awful though, there's blood everywhere.'

The door to her right was shut with a sliding latch keeping it in place, and Julie shoved it open. "Maggie..." Julie lifted a shaking hand to her mouth.

Her little sister was coated in blood.

But it wasn't hers.

CHAPTER FORTY-SEVEN

Julie

"Julie." Maggie's voice broke as she clung to her sister. Julie's shoulder was immediately dampened by her sister's tears. "He's gone." She cried. "He saved me but-" Maggie whispered, her whole-body trembling. Julie's eyes stuck on the body of a guard with a knife protruding from his throat. Not far from him, was the unmoving silhouette of Silver, his ice-blue eyes open and unblinking. A Star who'd shone for the last time. His words to Julie rang clear in her head. *I'm content with what has to happen now that I've had that chance...'*

He had known all along. Silver had chosen to love her sister over keeping his own life.

Julie felt acid scorch her throat as fresh tears stung her eyes. "Oh, Maggie, I'm so sorry." Julie cradled the back of her sister's head. This day had turned into one horrible nightmare that she simply could not seem to shake her way out of.

"Amor?" Maggie asked through raggedy inhales as she slowly pulled away from Julie.

"He's hurt, badly." Julie shut her eyes against the image in her mind. "I have to get him help."

"Go." Maggie cradled Julie's face. "Get him help and I'll stay with Silver." Maggie gave Julie one final hug before she knelt and pulled Silver's lifeless body into her grasp. "Hurry." Maggie ran her hand through Silver's matted hair. "It's not too late."

But it was too late for Maggie.

Tears flew behind Julie as she ran outside. Everything hurt. Her heart broke for her sister. It ripped when she realized Silver would never dance with Maggie again. It shattered entirely at the thought that Amor may have looked at her for the final time. The difference between now and the last time she'd run through this forest was that Amor had been right behind her, promising to chase her into eternity if he had to. Now, she wasn't even certain if he would be alive when she returned. "Hold on, Amor." Julie panted. The branches tore at her sleeves, ripping the remains of a blood-soaked skirt. If she could get to the stable she could find someone to help. It shouldn't be far, she'd walked this path before, she-

She found herself at the edge of a cliff.

As she began to turn around, her ring finger grew cold. Julie's soulmate string wavered, flickering between tangibility and mist.

Amor was leaving her.

"No. No. No. No." Julie grabbed onto it as it pulsed into tangibility for half a heartbeat and she kept pulling, wrapping it around her hand. "Amor, you can't do this to me." Julie crushed the tangle of fated thread to her heart. If hers could beat for his then let it. "Don't go." Julie stared in disbelief as black began to seep into it, draining the color and life from its knots. "Please, I just got you back..."

Her soulmate cord faded into nothing.

Julie crumpled. She didn't know where her screams ended, and the hollowness began. If this cliff bordered a canyon, she was certain the weight of her tears would form rivers to flood it. Julie wasn't sure how long she stayed curled into herself on the bitter rock. She felt lost and lonely. Empty, yet so full of pain she felt she may burst. Then the breeze whispered against her damp cheek, urging her face to lift towards the inky expanse of night as each glittering light watched her sorrowfully. *If you're ever lost, look up.'* Julie drew in painful breaths. "The stars grant wishes…" She whispered, slowly unfurling her curled limbs. "The all consuming, down-on-your-knees, heart aching, fists-bleeding kind."

Amor had said those very words that night in the tree. He'd told her those types of wishes could only stem from the worst type of pain…

And Julie's heart was irreparably broken.

"I wish to save Amor. I wish for his life to be returned to him!" Julie pulled herself to her feet. "Grant me this, please. It's the only thing I'll ever ask of you!"

The stars were silent. Did they not believe Amor's life was valuable enough to save? "You're wrong." Julie fought the tremble in her voice. "You're all wrong. Silver said everyone gets a second chance, no matter what they've done. Please, allow Amor a second chance." Julie dropped her head into her hands.

"So, you did learn something from me, after all." A low, gentle voice met Julie's ears. Soft, blue and white light glowed behind her eyelids. When she opened them, she would have sworn she was dreaming.

Silver.

"You're alive…" Julie breathed.

Silver chuckled, glancing down at his glittering white, blue, and silver clothes. "I am what I was always meant to be. Now, it's your turn." Silver extended his hand to her, his skin glowing in the dark. His feet were barely touching the edge of the cliff, like he belonged to the sky and every breeze of night.

"What do you mean?" Julie took his hand, and Silver helped her rise.

"Your gift was no accident, Julie." Silver set his hands on her shoulders and her tattered, stained emerald gown shifted, transforming into something else entirely. Black pants fed into deep crimson boots, the same color as the long-sleeved shirt and border of a glittering cloak that now draped over her shoulders. "You were always meant to be one of us."

"But Amor... is he...?" Julie searched Silver's eyes, fearful to answer the glimmer of hope breathing embers into the shadows of her hollow chest.

"Why don't you see for yourself?" Silver turned her hand over as something began to materialize on her finger. Julie gasped. Her soulmate cord was returning but it was different than before.

This one faintly glowed and its light pulsed steadily like a heartbeat. "Thank you. Thank you." Julie threw her arms around Silver's neck and held him tightly.

"You're welcome. Before I forget, you'll be needing these." Silver chuckled after they pulled away. In his hand, formed a sleek ebony bow encrusted with stardust made to sparkle like diamonds. "Perhaps, we can keep the poisoned arrows to a minimum."

"I think I can work with that." Julie adjusted the quiver over her shoulder. "And Silver..."

The Star tilted his head in question.

"You'll take care of my little sister, won't you?"

Silver opened and closed his mouth, confusion etched across his face. The Stars may know a lot of things, but Julie bet he hadn't predicted this. "You mean..."

"You both deserve that dance." Julie squeezed his hand before she let go.

"Thank you, Julie." Silver's unearthly blue eyes shone with gratitude. Luminescent cuffs that Julie hadn't been able to see before now cracked, light pouring from the gaps as they fell off him.

They shared one final look before Silver faded back into the night. Julie was left standing on the cliff, a fated bow in her hands, a quiver of arrows at her back and a soulmate string on her finger.

And she knew exactly how she would use all of them.

Chapter Forty-Eight

Julie

Julie's boots pounded against sandstone steps as she hurled her body down into the holding cell. "Amor?" She called, instantly spotting the stain of crimson seeping into the gaps of the uneven floor. A gentle tug on her soulmate string brought her attention to her hand. The cord floated up, stretching and scrawling until it formed intricate loops that looked like handwriting.

'I'm alright. Gone after Matthias. Be safe, Firelight.'

Julie's lips parted in surprise. Her thread shone brightly before flattening, erasing the words. But the message *had* been there. She could not recall a singular instance of using her Sight that ever showed a string morphing into the shape of words. She didn't know how to send a message back to him, and she had little time to figure out the intricacies of the new power thrumming in her bones. If Amor was after Matthias, then she needed to find Varian before he fled Seruvia. She dashed outside, feeling faster and stronger than ever before as she took to the roads. The cold night air replenished her lungs, instead of biting into her skin. Her vision stretched ahead of her, illuminating every shadowy crevice and darkened street. Even the stars appeared to burn more brilliantly.

This was what it felt like to be free.

A smile nipped at her lips as she climbed the belltower. This power belonged to her. These movements, each breath and step were hers and hers alone. Julie knew she wasn't invincible, but when she made it to the top of the tower overlooking every street below, she felt she could fly. Tendrils of ink-dark hair swirled around her shoulders as the wind danced near her frame. She crouched on the ledge. The moonlight illuminated her shadow with the curve of her bow and quiver slicing through it like an eclipse. "Where are you, Varian?" Julie murmured. The instant the thought was voiced, her eyes snagged on the stars to the western most part of Seruvia that trickled down to blaze the way. "Thank you." Julie breathed, gratitude causing her heart to swell.

The Stars glimmered in response. Julie took off down the bell tower, opting for the rooftops instead of the streets. She had to admit, she finally saw the appeal. Luminescent, blue drops of stardust formed footprints ahead of her, guiding her path and lighting the darkness. The footprints came to an abrupt halt next to a particular alleyway that a man driving a smaller cart careened toward.

Julie recognized that silhouette, those greedy eyes. *Found you.* She knocked three arrows into her bow, pulling the string back until the feathers touched the corner of her lips. This time, she was certain her aim would be true. The arrows were released from the bow, each imbedding themselves into the front wheel of Varian's wagon. The cart veered to the side, one wheel rolling away before clattering to a stop. "I'm afraid I can't let you leave." Julie landed onto the ground from above, her cloak flowing around her.

Varian hopped down from his broken wagon. "Well, somebody had a wardrobe change."

Julie raised her bow. "I have questions, and you will answer them."

Varian chuckled darkly, "A few shiny new toys aren't enough to scare me, though I applaud your efforts."

"Why are you working with Esterod?" Julie aimed the arrow directly at Varian's chest.

"The people need change." Varian shrugged, smiling as he sauntered forward. "And we will give it to them."

"By *we*, do you mean you and Matthias?"

"And others. Plenty of others." Varian stopped to her left, eyeing her from head to boots. "We have friends in high places." Without warning, Varian thrust his fist toward her stomach, with every intention of cracking her ribs. Julie was faster, swerving her body to the side to avoid the hit. She struck his temple with the elongated curve of her bow, blood pouring freely from the newly inflicted gash.

Varian flashed his teeth, lunging for Julie's center of gravity. Julie somersaulted backward, a reflex she hadn't previously possessed before the change. But Varian caught a fistful of the ends of her hair and yanked her head back, pinning her against his body with a large arm. "You shouldn't play with things you don't understand."

Julie's grip latched around her bow, unable to move her arms to raise it. "Neither should you." Julie reared her head back, aligning the back of her skull with Varian's mouth. A grunt of pain and strings of foul curses filtered from his blood-stained lips as she scrambled away.

Varian snarled, like a rabid wolf.

Wolves. She knew how to handle those. Julie threw herself into Varian's grasp, knocking him off his feet as they contacted the cobblestones. He twisted, rolling on top of her and knocking her arrows free of her quiver as they lay scattered around her head.

"I should have killed you when I had the chance." His hand curled around her throat and began to squeeze. Julie's fingers inched to grasp one of the fallen arrows.

"At least your sister got to enjoy the same fate I should have showed you." Varian dipped his hand into his pocket and withdrew a pure silver necklace with sparkling stars dripping from its chain. "We're all the same. The instant you have your first taste of power, you forget all about those who helped you get there." Varian's thumb dug harshly into her neck, causing Julie's vision to blur as the sight of the necklace made her hesitate. No, Silver would have gotten her. *He promised to take care of her.*

Julie bucked against Varian's vice-like grip, kicking out with her legs. It was getting hard to draw in enough breath to keep her lungs from spasming. "We are *not* the same." She threw what fleeting strength she had left into plunging the arrow into Varian's chest. He choked and sputtered on his own blood as he released her throat. Julie coughed, wheezing in spite of her mental demand that she shake it off. Varian doubled over, clutching his heart in agony before his movements slowed, then ceased completely.

"And I didn't forget." Julie told the corpse, fighting a cough. "Maggie's necklace had blue stones. You bought a fake to trick me." Julie's hair acted as a veil for her face as she bent, bracing her hands on her thighs while she worked to refill her lungs with oxygen. "When you love someone you notice those details." Julie's neck ached as she gathered her lost arrows into her quiver. She didn't want to think of how closely she'd come to encountering death a second time. She was alive, that was the most important thing.

"Bravo, bravo." Four slow claps echoed through the alleyway as a figure emerged from the shadows. "I have to say, little Dove, you managed to escape much farther than I gave you credit for."

The very sound of his voice sent ice trickling into her every vein. "Pierre." Julie's hand curved around her bow as he stepped free of the darkness, the moonlight casting an eerie bluish hue onto his... marred face.

"Oh, do you like my new look?" Pierre gestured vaguely to the charred half of his features. "You should, seeing as you are the one responsible for destroying my livelihood."

Julie's mouth felt dry. The Fate-granted power that roared to life in her spirit earlier tonight now lay quiet, simmering like dull embers in the face of a hurricane. "How did you find us?" *She couldn't climb the wall without a foothold, and Pierre blocked the only exit in the alley.*

"The same way a hunter finds all its prey, by tracking." He took a step forward, causing Julie to retreat one step back. "Rumors of my Seer in Seltor spread like wildfire. Though, you weren't long for that job, it seems." Pierre raised a mangled, seared hand towards her. "Then, I happened to come across the most delightful little apothecary selling a peculiar red ribbon all tied in a bow." Pierre tilted his head. "You know how I know that red ribbon was yours?"

Julie's back thumped against the wall, nowhere left for her to run.

"Because I gave it to you." His lips pulled back from his teeth and Julie caught the glint of a knife being withdrawn from his jacket. "I told you I would rip your feathers, Dove. And I always keep my promises."

"I don't know if you've noticed." A dark, threatening voice resounded through the alleyway. Julie's eyes snapped forward to the broad silhouette filling the entrance. "But she took those feathers and turned them into arrows."

Pierre's distraction as his attention diverted to Amor's approaching form was all Julie needed to crash her bow against the back of Pierre's skull. The ringmaster crumpled to the ground, landing at a misshapen angle made all the more grotesque by his burns.

"Amor." Julie dropped her bow and ran full force into his arms.

"I'm here." Amor's arms wrapped around her back and waist, crushing her to him.

"How did you know I needed you?" Julie's hand bunched up the material of his black shirt.

"I saw your message." Amor drew her left hand forward, eyeing the red thread.

"But I didn't send a message." Julie's eyes fell into his.

"Your heart did." Amor tapped her ring finger, tracing a line up her arm until his finger rested over her quickening pulse. "And I am done pretending that I don't hang on to every beat of it." Amor leant down, resting his forehead against hers.

"I'm so glad you came." Julie whispered, tangling her hands in the back of his hair.

"I'm afraid I can't stay long. Matthias got away, and I have to find him before it's too late."

"Can't we be selfish for once?" Julie didn't want to let him go, not so soon. Not after everything that had happened.

"All I've been is selfish, Firelight. But I promise, someday soon we will have our forever." Amor's hands cradled her face. His smile made Julie's heart ache from the sheer beauty and rarity of it.

"If you get lost, follow our string." Julie ordered, memorizing each fleck of gold and wave of emerald in his eyes to tide her over while they were apart.

Amor took her hand and lifted it to his lips. "I will chase it into eternity."

One Year Ago

"Are you certain this will work?" A disembodied voice floated from the shadows.

"Of course. My father was very thorough in his blueprints."

A sigh. "Your highness, with all due respect. This could break the world."

The raven-haired Prince's lips curved into a smile that highlighted teeth a little too sharp.

"I'm counting on it."

Chapter Forty-Nine

Julie

Julie set her bow against the wheel of her wagon, running her hand over the painted facade. Time had passed since the day she'd forced Amor to paint it. It was beginning to fade after such a journey, but it was nothing that couldn't be fixed. "You ready for a new adventure, girls?" Julie stepped in front of the wagon where Fiona and Pepper tossed their heads, almost in answer.

"Me too." Julie took a deep breath and sighed, petting Fiona's flank. Julie chuckled as she peered back at her cart, a traveling piece of her history that she knew by heart. She wouldn't be giving soulmate string readings anymore, at least not for a while.

"I got a reading here. The lady said my string pointed to the north but honestly I think she's just making things up." Someone spoke behind her and Julie whirled around.

"Maggie." Julie laughed, crushing her sister into a hug. "You're glowing."

Maggie grinned. "Perks of being a Star, I never need to light a lantern when I enter the room."

Julie squeezed her sister's shoulders. "I'm sure there are more perks than just that." She winked.

"Oh, you're right." Maggie tapped her chin. "The dresses are stunning."

"You wound me, *stella mea*." Silver snuck up behind Maggie and wrapped his arms around her waist, making Julie's sister squeal delightedly.

"I'm so happy to see you two. I wasn't sure you'd find me before I left." Julie watched them fondly.

Maggie shook her head emphatically. "We wouldn't miss it. And lest you forget we see everything, if you're ever in trouble I'll be there, quick as a flash." Maggie snapped her fingers to elaborate.

"Trouble? Me?" Julie asked dramatically. "I would never. Besides, now that Varian has been taken care of by yours truly, and Amor's gone after Matthias, I shouldn't run into anything my arrows can't solve."

"Speaking of Amor, have you seen him since...?" Maggie questioned.

A smile tugged on Julie's lips. "He'll always be around. Call it... intuition." Her eyes flicked to the cord attached to her hand, glowing, strong and vibrant.

Maggie took Julie's hands into her own. "Now, you listen to me. All our lives you were the one to protect me. You put my happiness before your own and you loved me in a way no one else could. Mama and Papa are incredibly proud of you. Call it... *intuition*." Maggie smirked. "Whatever you're going to face from here on out, never forget that you're the strongest woman I know. You've rewritten fate and bent it to your will. After you get to the bottom of everything... live one of papa's stories for yourself, okay?"

A tear slipped from Julie's lashes as she pulled her sister in close. "I already am." She whispered.

Julie's gaze flicked to Silver who looked into the shadowy forest and then back to them, a mischievous smile tugging on his lips. He lightly placed his hand on Maggie's shoulder. "It's time."

Maggie nodded, covering his hand with her own before looking back at Julie. "I love you whole, Jules."

Julie swallowed past the lump in her throat. "I love you whole too, Mags."

Her sister's smile rivaled every single star as she and Silver faded away into mist.

Julie closed her eyes and tipped her head back, letting the midnight wind roll over her skin. She savored every gentle sound of the forest, every twinkle of the stars above.

Something in the forest snapped and Julie's eyes flew open, scanning the woods. Ever since she'd become an extension of Fate, she was amazed at how well she could see in the dark. So well, in fact, that she could make out more than just a silhouette approaching her. She was pinned to the forest floor by a pair of the most startingly emerald eyes she'd ever seen.

"You're the fate-teller people are talking about?" He stepped out of the tree line, stopping just two feet in front of her.

"Yes." Julie said thoughtfully, setting her hands on her hips.

"Prove it." Amor's lips curved.

"If you want a reading, you're welcome to visit my wagon." Julie gestured to the cart behind her.

Amor put his hand in his pocket and withdrew something. "This should cover your going rate." He showed her the object. It was the feathered pen of crimson and gold. "You told me to rewrite our story, so..." Amor stepped around her, kneeling infront of the wagon wheel and lifting her bow. She couldn't see what he was doing, but she did hear the faint sound of scratching, like wood being carved. Amor then handed her the bow and Julie's heart melted as she read what he'd inscribed.

I love you, Firelight

"I love you too, Amor." Julie gently placed the bow down to throw her arms around Amor's neck. He wrapped his arms around her waist, his eyes settling on her lips. "I find myself in need of a traveling partner again. What do you say?"

"Well... the side of my wagon *does* need to be painted."

Amor laughed before stealing her breath with a kiss that made her knees weak.

Then a blast rolled through the land, cleaving Julie's heart in two.

Acknowledgements

In my debut novel, When You Return, I mentioned the 'Author' throughout the book. In every book I write, I will thank the Author of my life first and foremost. I want to thank my creator for everything, and for instilling in me both a passion to create and a love of writing.

I want to thank my parents for their unwavering support and love. I can never thank you enough for not only giving me the opportunities to pursue my dreams but also walking alongside me every step of the way.

Mama, you've taught me so many valuable lessons throughout my life. One that I will forever treasure is how you stressed the importance of following that which makes my heart sing. Thank you for cheering me on from my very first day. Thank you for raising me on a steady diet of imagination and fairytales. Thank you for the late-night talks and listening to me intently as I ranted about plot details, characters and life in general. When You Return and Our Poisoned Love are just as much your book babies. Thank you for being the best editor and loving these characters and their stories as much as I do. You taught me to never settle, and to dream big. You've always been my safe place, *I love you whole.* As always, there's no way I could do it without you.

Daddy, I can't thank you enough for your consistent encouragement, love, guidance and wisdom. You have worked so hard throughout the years so that I could pursue my dreams, and somehow always made time for me. You have been the best example of what a man of integrity looks like. You are and have always been my hero. Thank you for always believing in me. You also taught me the importance of patience, to be steady while the wings of my dreams get off the ground. I strive to live up to your amazing example every day. You are the best dad I could have ever asked for. I love you infinity.

To my amazing friends and family, I appreciate you more than you know. You are all so special to me. Thank you for the laughs, the support, the hours upon hours of conversations and inside jokes. It's been wonderful to embark on this journey with you, and I love you all so much.

And finally, for you, the reader. Thank you so much for picking up my books and going on these incredible journeys with me and my characters. Thank you for your kind messages, your unwavering support, your excitement, and for loving these stories as much as I do. *You* have made being an author so worthwhile.

Here's to the next chapter.

About the author

Isabella Ayubi is a YA fantasy romance author. Her debut series is the Soulmatism Saga, with the first two installments being When You Return and Our Poisoned Love. She graduated summa cum laude from Liberty University where she attained a BSBA in Digital Marketing and Advertising. When Isabella is not writing, you will often find her with a sketchbook in hand, walking the beach, or dreaming up new ideas for her next great literary adventure.

Also by

The Soulmatism Saga:

When You Return